DELETED: JACKSON AND MAGGIE

TESS THOMPSON

To Aunt Deb,

Thank you for all your support and love.

I love you!

Tess Thompson

4kids5cats
EDITIONS

For my first love, Eric Hansen,
who taught me how to write about love and made me an artist the
moment he kissed me in the rain on a Seattle street as the Blue's notes
wafted sweet around us.
No love is ever wasted.
Or forgotten.

CHAPTER ONE

Maggie

MAGGIE KEENE TURNED thirty the week she learned she'd been dead for twelve years. It started with a phone call from across the country and a hangover. Her phone squawked and vibrated in that darkest hour before dawn, when even the Brooklyn streets had quieted to a spattering of shouts and sharp horns and rumbles from battered cabs. She groaned as she reached across the bedside table for the abhorrent gadget. Why had she chosen the whistle ringtone? It pierced the very center of a person's brain. Which, at this precise moment, throbbed without any outside stimulus whatsoever. An empty plastic water glass fell to the floor and bounced across the room.

Finally, she found the phone and punched it into quiet submission. "Hello."

"Hello, Maggie?"

"Yes."

"This is Darla."

Maggie jerked upright, hard and straight. *Darla*. Her father's wife. *The Postmistress*.

"It's four in the morning." Vodka and perspiration seeped from her pores. Maggie wiped her forehead with the corner of the sheet.

"Your father's dying. He doesn't have long. He's asked for you."

"Asked for me?" Maggie repeated the question, dull and confused. "It's been twelve years."

"He wants to make amends," Darla said.

Amends?

"He's found God."

God? Viscous, acrid syrup boiled in Maggie's belly. She pressed her fingers against her mouth and swallowed.

"Will you come?" Darla asked. "Will you come home?"

"Home?" *Come home?* Cliffside Bay was no longer her home. She wanted to say that out loud, but instead a gravelly voice like Al Pacino in a bad gangster movie played in her mind. *The hard streets of Brooklyn, baby. That's my home.*

"Yes," Darla said. "Home to California."

The idea landed with a heavy thud inside her aching head. Go home. Could she? After all this time? Not for him. But for herself? Confront the past and gain the truth? Say what she wanted to say? Not redemption for the dying, but peace for her, the living? Closure. Answers?

Yes, answers. She deserved answers. This was an irrefutable fact. The injustice of it bored into her mind like a cancer. She would never be free until there was retribution—until he had to pay with something dear to him. Just tonight, on the way home in the cab, she'd been unable to keep the images of that day from crowding into the lonely spaces of her mind.

Her mother crumpled at the bottom of the stairs. Her father teetering above with the bag in his hands. Jackson tugging at her arm, his face the color of an oyster's pearl and his voice an octave too high.

Would this be her last opportunity to get her father's confession?

Below, from the street, a horn blared a staccato warning.

"I'll come," Maggie said. "But not for him." *I'll get him to tell the truth.* Before he's whisked off to hell, he would affirm what she already knew. He murdered her mother and baby sister. He would tell her where her newborn sister's body was hidden. And finally, Maggie would bury the sweet baby that hadn't had a chance to live next to their mother.

"It's the right thing, Maggie."

"The right thing? For whom?"

"You don't know what you think you know. You were always too big for your britches." Darla and her Texas sayings. Maggie had forgotten how self-righteous the Postmistress was.

The thick, bubbling hatred stewed in Maggie's stomach. "You don't get to say one word about me or my life. Not after what you did—what you helped him do."

Darla cleared her throat. She must still smoke. An image of cigarette smoke wafting around Darla's pocked face flashed before her eyes. When had Maggie last seen her? A week before she left, waiting in line at the drug store. They'd pretended not to see each other. "What do you think he did exactly, Maggie?"

Out of Darla's mouth, *Maggie* sounded like a curse word. *Maggie.* She'd learned once from one of Lisa's boyfriends—the sales guy—that you should insert someone's name into conversation because it made them feel seen and heard. The technique was good for selling things or picking up chicks in a bar. It had worked on her best friend Lisa. For a while, anyway.

Darla repeated the question with even more scorn in her voice this time. "What do you think *we* did, Maggie?"

"You know."

"There's something I should tell you," Darla said.

The line went silent. Maggie waited. Had they lost the connection?

After several dead seconds, Darla spoke. "Never mind. Best it waits 'til you get here."

"It'll be a few days," Maggie said. *I'll have to rummage up the cash for a plane ticket.*

"He's old. Sad and remorseful. You'll pity him now," Darla said.

"I won't." Maggie hung up and resisted the urge to toss her phone across the room.

She collapsed back in bed and stared at the ceiling. It was her birthday in a few days, but her friends had taken her out tonight. They'd gotten all dolled up with perfectly applied makeup and dotted perfume behind their ears and worn little dresses that barely covered their behinds.

Maggie groaned again as the night rushed back to her. The club. Dancing. Birthday drinks, pink and festive in their fancy glasses. *Clearly overserved.* All of them spilled into cabs an hour before closing time, still giggling.

What a night, though. *To the future,* they had roared as they toasted and spilled and laughed and danced. They'd promised one another, for tonight, no thoughts of auditions or callbacks or diets for this gaggle of chorus girls. Just a pounding bass and those overpriced drinks they'd pretended they could afford and had no calories. They were actresses, after all, and the whole "as if" scenario from Sanford Meisner could be used for more than acting. Denial was a wonderful thing. Until rent came due. Until you got on the scale.

Now, though, reality fermented in the murky pit of her stomach where the black syrup remained. The angry scar on her left knee itched, reminding her that her story was officially over. *No more dancing professionally,* the doctor had said with a click of his pen. *I'm sorry.*

Sorry? That was all he could come up with? He could have at least added her name at the end of the sentence. I'm sorry, *Maggie.* I'm sorry for your broken heart and your ridiculous dreams and your empty bank account, *Maggie.*

What he'd actually said was much less sympathetic. "What did you expect? You started ballet at three years old. That's a lot of years abusing your body. It's time to retire from dancing."

Retire? From what? Working in a bar and taking endless dance and acting classes and auditioning for chorus roles? Was this a career from which to retire?

Thirty years old. Dreams a bust. Twelve years in the Big Apple and nothing but the calluses on the bottoms of her feet and the stage name *Marlena Kassidy* listed under "chorus" in a handful of theatre programs to prove she'd ever been here.

Other than her friends. She'd figured the phone call just now would be one of said friends. The most likely candidate being Pepper. She'd decided to stay for another round when they left the club and Maggie figured she was stuck somewhere without cab fare. Or, crying into her vodka-soaked pumps about the former boyfriend she'd run into that night. Or, God forbid, panicked in a urine-splashed jail cell after a moment of lapsed judgment.

Maggie was always the one they called. Even on her birthday. She could figure a way out of a mess or an empty pocketbook like no one else. *Like a boss*, as Pepper was prone to say, which always made Maggie giggle. Pragmatic and sensible, able to get right to the heart of a thing—that was her. It was the small-town-girl vibe, they always said. She was kind, fanciful, and still had the right answer to comfort a friend, despite living as a New Yorker for twelve years.

Come to my place. I'll pay the cab from my "mad money" when you arrive. He's not worth crying over, sweetie. I'll make pancakes and mimosas and we can watch Rent *until the sun rises.*

Maggie's mother had called it *mad money*. And, like her mother, Maggie never had much, mad or otherwise. But that didn't keep a girl from taking care of her own. There was always an extra shift behind the bar. Or two.

She stared at the ceiling. Her mind raced like the rapid beat of a club song. She wouldn't be able to fall back to sleep. Not after that phone call. *Just get up. Play guitar. Work on a new song.*

5

Maggie stumbled to the bathroom and stared at her reflection in the mirror. She'd fallen into bed still wearing her dress and thick makeup. Her long, red hair hung in a tangled mass down her back. Smeared black eyeliner and mascara blotted out the freckles on her cheeks. The ocean blue dress, once so perky and boastful, hung in wrinkled and disheveled defeat.

Like me.

Maggie scrubbed her face with soap and hot water. Steam rose from the sink and soothed her tired eyes. She swallowed a few ibuprofens and changed into leggings and a soft t-shirt, then wandered out to the front room. Lisa was asleep on the couch, still dressed from the evening in her little black dress. One of her shoes rested listlessly on the coffee table, speckled with sticky drops of a Cosmopolitan.

Since Whiskey broke up with her, Lisa had been sleeping on the couch instead of in her bedroom. Maggie didn't need to ask why— nor the reason for the French language lessons or the shortening of her once waist-length hair. They'd been friends since their theatre days at NYU. There wasn't much they hadn't been through together, most recently a jerk who called himself Whiskey. *Whiskey,* for heaven's sake. Maggie knew his real name was John. A stealth peek at his driver's license had revealed that dirty little truth. No one in this town could admit to what and who they really were.

Who was she now? She wasn't sure anymore. Beneath her exterior made of dance muscles, expensive haircuts, and thrift store clothes—always better to pay for a good haircut than clothes—was she still a small-town girl?

Fear rumbled down the back of her neck and settled in her chest, blinking like an errant traffic light. She imagined her father, dying in a hospital bed, shrunken and sick. Were his strong, mean hands and cutting words still able to hurt her, or had looming death squashed his venom? Could she summon the courage to do what needed to be done?

And what of the rest of them? Those who had betrayed and abandoned her? The ones she had believed would always love her unconditionally? What of them? *That* script had taken a cruel turn. Jackson and Zane, and Doc and Miss Rita were as much a façade as the sets in a theatre production. How easily they were pushed over and dismantled.

All these years she'd stuffed the pain inside, focused on her new life and her goals.

A glorious life.

Not a glorious life. A hard life.

This turning thirty was turning her into a real crybaby. She spoke in a silent, stern voice to herself. *Buck up. You're going home. You do what you have to do and get out. Once that's done, you can and will figure out what to do with the rest of your life.*

But first, she might have a good long cry.

No. No more crying. She'd cried enough self-pitying tears for a lifetime over the past few weeks.

Maggie slipped Lisa's other shoe from her foot and set it next to its mate. She covered her friend with a blanket. Lisa stirred and mumbled something in French.

Maggie shuffled over to the front window. Her reflection was ghostlike in the glass, the details of her appearance obscured, other than the outline of her slender figure.

The phone call had opened a door inside her mind. Memories surfaced in images that played on the window. Surfing next to Zane. Dancing under the full moon in Jackson's arms. *Jackson Waller.* How was it possible that her heart still ached at the thought of him?

She placed her hand on the glass and whispered his name as if he were merely outside waiting in the gloomy night. Where was he now? Had he become a doctor like he'd planned? Or were his dreams like hers? Unattainable? Silly to him now that the reality of the world had swallowed all sense of self?

No, not Jackson. He would have done what he said he would. Singularly focused on whatever he wanted. Until he wasn't.

It would be easy to find him. Everyone knew a quick social media search would pull him up in an instant. Years ago, she'd vowed to keep his memory separate from her new world. This was a different life, a different Maggie. New York Maggie hadn't loved Jackson Waller all her life, only to have him break her with his dismissal. Not even Lisa and Pepper knew his last name. She couldn't take the chance that they might decide to look for him. When and if the pain of their parting ever subsided, she would free him from the cage and allow the remembrances to inform the present. Until then, she kept him locked away, like a box of photographs she knew existed but that she would not open.

Maggie grabbed her guitar and sank into the faded armchair they'd rescued from the street, deleted from someone's home for a newer, trendier model. She and Lisa had reupholstered it in an optimistic yellow. More precisely, Lisa had. She was from the Midwest and her mother was a home economics teacher, so she knew how to do useful things like cook and sew and decorate.

Maggie strummed a few chords. Usually she could think better when she played her guitar. While she recovered from her knee surgery, she had written songs with a focus and speed she'd never had before. Lyrics and tunes had come in abundant clumps of inspiration. She had to wonder if her idle body had somehow lent her brain its energy. The songs were pretty good. Maybe. Who knew, really? She'd thought there was no way she could fail until she arrived in New York and ran smack into the cement of reality.

Unlike her friends, she no longer believed tomorrow would be better. She knew after yesterday's appointment that it would not be. She had told no one, not even Lisa, about her doctor's visit the previous afternoon. Since her injury and subsequent surgery, a persistent thought had snuck in like a snake and wrapped its reptilian muscles around her neck. Was it time to leave New York?

The problem was this: who the heck was she if not a chorus girl looking for her big break? All these years she'd sacrificed every-thing to *make* it, and she was no further ahead than when she'd arrived at eighteen. It was time for a new chapter. If only she knew what that was.

A more traditional life? Marriage and children? A family of her own? These blessings would be welcomed, but how did one find them?

While Lisa and Pepper were in a constant search for *the one*, Maggie had never bothered with men. After college there had been a few men she'd dated casually, but no one important. No one who could push away the memory of Jackson. She told herself it was because of her ambition and focus. No time for men. However, the truth was—no one would ever compare to Jackson. She would never love another man like she had him. If she couldn't have that kind of love, she'd rather have none.

Was her summons home a sign? Should she go back to California and try her luck in Hollywood? She could change the direction of her career away from theatre to television and film.

The truth, Maggie.

The idea of Hollywood left her cold and exhausted. Without dancing, performance had lost its hold on her. She loved to sing, but her voice was more suited to popular music than the operatic style of musicals. It had only taken her twelve years to admit *that* truth.

God, she was tired of hoping. She plucked a melody on the strings of her guitar. The sympathetic notes reverberated in the quiet room.

From the couch, Lisa stirred. "What time is it?"

"It's just after four. Go back to sleep."

"What happened?" Lisa asked.

"You passed out before I could get you into your pajamas," Maggie said. "As did I."

"I barely remember stumbling up the stairs. Oh no, did we pay the cab driver?"

"I took care of him. You want water?"

"And an aspirin? I feel like death."

Maggie set aside her guitar and went to their kitchen. Kitchen being a loose term, as it was more like an *area*.

Lisa was upright by the time Maggie came back with the water and painkillers. She did her nurse-like duty, then plopped back in the armchair.

Lisa drank the entire glass of water, then swept her blond curls back from her face and wrapped the blanket around her shoulders. "I'm afraid to ask what the doctor said yesterday. I know it's bad because you didn't say anything before we went out."

"He said the surgery healed nicely, but it won't stay that way if I keep dancing professionally. The strain on my knee is too much, unless I want to live a life with constant pain and subsequent surgeries."

"Crap." Tears welled in her friend's eyes.

"I know."

"What does this mean?" Lisa's eyes looked like a baby doll's when she cried, round and glassy blue.

"Plan B, I guess."

"What *is* that?" Lisa asked.

Maggie picked up the guitar and plucked a few notes. "I got a call tonight. From home. My dad's dying." She needn't provide any further information. Lisa knew what that meant.

"Oh, God."

"I have to go see him. It might be my last chance," Maggie said.

"You have to try, at least." Lisa wiped under her eyes with the corner of the blanket.

"I just want him to tell me where the baby's body is." Maggie's voice quivered. She strummed a chord on the guitar to gather herself. "Jackson's dad left no stone unturned twenty years ago. Whatever my father did with her, we'll never know unless he tells me."

"Do you want me to come with you?" Lisa asked.

"You know you can't." Money, for one. Money, for two.

Lisa drew her knees up to her chest. "Why do I feel like you won't come back?"

"Because I probably shouldn't. I don't know who I am without dance. But I need to find out." Right then she craved the shelter of sycamore trees and the scent of the Pacific.

Home. She had to go home.

Lisa looked toward the window, picking at the skin around her thumb like she did when she was troubled. "I got a call this morning from my mom. My twin brother and his wife are having another baby. A girl this time."

Maggie waited for her to continue.

"It got me thinking about all the stuff I've missed since I left home and moved to New York. All the birthdays and Christmases —I missed the birth of my *twin's* little baby once already and I'm not sure I want to miss the next one. I want to be Aunt Lisa." She smiled. "Cool Aunt Lisa who speaks French. Not loser Aunt Lisa who can't afford the plane fare to come home for Thanksgiving. Not delusional Aunt Lisa who lies to herself and everyone else about how great things are going here."

"Everyone but me. I know," Maggie said. "And I love you no matter what."

"I know you do. I saw some of your songs on the table this morning. They're good."

Maggie flushed, embarrassed. "Maybe."

"I know they're good. You should do something with them. Your voice is special. You know that, right?"

"You know you're a great actress?" Maggie asked.

"I am, yes."

"You are." She *was*. As good as anyone out there. Not to mention, Lisa was a classic beauty, like a movie star from the forties with an hourglass figure and eyes the colors of sapphires.

Maggie was *not* a classic beauty. Not with her flat chest and white skin and freckles that covered every inch of her body.

"But it doesn't matter," Lisa said. "Every single day a new busload of girls as talented as we are show up. They're fresh and young and their hearts haven't been broken a thousand times already."

"What're you saying?" Maggie asked.

"I'm saying I want to go home. I want to live in a home with a real kitchen. I want to know people who are doing interesting things outside of the theatre. I want to find a nice man who doesn't pretend his name is an adult beverage."

Maggie laughed through her tears. "But what will we do?" She gestured toward the window. "We don't know how to do anything but be chorus girls."

"And bartenders."

"And waitresses," Maggie said.

"I always told myself I'd give it ten years and if things hadn't worked out by then, I'd think about Plan B." Lisa wrapped the blanket tighter around her shoulders. "It's been almost twelve years since the first day we met in Professor Yang's drama class. We've given it a good try, but it's time to find another path, another way to live."

"I'm scared," Maggie said.

"Me too. But we're going to have to trust that we'll figure it out along the way," Lisa said. "You go home to California. Pepper and I will pack up or sell anything you don't take with you."

"Really? You'd do that for me?"

"Maggie, we've been friends for what feels like a lifetime. Anyway, we're paid up until the end of the month. That'll give me time to sort through stuff. It's not like we have any furniture worth taking with us."

"What about this chair?" Maggie asked. "The color's so optimistic."

Lisa chuckled. "That chair is like us—looks good on the outside, but a wreck underneath."

"That's a good song lyric."

"It's time to go home and get our insides fixed up," Lisa said.

Home. She would go home to Cliffside Bay and settle her scores. Not to live, obviously. Not after what had happened with Jackson, not after the betrayal of everyone she once loved. But *somewhere* in California might work. Or maybe Oregon. Washington State? A place with pines and sycamore trees. A town where the briny scent of the Pacific would soothe her disappointment.

"Once I get settled wherever, you have to come see me," Maggie said.

"Absolutely. And you can come to Iowa."

"I've always wanted to go to Iowa."

"Liar."

CHAPTER TWO

Jackson

THE SUN HAD not yet peeped up over the eastern mountains when Doctor Jackson Waller parked in front of Cliffside Bay's only market. A woman in the park across the street caught his attention. His stomach lurched. *Maggie* stood under the birch tree. Dressed in running pants and a sweatshirt, she bent at the waist and touched the dewy grass with the tips of her fingers. Long red hair covered her face.

"Maggie." He whispered and leapt from his truck. *Maggie. His Bird.* It was her. It had to be her. His feet pounded the concrete, loud in the quiet of the morning. He reached the mailbox at the edge of the grass and stopped. His breath lurched. He leaned with both hands on the cold metal of the mailbox. Not Maggie. Not even close. This woman had legs sturdy like old-growth forest, not lean dancer legs.

He expelled air from his tight chest and a strangled sob drowned out the song of a sparrow in the birch tree. The woman looked up at him and staggered backward. He'd frightened her—staring at her like he'd seen a ghost.

He'd frightened himself. This was not Maggie. No freckles scattered across a narrow nose or a birthmark on her neck in the shape of Italy. This woman had blue eyes, not the green of a mountain lake.

My God, he was slipping into insanity. Having visions. Seeing ghosts. More specifically, he was seeing Maggie. Everywhere. Not like before, when it happened maybe once a year. Since he'd moved home to Cliffside Bay six months ago, his visions had grown to daily occurrences.

Two days ago, he'd been sure it was Maggie holding a dress to her torso outside the women's boutique. Yesterday, he'd seen her in the bookstore with her head bent over a journal. All it took was one close look at the women's faces to realize it was only red hair they had in common with Maggie. And yet, in that first split second, he'd believed it was her.

His brain knew the truth. Maggie Keene, love of his life, had died in a car accident on her way to college in New York City twelve years ago.

But his heart had eyes too. They were made of hope and denial. They saw what was not there.

Damp with sweat, he apologized to the woman and slinked across the street to the flowers.

As the sun rose in the eastern sky and shot beams of golden light over the rolling hills, he stood between buckets of flowers outside the food market. To the west, fog hovered over the Pacific, eliminating the view of the beach and water. It would be hours before the mist conceded to the warmth of this late-June day and dissipated. Around noon, as if the dampness had never existed, the sky would transform into a deep blue and the long strand of beach would fill with umbrellas and children and dogs and picnics.

But at daybreak, the drowsy town dozed. It seemed to Jackson that the world at this hour was conversely dejected and hopeful.

Other than wetsuit-clad surfers who rode waves down at the long stretch of beach, the bustling movements of the grocery store staff was the only pocket of activity. Shades covered the windows of the rest of the storefronts along Main Street, including the bookstore, Violet's shop of refurbished items, Zane's bar and grill, a surf shop, Miss Rita's dance studio, as well as Jackson's medical office. *Doctor Jon Waller and Doctor Jackson Waller.* Father and son. Like Jackson had planned all his life.

Many early mornings since his return to town, he met Zane for a surf. They would head down to the beach with their boards like they had when they were young and ride the waves as if they still were. Today he would not surf. He had other business. Flowers and the cemetery. Today Maggie would have turned thirty. And, today, like every birthday since her death, Jackson would lay ranunculus on her grave.

Clayton, the floral manager, despite being in his late seventies, had arrived before dawn with the daily allotment of locally grown flowers. Now, he stood to the side as Jackson chose a pale pink ranunculus from the bucket. The intricacies of the ranunculus were surely some of God's finest work. Their petals were like layers of the finest crepe paper and reminded Jackson of ballerinas' tutus. They were perfect for Maggie.

He examined another before adding it to the bunch cradled in his arms. Only the best would do.

Just inside the door, Martha wriggled her plump fingers at Jackson as she prepared her organic coffee stand for the wave of locals and tourists who would soon invade. If sympathy could be expressed through the wriggle of fingertips, Martha was your girl. The produce manager, Fred, an old friend of Jackson's father, paused between apple stacking to tip his hat. Also in sympathy.

They knew why he was buying flowers at the crack of dawn. They even knew why it had to be ranunculus. Clayton had likely picked them that morning for just this purpose.

Ranunculus, once grown in his mother's garden, were Maggie's favorite. Everyone in town knew this. Everyone in town had grieved with him when they'd lost her. They didn't pretend she'd never existed like so many did when presented with death. Not here. Here they still talked about her. How talented she'd been. How beautiful. How sad it was that she was plucked from the world so young.

Clayton's 1970s beater of a pickup truck was parked in front of the store. Muddy tires told the story of its morning adventures to the flower farms.

"How's your truck holding up, Clayton?" Jackson asked.

Clayton took off his hat and brushed his hands through wild white hair before answering. "Heck, she's as good as she ever was. The old girl and I do our runs out to the flower farms every morning like we always have."

"Ever thought of treating yourself to a new truck?" Jackson already knew the answer, but it was fun to ask Clayton just to hear his rote response, followed by the lecture of the demise of practicality, thanks to the younger generation.

"No need to replace something that isn't broke, Doctor Waller. Your generation needs to learn that."

"We sure do, sir." Jackson smiled as he handed Clayton the bunch of chosen flowers. "Every time someone calls me Doctor Waller, I want to look behind me to see if my dad's there."

"Well, that's you now, son. We're real proud of you too. Speaking of your dad, I saw him golfing yesterday afternoon with Janet Mullen. I gather they're an item?"

"You're correct, sir."

"Never too late for an old dog, I guess. Not that I'd know. Harriet and me been together since we were eighteen years old. We figure we're the lucky ones, loving so young and for so long." Clayton wrapped the flowers in brown paper. With his shaky and weathered hands, he tied a pink bow around the cone-shaped container. Pink for Maggie.

Jackson grabbed money from his wallet, but Clayton pushed his hand away. "Not today, Doctor Waller."

Jackson knew better than to argue. "Thanks, Clayton."

"You tell Maggie I said hello."

"Will do." He bit his bottom lip as he jogged to his truck. Once inside, he rested his forehead against the steering wheel and gulped air. He would not cry. *Not today. Please, not today.*

The first time he'd thought he'd seen her was just a year after she died. On a busy street in Los Angeles, he'd spotted her waiting for a bus. He'd called out her name. When she didn't respond, he'd touched her shoulder. The stranger had turned and glared at him, afraid of his unwanted touch. Like today, he'd backed away, apologizing. It was not Maggie, but a cruel imposter.

For God's sake, she'd been dead for twelve years. Twelve years!

He was a doctor, a healer. Yet, he was sicker than any of his patients. Many people who'd lost a spouse or lover, especially when they were young, couldn't even recall their face. Not him.

What had Clayton said about his wife?

Lucky ones to have loved so young and for so long.

I thought that was you and me, Bird.

* * *

Ten minutes later, Jackson knelt on the damp grass and brushed the dust from Maggie's tombstone with his free hand before placing the flowers in the vase he kept there. It was empty of the ranunculus he'd brought several weeks ago, on the twelfth anniversary of Maggie's death. Zane must have been out to tidy up between then and now. They never spoke of it, but he knew Zane visited Maggie often too.

With his index finger, Jackson traced her name.

Maggie Laura Keene

June 27, 1987 – August 7, 2005

Our Songbird.

Jackson had nicknamed her Songbird when they were little. Over time, it morphed to just Bird, which he interchanged equally with Maggie. When they were teenagers, she used to tease him that he only called her Bird when he wanted to kiss her.

Fog hovered between pine, eucalyptus, and sycamore trees. A sparrow hopped between tree branches, singing. She would have loved a morning like this.

He arranged the bouquet so that each marvelous flower was shown to its best advantage, like ballerinas on a stage.

Sometimes he spoke out loud to her. Not today. Today his heart was so big and sore that it took up every ounce of energy just to breathe.

Thirty years old. What would she be like now? Would she have forgiven him for sending her away? Would she have ever gotten past the cruel and selfish way he'd ended things between them?

Would you, Bird?

Her answer seemed to drift up from the sea and rustle through the pines.

I would have, Jackson. It was a silly fight. We would have been back together by Christmas.

If only he hadn't made an ultimatum that night, she would be alive and by his side.

Either stay in California with me or we're done.

The last words he'd ever said to the girl he'd loved all his life had been cruel. He'd never had the chance to say he was sorry and beg for her forgiveness. He lived with that every single day.

She'd chosen her dream over him. Who could blame her? She'd seen him for who he was.

I never thought you could be this selfish.

Her father, Roger Keene, had been the one to tell them she was dead. His name was in the databases as "next of kin" instead of Jackson's parents, who had raised her from the time she was ten years old. That bitter irony was lost on no one. The bastard had pounded on the Wallers' door two mornings after Maggie drove out of town. *She's been killed in a car accident,* he told them. Somewhere in Kansas she'd lost control of the car. The police had suspected she'd fallen asleep.

Roger Keene had been the one to go to Kansas and collect her ashes. He'd been the one to arrange for her urn to be buried in the family plot next to her mother. There was nothing Jackson or his father could do. They were only her family by love, not blood. Jackson balled his fists, remembering how Roger Keene had played the grieving father at Maggie's memorial. As if he'd had anything to do with raising her. As if he'd ever loved anyone but his narcissistic, brutal self. In further irony, the bastard was still alive. Sick and dying, but alive. *May he rot in hell.*

Jackson tugged at a tuft of overgrown grass at the edge of the tombstone and tore it into bits. The lazy groundskeeper should use clippers. This plot should be kept tidy and beautiful.

His gaze moved to Maggie's mother's tombstone. At least her father had put Maggie next to her mother. *Mae needs a flower too.* He placed one from the bouquet over her grave.

Oh, Bird. I still miss you so much. I'm afraid I'm insane.

He hadn't even confessed to his therapist that his Maggie sightings had become a daily occurrence. How much longer could he keep Sharon waiting for a proposal? How much longer until Maggie no longer filled his restless dreams at night?

The sparrow hopped from the tree and landed on the top of the tombstone. She chirped at him. Did she sing *move on, move on, move on*?

Happy birthday, sweet Bird. I love you. Say hi to my mom.

* * *

Jackson had a good poker hand. In fact, it was a great hand. A full house. He couldn't remember the last time he'd been up during a Dog's poker game. Not that they played often now that they were adults. They'd come a long way from the geeky underclassmen at USC assigned to the same dorm room who'd named themselves the Dogs after the famous painting of dogs playing poker. With time had come responsibilities. What had been a weekly game during their college days had become more like a once-a-month game at best.

He looked around the table to gauge the others' hands. *Not much to see.* Almost twelve years they'd played poker together and he still couldn't read his friends' faces.

Brody never allowed his expression to show anything but a competitive intensity, perfected during his time on the football field as the quarterback for San Francisco's professional football team. He loved to win and would do almost anything to do so, on or off the field. His fiancée, Kara, called it his *game face*: glittering eyes, mouth set in a straight line with his square jaw clenched. The rest of the Dogs called it "resting douche face." God forbid any of them would ever give one of the others a compliment without some form of mockery.

Truth was, Brody was the heart of their group. Without him, Jackson suspected the entire dynamic would fall apart. He was a born leader and, whether any of them liked to admit it, good-looking, smart, *and* humble. Kara said no one should be given that much talent and beauty in one lifetime. Whether it was fair or not, the man recently threw a sixty-yard pass to win the Super Bowl.

His twenty-million-dollar-a-year contract helped him build this house that overlooked the ocean. Not only had he built suites for his mother and their longtime housekeeper, Flora, but he'd also made sure to build a man cave for the Dogs' poker games and to watch sports, including Brody's games during football season. With dark walls and bulky, masculine furniture, the room was like a commercial for bourbon and tobacco. In one section of the room, a wraparound sofa faced a giant, flat-screen television. On the other end, a round table with five chairs had been custom built for the five Dogs.

Tonight, the scent of the sea and freshly cut grass drifted in through the open windows and mingled with the smells of leather and expensive booze. Brody and Kyle each had a tumbler of Glenlivet scotch. Zane sipped from his usual vodka on the rocks with a squeeze of lime. Jackson had a glass of a Paso Robles Cabernet. Yes, he was a wine snob, which could be blamed on his father.

"I raise you one," Jackson said.

"Good hand, Doctor Waller?" Brody tossed in two chips. "I raise you another one."

"It's creepy when you call me Doctor Waller," Jackson said.

"You sound like you have a crush on him," Kyle said. He also tossed in two chips.

Brody smiled. "I *do* have a crush on him." When Brody smiled, his face transformed from intense to striking. He'd been doing a lot of smiling since becoming engaged to Kara.

"Doesn't the whole town? Oh, Doctor Waller, can you look at the rash on my arm?" Zane fluttered his eyelashes as he slid two chips across the table and into the pot. "I think you need to rub some ointment on it. Maybe back at my place?"

"Aren't you talking about yourself, Shaw?" Jackson asked. "You haven't deluded yourself into thinking women are coming into The Oar for the food?"

"You know it's my food," Zane said. "My rock-hard abs are just a bonus."

Jackson looked at Zane. One hand held his cards. The other rested on the table. No movement. Zane could keep a stoic expression while riding the toughest wave, and he ran his bar and grill without ever breaking a sweat. In addition, truth be told, his restaurant's food was fantastic. That said, he was a terrible poker player. He gave himself away when he had a good hand by tapping his fingertips against the tabletop like a miniature drum roll. Every single time. In typical Dog style, no one had ever pointed this out to him, which is why he hardly ever won a game. When he did, it was usually for a small pot. They knew to fold when they saw those fingers start to tap.

"I raise you," Jackson said. Three chips. This was going to cost him if someone had a better hand.

"It's definitely Zane's pretty face bringing them into the bar," Kyle said. "Did you see that group of girls at the back table last night? Every time you walked by, I thought the brunette was going to faint."

"I heard one of them squealing about your eyes," Brody said, matching the bet. "She called them turquoise, as if that's a real eye color."

Zane rolled his said turquoise eyes as he tossed more chips into the pot. "You guys exaggerate. Plus, those ladies were barely old enough to drink, which makes them too young for us."

"Twenty-one's legal, man," Kyle said.

"We're thirty, in case you've forgotten," Jackson said.

"I refuse to acknowledge this blasphemy," Kyle said. "Anyway, age is merely a number."

"Have you heard of the Peter Pan syndrome?" Brody asked. "You might look into it."

"I never look into anything called a *syndrome*," Kyle said.

Jackson studied Kyle. What kind of hand did he have? The jerk almost always won.

Kyle raised an eyebrow and winked at him. "You know you can't read me for crap."

"I can," Jackson said. "Like a book."

"No one can read me. Years of dedication and practicing my poker face in the mirror has made me who I am." Raised in poverty, Kyle was making up for it in adulthood by buying up half of California as a real estate developer. His latest venture was a new resort here in town.

"That's probably true," Zane said. "As much as it disgusts me to imagine how many hours a day you spend looking at yourself."

"Hold on there, pretty boy," Kyle said to Zane. "I recall a certain roommate who used to spend hours fixing his hair."

"That's a lie and you know it." Zane grinned and pointed to his sun-kissed blond curls. "This is just natural beauty."

"You *are* pretty," Kyle said. "If only you'd use your good looks for good. Me, I use mine to give pleasure to as many women as I can."

"Oh, brother," Brody said as he rolled his eyes. "That's where you're wrong. Giving pleasure to one woman—*the* woman is where it's at."

"And deny the rest of them?" Kyle ran his hands down his muscular torso. "That would just be cruel."

"No one likes a braggart," Jackson said. Kyle *wasn't* bragging. His angular face, patrician nose, and dark blue eyes that glittered with intelligence and curiosity caught women's attention. However, it was his utter self-confidence and wit that made women fall into his arms without a thought to the heartbreak waiting around the corner the moment they hinted of any real feelings. Kyle was a cad of the first degree.

"You *do* look better now that you pay someone at Nordstrom to dress you," Zane said.

"Rachel is her name and she's very clever," Kyle said.

"She'd have to be, given the raw material," Brody said.

When they'd first met as freshman at USC, Kyle had been skinny and nerdy. Now, a dedication to fitness and a personal shopper at Nordstrom had transformed him from nerdy to smoldering.

"Very funny. Zane, you should call Rachel immediately for help," Kyle said. "If you ever want to dress like an adult instead of an overgrown surfer dude."

"I will never dress like an adult again," Zane said. "I burned my suits when I left L.A. I have no interest in looking slick."

"Except for my wedding," Brody said.

"Right. For Kara, I will make an exception," Zane said. "It's not every day I'm asked to walk a beautiful bride down the aisle."

"I'm not slick, by the way. Some woman called me wolfish the other night," Kyle said.

"Wolfish? I don't think that was a compliment," Brody said, laughing.

"Really? I liked it," Kyle said. "It made me feel dangerous."

"Speaking of dangerous, it's time to face the music, boys." Jackson displayed his poker hand on the table. The Dogs made various noises of disgust.

Jackson smiled as he scooped the winning chips into his pile. "It's fun to win."

"It happens so seldom, though," Kyle said.

"Maybe this is the start of a new chapter for me," Jackson said. Four of the five Dogs were here, which lifted his spirits. Lance, Brody's younger brother, was the only Dog missing. He was in New York working on Wall Street. Hopefully, they would see him next month for Flora and Dax's wedding. Although, no one could win against Lance. He had a photographic memory and Jackson suspected an ability to count cards. If Lance were a less ethical man, he would be in Vegas right now beating the house.

A new chapter? That's what he needed. But could he make one?

"You okay, buddy?" Zane asked him.

Jackson looked up. "Me? Sure, yeah. Fine."

"We know what today is," Brody said. "You doing all right?"

"It's okay if you're not," Kyle said.

Jackson looked at him, surprised. Kyle was usually the first to run when a conversation turned serious. "I'm struggling a little." *The understatement of the century.* "She would've turned thirty today."

"Yeah, I know," Zane said.

"I should be better than I am," Jackson said. "No one grieves this long unless they're a little screwed in the head."

"You loved her very much," Brody said. "And today's her birthday. I understand, now that I love Kara. To lose her might kill me."

"It's been twelve years," Jackson said.

"What does your therapist think?" Brody asked.

Jackson shrugged and sipped from his glass. The wine tasted bitter tonight. "She thinks I've never fully believed that Maggie was dead, therefore I haven't moved on like I should."

"What kind of half-cocked theory is that?" Zane asked.

"Right?" Kyle said. "You know she's dead. You just wish she wasn't."

"Anyway, there's no instruction manual on grief," Brody said. "I still miss my dad every single day."

The urge to confess his fears trampled all reason, all self-preservation. If he could tell anyone the truth, it was the Dogs. "I've been seeing her everywhere. Since I moved back here. Any woman with red hair—my mind thinks she's Maggie. This is not normal, guys."

"It's just because you're back here," Kyle said. "When I went home a few years ago, it felt like my mom was around every corner. And she's been gone a long time."

"Sure. It's all the memories here," Zane said. "Stirring things up."

"The ring I bought for Sharon's been sitting in my desk drawer for months," Jackson said. "I need to ask her. She's *expecting* me to ask her. The longer I put it off, the less fair it is to her."

The room went silent. No one would meet his gaze.

Finally, Zane spoke. "There's no rush. No timeline."

"Proposing to her isn't going to make you miss Maggie any less," Kyle said.

Again, Kyle surprised him. What did he know about missing someone?

"It might," Jackson said. "Like a line in the sand for my mind. I love Sharon. She's amazing. You all know that." Sharon Fox was a research doctor who looked like a supermodel. She loved Jackson despite how he'd strung her along for years. Heck, they'd been friends for six years before she convinced him to become involved romantically. "She's hung in there for a long time."

"What about her job in L.A.?" Brody asked. "I thought she didn't want to move here."

"She told me she will—*if* there's a ring on her finger," Jackson said. "She'll commute to a university in San Francisco once she secures another position."

"I don't think she'll like it here," Zane said.

"What's not to like?" Jackson asked.

No one spoke for a few seconds. Kyle plucked strips of the paper label from his beer bottle. Brody drank down the entirety of his scotch. Zane clasped his hands behind his head and stared at the light fixture that hung over the table.

"What is it?" Jackson asked. "What's wrong?"

"We want you to be happy," Zane said.

"I want that too," Jackson said. *I don't want to slowly lose my mind.* "Sometimes I wonder if coming back here was a mistake."

"No way, man. This was your plan since we were kids," Zane said.

Maggie was my plan, too. And look what happened there.

"Maybe you're right. It's just being back here. All the memories." Jackson smiled to assure them he was fine, but his dry mouth stretched painfully against his teeth.

"They'll fade," Zane said. "I'm sure of it."

"I'm going to marry Sharon. I owe her that much," Jackson said. "And I need to know you guys are on my side."

"Of course we are," Kyle said. "Thick and thin, like we always promised."

"No matter what," Brody said.

"Sure. Whatever you decide, we'll get behind it a hundred percent," Zane said.

Kyle raised his glass. "To the Dogs. We have one another's backs. No matter what goes down."

"Always," they repeated as they clinked glasses.

"Now somebody deal," Kyle said. "I'm in the mood to win."

* * *

The next day, Jackson finished putting the cast on three-year-old Dakota Ellis's arm. "All done, buddy. You did a fantastic job of staying still."

Dakota grinned. "Mommy said to."

His mother, Violet, sat in the chair with the same worried expression they'd come in with, even though her son's tears had long since dried. Jackson knew a thing or two about worry.

"Now, off you go. Ask Nurse Kara for a lollipop while I talk to your mom for a minute," Jackson said as he scooped the little boy off the table.

Dakota headed out the door, staring at his cast.

Jackson turned back to Violet. "There's no need to look so worried. He'll be good as new in a month."

"It's not that so much as, well, I'm struggling. Money-wise."

"Is business slow?" he asked.

Violet owned a shop in town that sold goods made from refurbished items, like tires into purses and so forth. Jackson had bought a bracelet made from chicken wire for Sharon. It had not gone over well.

Violet also headed up the committee in town with a sole purpose to protect the historical parts of town from development.

"My rent at the shop is too high compared to what I'm able to sell things for," Violet said. "If my parents hadn't moved to their vacation place in South America and left me their house here, I'd be in deep trouble. Still, with self-employment taxes, property taxes, not to mention the price of health insurance—I'm barely making it. A broken arm wasn't in the budget." Violet's bottom lip trembled. "Do you guys have payment plans?"

"We *can*, but insurance will cover most of this," he said.

"Not *my* insurance. My deductible's six thousand dollars before they pay a dime. I have to pay over five hundred a month for our premiums, and I make too much to get a government subsidy for Dakota." She wiped under her eyes. "I'm sorry. I'm just so tired."

"Don't apologize." How was she supposed to get ahead when the system was rigged against her? "Anyway, you're in luck. We happen to have a special running this month on little boy's broken arms. They're free with a purchase of a lollipop."

"Jackson, no. I can't take your charity."

His mother, who had run the office when Jackson was a kid, had conveniently forgotten to bill people for visits if she knew they were struggling financially. "You let me know when things are looking up and we'll bill you then."

"I won't forget," she said.

"I'm not worried."

Violet tucked her long, honey-hued hair behind both ears and lifted the corners of her mouth in a sad smile. "It's been a rough few years." Despite it all, Violet was even prettier than she'd been in high school, with hair the color of honey and small, delicate features. As Kyle had pointed out the first time he was introduced to her, she had a beautiful figure, thanks to yoga. Although, *beautiful figure* wasn't exactly how Kyle had described her. He'd said something more along the lines of *sizzling hot body*, if Jackson recalled correctly.

However, Kyle's admiration of Violet was short-lived. She was a zealot when it came to their little town, crusading to keep the town historically pure, which created a massive conflict with Kyle. She did not approve of new construction, especially a large resort, and was not shy about expressing her displeasure. Usually with a picket sign.

"How's Sharon? Have you convinced her to move here yet?" Violet asked.

"She's been pretty clear that a proposal equals her commitment to moving." He kept his voice light.

"Well, it's a big step," Violet said.

"Yes. It is. Very much so." He cringed at the uncertainty in his voice.

"I'm happy for you."

Jackson scratched his neck under the stiff collar of his button-down shirt. "What about you? Are you seeing anyone special?"

"No. I have Dakota, so you know, not much chance I'll attract anyone decent. Way too much baggage."

"Everyone has baggage. Don't give up on love. You're a catch, with or without your adorable boy. Some guy's going to be lucky to have you."

Violet rose from the chair and smoothed the front of her cotton sundress. "Thanks, Jackson. I didn't realize a pep talk was an additional service you provide."

"Anytime. Now go open your shop. Town's practically crawling with tourists today."

After he escorted Violet out to the lobby, he went into his office and opened his desk drawer. A small box nestled next to freshly sharpened pencils. He opened it; the diamond ring sparkled under the lights. *Just do it.*

His pulse quickened to the pace of a hummingbird's wings. Sharon was a good woman. Even if he had to keep reminding himself, he was a lucky man. Nothing good ever came from his overanalysis. Or did it? Never mind. He must stop this nonsense.

It was time. He had to propose to Sharon and make it official. Time to grow up and start a family. Move forward with someone else. Finally.

* * *

For lunch, Jackson and Kara ate sandwiches in his office. Jackson had his feet up on the desk. Kara sat in the armchair across from him with her food spread out on her lap.

Their former nurse had retired. Jackson suspected due to the young Doctor Waller's presence. She hadn't liked change, which was just fine with him. He and his father had jumped at the opportunity to hire Kara, not only because she was engaged to Brody, but because she was great at her job. Additionally, because she was a nurse practitioner, it allowed the elder Doctor Waller to reduce his hours. Therefore, freeing his dad up to spend time with his new girlfriend.

His new *girlfriend*, Janet Mullen, formerly known as Brody's *mother*.

Jackson tossed a baby carrot at Kara. "This is the official end of your first month. How does it feel?"

Kara caught the carrot and held it between two fingers like a baton. Her engagement ring glittered under the lights. Apparently, rich football players like Brody could afford diamonds the size of a small country.

Brody hadn't hesitated to propose. He hadn't kept a ring hidden in his desk drawer for months.

"It feels fantastic to be back at work," Kara said. "I didn't realize how much I missed it. Even though this is quite different from my old job in Philly."

"Not the same as a trauma unit in a big hospital?"

"Not quite. Brody's happy to have me out of the house. I was driving him crazy."

"Impossible."

"No, for real. I've been a bit obsessive about the wedding plans. Surprise. It turns out I'm a control freak when it comes to my own wedding."

Jackson smiled as he opened a container of hummus. "I can't imagine he cares one way or the other about the details."

"That's the problem. I can't get him to engage about colors or flowers or anything. Other than he wanted all the Dogs to be in the wedding party, he couldn't care less what I do."

"The Dogs guarantee a fun party," Jackson said.

"*Honor* guarantees a fun party," Kara said.

"Until it dips over into chaos." Honor was almost an honorary Dog. She'd been Brody's assistant for over five years. Although feisty, opinionated, and bossy, she was fiercely loyal to all of them. Jackson suspected that her childhood in foster homes had a lot to do with her fervent protection of the people she thought of as family.

"Any luck on finding a house?" Kara asked. Cliffside Bay rarely had houses for sale. The past few months had been no exception.

"No, and I need to find a house of my own. I think my dad wants to propose to Janet," he said.

"I think so too," Kara said.

Even his dad was moving on.

"With Flora moving out to live with Dax and Janet moving in with your dad, we're going to have an empty nest," Kara said.

"You can fill it up with babies, maybe?" Jackson said. He wanted to fill a house with babies.

"Maybe. Not right away. I want Brody all to myself for a while longer."

They munched on their lunches in compatible silence for a few minutes before the conversation turned to Flora.

"Are you bringing Sharon to Flora and Dax's wedding?" Kara asked.

"I'm not sure. She might have to work." Had he even mentioned it to her? "Why?"

"Flora said you hadn't RSVP'd yet."

"I didn't? Shoot, tell her I'm sorry. I'll get it in the mail today," Jackson said.

"Good because Flora's worried about you. She said it's not like you to forget a detail."

Flora was too smart. She was the Mullen family's long-time housekeeper and was like a second mother to Brody and his younger brother Lance. When Brody's father died, Flora and Janet had agreed to move to Cliffside Bay and live with Brody.

"Cameron's giving Flora away. I'm making sure to wear water-proof mascara," Kara said. "For their wedding and my own."

After a health scare, Flora had decided to look for her high school sweetheart, Dax, and the baby she'd been forced to give up when she was only sixteen. She found them both. Cameron Post, their son, was in his forties. Dax Hansen was a widower with one daughter, Mary. It took a matter of days for Dax and Flora to fall back into love. Now they were getting married in the church in town and planned to move into a house on Brody's property for part of the year. The rest of the time they would live in Dax's house on the Oregon coast.

"It's wedding season around here," Jackson said. First Dax and Flora, followed weeks later by Kara and Brody. Soon his father and Janet would marry. Would his wedding to Sharon be the third or fourth of their group of friends? Why did that thought not fill him with excitement?

"Brody told me you're going to propose to Sharon," Kara said. "She's smart and beautiful. I hope you will be as happy as Brody and I are."

"Thanks. The Dogs didn't seem too keen on the idea at our poker game last night."

Kara fiddled with the silver bracelet she wore on her wrist. "Well, you boys are sometimes in one another's business a little too much. It's sweet."

"Sometimes annoying."

Kara smiled. "Listen, if you feel it's right with Sharon, then no one should tell you otherwise." She tapped just above her chest. "You're the only one who knows your heart. Whatever you decide, we're all here. The Dogs, Honor, me."

"Thick and thin," Jackson said. "That's what we've always agreed on. Even if we are a little too much in one another's business."

"You guys really are." The corners of Kara's brown eyes crinkled as she laughed.

"Why is that funny?" Jackson grinned.

"No reason, boss. No reason at all."

CHAPTER THREE

Maggie

MAGGIE'S RENTAL CAR smelled of cheap plastic and the remnants of the last occupant's cologne. The cloying scent clung to the seats and the inside of her nose, as if she had a companion riding shotgun. Except there was no companion.

Stop your whining. You're fine alone.

She knew every twist, turn, and bump of the coastal highway that took her from San Francisco to Cliffside Bay. Time had passed, yet the turns of this road remained unchanged. Her eyes filled as the pain of regret, like a hundred porcupine quills, stabbed her. Why had she left? Had she made the right decision to leave Jackson and the only home she had ever known to chase the tail of a dragon? Had a part of her remained here, like a ghost that forever surfed the waves or danced in the sea breezes?

A few minutes later, Maggie reached the boomerang-shaped curve in the road and turned from the two-lane highway into the town of Cliffside Bay. She did not need to look for signs indicating the way. There were none anyway. Visitors were not welcome. The state of California diligently put road signs up to communicate with the intrepid traveler. As soon as the state put them up, the residents took them down, always in the middle of the night without leaving so much as a trace of evidence. Still, tourists found the seaside gem and passed it on to others, along with specific instructions on how to get there.

Cliffside Bay. A town who wished to be hidden from the world like Sleeping Beauty's castle. If only people would stop talking.

The late afternoon sun hovered high on the horizon and beat down on the waters of the Pacific. She slowed the vehicle and adjusted her sunglasses that had slipped down the narrow bridge of her nose. Not much had changed. Buildings battered by damp sea air lined the main street. A church marked the beginning of town, painted brilliant white and adorned with a steeple that hosted more resting seagulls than the pews hosted sinners. Once upon a time, she'd imagined her wedding to Jackson would take place there. Back when she was young and stupid.

A hardware store next to a laundromat, owned by the Wilsons, nestled between a group of eucalyptus trees. The post office, a bookstore, the library, and a small park took up the middle section of town. Fresh flowers covered the sidewalk in front of the local grocery. Would there be ranunculus? Did Clayton still drive his beat-up truck out to the flower farms in the early morning hours?

Zane's dad's bar, The Oar, a local fixture since the turn of the century, had been given a facelift since she'd left. When she'd worked there in high school, the building had only a few windows and a weathered awning that might collapse at any moment. Now, picture windows that doubled as doors opened to the street. Patrons spilled out onto the sidewalk, dining at tables under blue umbrellas. One could always tell the tourists by their sunburned backs. Locals were some shade of tan with hair and clothing bleached from the sun.

Was Zane's father still the owner? Was Mr. Shaw alive? She'd been gone so long, she suspected many of the people she knew had either died or moved along.

Doctor Waller's face flashed across her mind. At Lily Waller's funeral, he and Jackson had sat together in the front pew of the church with their heads bowed as Maggie sang "Carolina In My Mind," Lily's favorite. Maggie had sung it to Lily dozens of times when she was sick. *One more time, Maggie. Just until I fall asleep.*

Jackson Waller. He remained in her imagination as clearly as the day twelve years ago when they'd said goodbye. He had eyes the color of the ocean on a sunny day and golden curls that fell over his forehead. His muscular surfer body had burned under her innocent touch back then. Their angry last words haunted her. He would not go. She could not stay.

Never mind that. I am here to say goodbye, not to remember.

The memories rushed in as she came upon the old-fashioned pharmacy with faded signs in the window that said, "No Skateboards" and "Clothing Not Optional." How many afternoons had she and Jackson sat at the counter having sodas when they were kids?

In high school, bonfires on the beach had been their entertainment of choice. Maggie would play her guitar and sing. After each song, Jackson would wrap his arm around her shoulders and beam with pride. *My Bird.* Maggie, the future Broadway sensation. How she'd believed in herself back then. She'd seen herself through the eyes of Jackson and Zane, one her love and the other her best friend—the three of them fueled by their dreams and one another and the surf and music. And love.

Don't think of it or him or anything else. You have a job to do. Get in and get out.

Miss Rita's dance studio was next to Doctor Waller's office. Curtains were drawn over the large front windows to keep the sun from warping the wooden floor. Was it Miss Rita's in name only now? Had Rita, her former mentor, retired or moved away? Did a new owner teach the children ballet and fill their heads with dreams of Broadway? It stung, even after all these years, that her letters to Miss Rita had returned unopened.

After Maggie left, everyone deleted her from their lives. Like she'd never existed, simply because she dared to go after her dream, dared to leave them. Even Zane. Other than Jackson, his betrayal had hurt the most.

She swallowed the bile that rose to her throat. Every person she'd ever loved had sided with Jackson. His dream they could support. Hers, not so much.

As she drew nearer, she saw that the doctor's office sign now said: Doctor Jon Waller and Doctor Jackson Waller. He *had* done it. Jackson was his father's partner. She should be happy for him. She really should. It had been twelve years, for heaven's sake. She was a child when she loved him. An eighteen-year-old knew nothing of love.

He was probably married by now with little children, like they'd planned. Maybe he'd bought the house they'd always wanted. How stupid she'd been. The way they'd stood outside the gates of the Arnoult house and dreamed of their life together embarrassed her now. She bet he had it with someone, though. A man like Jackson wasn't single at thirty.

She was six years old when Tyler Mueller tripped her on the playground on the first day of grade school. "Ugly redhead," he said before kicking her in the gut. By the time she rose crying from the muddy ground, Jackson had directed several pointed punches to Tyler's nose. As Tyler covered his bloody nose with his hands, Jackson offered his to Maggie. "Come on, Maggie Keene. I'll walk you home."

They'd walked home holding hands. He'd told her funny stories. She couldn't remember what they were, only that they made her laugh.

When they'd reached her house, he gazed at her with those big blue eyes of his. "Don't you believe for one second what Tyler Mueller says. You're the prettiest girl in the whole world. I'll come by and get you in the morning for school."

She'd glanced nervously at the front door of her house. Jackson must not know about her father. How he hit them for any small thing. A boy coming to the house might be one of the small things.

"I'll meet you on the corner." She pointed to a half block up the street.

From that day forward, he had walked Maggie to and from school. From that day forward, Maggie loved him.

Coming back to this town was not going to help rid her mind of the memories. The faster she could get out of here the better.

Push it aside.

She drove another block. Her stomach turned at the sight of her father's house, tucked behind scrubs and a tall fir tree. She slowed the car as her pulse quickened. The house had been in her mother's family since the day it was built in 1901. Painted white with green shutters, the outside was almost charming, despite its obvious neglect and decay that had made it shabby and concave, like an old woman's face that had fallen from years of sun and sorrow.

The yard lay in shambles. Uncut grass had thinned in spots, yellowed in others. Unruly branches of scrubs stuck out this way and that, like little boys' hair after a long summer of playing. Empty flowerpots, cracked, weathered, or in various states of disintegration, made a haphazard pattern on the steps of the porch.

Shaking, she turned her eyes back to the street and pulled away from the curb. My God, she was still afraid of him. Thirty years old and the thought of him chilled her blood.

Maggie parked in the public parking lot above the long strip of beach. She wanted to see the bench. Just briefly and then she would go do what she had to do. As she crossed the lot to the bench, she squinted into the unforgiving afternoon sun. June in Cliffside Bay—the height of beach season. This, too, had not changed. Umbrellas dotted the beach. Kids dug in the sand. Adults lounged in chairs or on blankets. Surfers rode waves. Boogie boarders screamed with delight as they plummeted to shore.

Maggie opened her arms and threw back her head as if she were a mermaid waiting for her human lover to return. Sea breezes tossed her long hair about her face. Sun warmed her sinewy arms as she breathed in the briny scent of her childhood, of home.

She trailed her fingers across the engraving on the back of the bench. *M.K. + J.W.* She'd kissed Jackson so many times right here at the end of this bench, where a knot in the wood made a spiral like the peace symbol.

Maggie sat and tilted her face to the sky, knowing sun wasn't good for her skin and would no doubt double her copious freckles. It no longer mattered what she looked like. There would be no more headshots, auditions, or opening nights.

Such a crybaby. Face the music. She rose from the bench. Her father must be faced. But first, the cemetery. She'd stop at the market and pick up flowers for her mother's grave. Was Clayton still the flower man? *Cliffside Bay, I've missed you.*

The breeze stole her sigh. A seagull cried a long, mournful note against the percussion of the crashing waves. Had she heard someone call her name? She turned, but there was no one there. A man hidden behind a surfboard ran down the slope of the cement boardwalk to the beach.

In an instant, her last night with Jackson came rushing back.

That night a full moon was high over the sea. Eucalyptus mingled with salty air.

"I want you to stay here. For me, Bird. For us."

"I can't pass up the scholarship to New York. It's wrong of you to ask me."

"Our dreams aren't compatible. Did you ever think of that?" he asked.

"Don't you love me anymore?" she whispered, tears sliding down her cheeks to find a resting place in the collar of her leotard. "Did you ever love me?"

"Love doesn't mean it's meant to be." His voice sounded strangled and unfamiliar, almost clinical. Below them, waves crashed in a pitiless rhythm. The sea didn't care if hearts splintered and broke. "Just like someone can die from lung cancer who never smoked a day in her life."

"Jackson. I know you're hurting." *I'm motherless too.* Who was this stranger? This angry, young man? He was not her Jackson. Not the boy who had defended and cherished her.

"Go to New York. Go live your dream without me."

"Jackson, no. I can't leave like this. Please, don't be this way." She reached for his hand in one last, desperate attempt to stall him —to remind him with her touch that they'd loved each other for a lifetime already. But he jerked away, leaving only the dark night between her fingers.

"If you go to New York, we won't make it. You'll change. I'll be your past, not your future," Jackson said. "Either stay in California with me, or we're done."

"I never thought you could be this selfish," she said.

"Well, I am." He slipped into the night. To this day she could not hear a car engine roar to life without catching her breath. *The sound of goodbye.*

She'd spent the last twelve years learning how to let go.

Apparently, she was a slow learner.

CHAPTER FOUR

Jackson

JACKSON TOSSED HIS surfboard onto the wet sand and fell to his knees. *No, no, no. It wasn't her. It was not her.* He pressed his forehead into his surfboard. It had happened again. As he grabbed his board from the back of his truck, his eyes had been drawn to a woman standing by the bench. Her back was to him, so he could not see her face, but her slender, graceful body and long, red hair was so like Maggie that he'd stopped and stared. Had he said her name out loud?

God, he had. What was wrong with him? Was this the slow descent into madness? Is this how it happened?

A wave larger than the rest broke near him. He held onto the surfboard and dug his toes into the sand as the wave tried to pull him out to sea. His chest squeezed tight as he gasped for air. No surfing today. He would go home and talk to his dad or call Brody. Anything to keep this spiral from pulling him into the dark abyss.

He stood and held his board like a shield over his torso and looked back to the grassy cliff where the bench told his young love story in the crevices of its wood. The woman was gone. Had she even existed or was he now seeing Bird where there was nothing but empty space? Stepping back from the water, he set his board aside and slipped out of his wetsuit. The sun on his back would warm him, stop this shaking. Heal him.

He sat with the sun on his back until the pounding of his heart returned to its usual dull thud. Around him, children shouted with glee. Smiling dogs chased the surf. A young mother fixed sandwiches under an umbrella. Teenage girls in bikinis tossed a Frisbee back and forth. An elderly couple passed by, arm in arm, sunhats shielding their delicate skin from the afternoon rays. All of them alive. Going about the business of living. He was chasing ghosts.

I need help.

When he got to the parking lot, he tossed his surfboard into the back of his truck and drove up the street to his office. It was Saturday. The parking lot was empty. He didn't bother to lock his truck. No time to waste. He unlocked the back door of his office and strode down the hallway. He yanked open his desk drawer and grabbed the box with the engagement ring in it. Tonight, Sharon would come for dinner. Tonight, he would propose. Enough insanity. *Enough.*

At his dad's house, he left his board in the garage and hung his wetsuit on the railing to dry. He stopped to hose the sand from his legs and feet before climbing the stairs to the deck.

"Jackson, is that you?" It was his father, calling from inside the study. The windows were open. Jackson could make out his shadow through filmy curtains. He was in his favorite chair, probably reading.

"Yes. Going to take a shower." He entered the airy kitchen. A heap of lemons in his mother's favorite blue bowl adorned the table. A pile of mail was next to it, left by the housekeeper. *Go about the business of living.* He rifled through the mail. Nothing of note caught his attention, other than a travel brochure for France. Was his father thinking of taking Janet to Europe? The last vacation they'd taken was to Italy before his mother got sick. The idea settled like a spiny ball inside his chest. A breeze from the open window mingled with the scent of lemons. A memory slipped through the passage of time. *Lemons. Italy.*

He was sixteen again. His mother wasn't sick. It would be a year before they knew about the cancer. His father had surprised his wife, Jackson, and Maggie with a trip to Italy. For two weeks, they stayed in a hillside village that overlooked the Mediterranean.

It was late afternoon and everyone else had wanted a nap, so Jackson had taken the winding stairs down to the water and swam with the brightly colored fish until his eyes stung from too much salt water. Half way up the stairs to their rented apartment that seemed carved from the hillside, he stopped to catch his breath. Late afternoon sun toasted his bare shoulders. Salt water crystalized in the coarse hair on his arms. A gasp rose from his chest at the beauty that stretched out before him. Even after a week, it made his knees weak to see the color of the water.

Rested, he tore up the stairs. With a suddenness that surprised him, he yearned to see Maggie, like it had been days not hours since he was last with her. Maggie reclined on a chaise under the shade of a blue awning. An open paperback on her chest covered the top of her purple bikini. Her pale skin was flushed pink from heat and sun.

"Did you bring me a fish?" She smiled in that slow way, with that mouth that was like a pink rose. He was mad for her. Practically sick with love. If only he could tell her the truth. *I'm in love with you. I always have been.*

"No, they were too fast for me." The gray stone of the patio felt pleasantly coarse under his bare feet as he crossed over to her. "Plus, I didn't bring a spear."

"No spear? How American of you."

"I'm sorry to disappoint you." He grinned as he sat on the end of her chaise. The shade soothed his scratchy eyes.

"Well, we'll have to be satisfied with bread then." She brushed her white, slender throat with the tips of her fingers. "Italy's making me fat. Miss Rita will be disgusted with me by the time we get home."

He raised an eyebrow. "I don't think you have much to worry about." She was too slender, despite the muscles that formed almost every inch of her. "You've gotten more freckles since we've been here," he said.

"Don't tell me. Just pretend they're not there."

"I love them. They're like a sky filled with nutmeg stars."

"That's a terrible metaphor. Stars aren't the color of nutmeg."

"They should be." He scooted closer to her. "How about this? The sea's almost as beautiful as you, but not quite."

"You can't compare a girl and the sea," she said. "It's not fair."

"To the sea?"

"Yes, right." She smirked and sat up straighter, then crossed her legs. *Crisscross apple sauce, like in their first-grade class.*

"Do you really think I'm beautiful?" she asked. "Not like from one friend to the other, but the other kind. The other kind of love."

"Bird, don't you know? Don't you know how I feel?"

"I don't know," she said. "I only know what I hope."

"What is that?"

"That it's the other kind of love. Not pretend like when we were kids and we'd talk about getting married and living in the French house, but for real."

"I've never pretended. I've always known. It's you and me, Bird. Not like other people."

"You love me?"

"Yes."

"Good. Because I love you too."

He would kiss her for the first time right here with the scent from the lemons and the sea. "May I kiss you?" he asked.

"You don't have to ask," she whispered. "Just do it."

He placed his mouth on hers. What did one do? Wriggle their lips from side to side.

But he needn't have worried. Girls must have instincts about these things because Maggie wrapped her arms around his neck and opened her rosebud mouth just slightly and suddenly they were kissing. Gently, like the fluttering of butterfly wings.

"You taste like the sea," she whispered against his mouth.

"You smell so just unbelievably good."

"That's the air," she said, laughing.

"No, it's you. I can't even describe how you smell. Not even with those fancy adjectives on our SAT study guide."

"You're hopeless."

From inside the apartment, he heard the faint sound of his mother and father's laughter coming from the kitchen, followed by the pop of a wine cork.

If heaven were a moment, it was this.

Now, he came back to purgatory.

* * *

Jackson showered and then dressed in nice jeans and a button-down shirt in his childhood bedroom. It still had a single bed, although the sailboat wallpaper had been replaced with light blue paint. Leaning closer to the mirror, he noticed his eyes were blood-shot. He reached for the eye drops next to his wallet.

Jackson kept his hair cropped short. The sun had bleached it to the color of wet straw since he'd been back in town. However, there seemed to be less of it these days. Either that, or his forehead had grown larger.

His cell phone blinked with a message from Sharon.

Just landed in S.F. Will be there around 8:00.

He tugged on the collar of his shirt, suddenly warm.

Jackson typed a message back to her. *Great. I'm taking you to dinner.*

Seconds later, another text arrived. *Someplace nice? I hope.*

There was only one place in town. *The Oar.* She knew that. *Fantastic.*

It was possible to convey sarcasm via text.

How about dinner in, then? I can make steaks.

Better.

Her snootiness *did* bother him. It worried him, too. Despite the beauty of their little town and the impressive beach, this was a small place with people dedicated to living simply. Would she fit in? Would she hate it here?

He sighed and rubbed his eyes. Was Sharon not the right woman? Yes, she was. Of course, she was. *Put the worries aside. I made the decision.* He was like this, fretting over the smallest things until he was paralyzed with indecision.

His therapist thought that he hadn't grieved Maggie properly when he lost her and that was why he couldn't seem to let go. Sharon, though—she was alive and she wanted him.

He sat on the edge of the bed, staring at the phone. *Stop panicking.* He knew when he proposed that there was no going back. This was the right step. She was the right woman.

It was way too warm in this small room. He tossed the phone aside and stretched out across the length of the bed and stared at the ceiling. The glow-in-the-dark stars his mother had pasted there when he was a little boy still remained. This room was like him— unable to move forward in time. Photographs of Zane, Maggie, and Jackson from high school were still tacked onto the cork board over his desk, their corners curled from time into cruel smiles.

Maggie at a dance recital, wearing a flowing skirt and leotard; he and Zane on the beach with their surfboards; the three of them in their graduation gowns.

Photographs. There was a box in his desk drawer—a Pandora's box of pain he avoided. For twelve years they'd sat in the drawer. He never looked at them. His therapist disagreed with this approach. To move forward, she had said, you must embrace both the good and bad memories of your past.

How was he to move forward when all he wanted was to fall back into the past?

He crossed the room and jerked open the desk drawer so hard it fell on the floor. Like ripping off a bandage, he lifted the lid of the box and tossed it across the room. On the top of the stack was a photograph of Maggie and her mom. They both smiled into the camera, but Mae's eyes were flat and dead, like a woman who had given up on life.

Maggie was eight in this photo. He knew because she had bangs that year and her two front teeth were missing. Freckles covered her nose and face; her skinny arms were wrapped around her mother's neck.

The next was a photograph of the two of them sitting side-by-side on the couch. Maggie's head leaned against Jackson's shoulder as they grinned into the camera. Another was of the two of them walking to school holding hands on what looked like the first day of school, given their shiny, new backpacks. He remembered that backpack—fourth grade. The year before Mae was killed.

On the way to school, she would slip her small hand into his rough one. When they were teenagers and so in love—it didn't matter where they were—if they could get away with it, some section of their bodies touched.

He put the photos back in the box. No more for tonight. His therapist was wrong. Remembering the good times only made him feel worse.

Jackson picked up the ring box from the dresser and shoved it in the pocket of his jeans. There would be no more visits to the cemetery. No more pining over a dead girl. Today had proven that what he needed was an intervention. He intended to give himself one in the form of one very much alive fiancée.

His dad looked up from his book as Jackson entered the study. "How was the surf?"

"I didn't go in," Jackson said.

"Why?" His dad looked good for sixty, with salt and pepper hair, deep brown eyes, and a smile that had the power to reassure even the sickest of his patients they were going to be fine. Lately, he had a new spark in his eyes, courtesy of Janet Mullen.

Jackson didn't answer. He went to the liquor cabinet and poured himself a two-finger scotch and downed it in one gulp.

"Son, you okay?"

He poured another scotch before sinking into the armchair across from his father's, cradling the glass of scotch in the palms of his hands.

"Jackson?"

"I'm tired." Jackson leaned his neck against the back of the chair and looked up at the ceiling.

"I know it's a tough day for you."

Jackson's eyes stung from unshed tears. "I think I'm going crazy."

"What do you mean?"

He sat up straighter as he glanced over at his father. Late afternoon light leaked through the wooden shades and made patterns on the hardwood floor. For the first time since he walked in the room, he noticed a decanted bottle of wine and two glasses on the coffee table. His father's only indulgence: good wine and the cellar to store it in. "I'm sorry, Dad. I didn't see you'd opened wine."

"It's nothing. Some evenings, a man needs a scotch."

Jackson nodded and drank from his glass. "I see Maggie everywhere." He called her Maggie when he spoke of her now. Bird gave him away.

"You mean, you think you see her and then it's not her?"

"That's right," Jackson said. "It used to be once a year. Then, it stopped. But since I came home, it's increased. I thought I saw her standing by the bench today. I swear to God, I thought it was her. I might have even said her name."

His father set aside the book on his lap and poured himself a glass of wine. "It's to be expected on a day like today, wouldn't you agree?"

"It's every day, Dad."

"Have you talked to your therapist about it?"

Jackson downed the rest of his scotch. "No."

"The memories are fresher here."

"It's been twelve years. I mean, seriously, what's wrong with me?" Jackson asked.

"I used to see your mother everywhere too."

This was new information. "When did it stop?" Jackson asked.

His father rubbed the finger where his wedding band used to be. "I can't remember. I only know it's been a long time since it last happened. Perhaps I finally stopped looking."

Stopped looking? Did that mean that he was still looking for Bird, knowing she was dead? Perhaps he *was* certifiable.

"I'm asking Sharon to marry me tonight, Dad. Enough's enough."

"You sure?"

"It's time to move forward. If I don't, I'm not sure what's going to happen to me."

They were interrupted by the sound of someone knocking on the patio door. "Hey, you guys home?"

Zane. Jackson yelled for him to come in. "We're in the study."

Seconds later, Zane stood in the doorway, holding a woman's sweater in his hands. "Sorry to barge in, but I told Janet I'd swing by and deliver her sweater to you. She left it at the bar last night."

"How kind of you," his dad said. "Care for a drink?"

Zane shuffled his feet. "Nah. I want to go out to see Maggie before it gets busy at the restaurant."

Jackson turned away. A hive of bees buzzed inside his head. Or was it real?

It was real, unlike his other visions. A bee was trapped between the glass and the wooden shade. He went to the window and lifted it, then opened the window all the way. The bee flew out and up toward the blue of the sky.

"How's business?" His dad asked Zane.

"We've had a good summer so far. Hope it stays that way," said Zane. "I worry pretty much all the time, but so far so good." He raked a hand through his blond hair. Bird used to say they looked like brothers. "Running this place is making me an old man."

Zane had taken over from his father a little over three years ago. He'd added forty microbrews and spruced up the inside and outside and changed the menu to attract a younger crowd. To the horror of the old-timers, people were coming to town not only to surf but also to go to Zane's restaurant.

Zane stretched his arms over his head. "I better run. I stopped by to see my dad this afternoon, so I'm running late as it is."

"How's he doing?" Jackson asked. Zane's father was in a memory care facility just north of town.

"He has good days and bad. Last week he almost seemed like his old self," Zane said. "Today he didn't recognize me. But, you know, he's still polite and thoughtful, so he pretends like he does."

"Sorry to hear that, Son," said his father.

"Yeah, well, what're you gonna do but carry on, right? You taught us that, Doc. But hey, I have to run. I'll see you two cats later. No need to walk me out."

After Zane left, Jackson poured them both a generous glass of wine and took the chair just vacated by his friend. The wine tasted of blackberries with a slight tobacco finish. Before he could take a second sip, Kyle arrived. Dressed casually in shorts and a t-shirt, he set a bottle of wine on the coffee table. "Found a new one I want you to try, Doc."

"Great. What brings you over?" his dad asked.

"I have news. But first I need a glass of vino," Kyle said.

Jackson grabbed another glass from the bar and poured a generous amount for his friend.

Kyle accepted the glass with a grateful smile. "The weekend couldn't have come soon enough. I'm losing sleep over this damn project. Not to mention that Violet's out there with her band of protestors every day."

"Still?" His dad grinned and shook his head. "They have stamina. I'll give them that."

"There's only four of them," Kyle said. "But they're out there every day with their picket signs. I swear, that woman has it out for me. She hates me."

"That's not true. She just hates what you're doing," Jackson said.

"No, she hates *me*," Kyle said. "I'm offensive to her in every way. Anyway, enough about that. I have big news. I might have found you a house. Let me start by saying, it needs a lot of work, but the potential is huge."

"A lot?" Jackson asked.

"You remember the documentary of the two sisters who lived together in that old house in New England and basically ruined it?" Kyle asked.

"Grey Gardens?" his dad asked.

"They were some relations to the Kennedys, isn't that right?" Jackson asked.

"They were cousins of Jackie," his dad said.

"Yeah, well that's what the house looks like," Kyle said. "The old lady who lived there for the past twenty years pretty much Grey Gardened it up. It needs massive cosmetic work."

"Wait, are you talking about the Arnoult house?" His dad sat forward in his chair.

"Arnoult? Right, that's the name of the owner," Kyle said.

"So, it *is* the Arnoult house," said his dad.

"From what I gathered, the heirs have wanted to sell, but the elderly aunt was living there," Kyle said. "She recently passed. The kids described her as eccentric. That's a nice way of putting it. The house is a wreck."

"What a shame," his dad said. "Lily and I went to dinner there once. When we were there, it was still glorious. The swimming pool and grounds reminded me of something out of Great Gatsby."

Jackson listened to the exchange in stunned silence. The Arnoult house was for sale. How could this be? It was Maggie's birthday and the house they'd dreamt of owning someday was for sale? Was it a coincidence? Or, was this Maggie's way of sending him the forgiveness he craved?

"Maggie and I used to ride our bikes up there," Jackson said. "And peer through the gate."

"You told your mother you'd own that house someday," his dad said. "I'd forgotten that."

"It's not even listed yet, but the selling agent's a friend of mine," Kyle said. "He knew I was looking for a house for you. If you want it, we can make an offer before they put it officially on the market."

Jackson wandered over to the window. The filmy curtains moved in ripples from the evening breeze.

The Arnoult house. He had to see it. Now.

"Let's go out there and take a look." The tremor in his voice betrayed him.

"You got it," Kyle said.

His father set aside his glass of wine. "I'm coming too."

* * *

Jackson sat in the back seat of Kyle's car as they drove up to the gate of the Arnoult house. At one time, an emblem of an eagle had adorned the center. When both sides were open, the eagle separated into halves, but came together when closed. Now, one of the wings had rusted and fallen loose and hung crookedly, like the broken wing of a living bird. Jackson looked away. Gates could be restored or replaced. The broken wing meant nothing. He could not look for signs in everything.

His father, in the passenger seat, looked up from the real estate listing sheet. "No lock on the gate?"

"It rusted away years ago. Sea air wreaks havoc on metal," Kyle said as they drove through and into the property. "Honestly, I was surprised the house didn't have squatters living in here."

"Wasn't there an old story going around that the house was haunted?" his father asked.

"When I was in high school, that was the story," Jackson said. "But Maggie and I always figured that was a rumor sent around from the family to keep pesky kids from breaking in."

The driveway, once graveled, was now plagued with potholes. Overgrown meadows peppered with wildflowers swayed in the slight breeze. "There used to be horses," Jackson said. "They kept the grasses short."

"The house and gardens have deteriorated," Kyle said. "No question. Just remember that surface damage is easily fixed. Under the cosmetic issues, this house was built to last."

The car bounced in a deep pothole. Jackson's heart had jumped between his ears and seemed to race as they reached the house.

Maggie had thought it looked like the French chateaus they'd seen in photographs. Jackson agreed with his father. The house and grounds reminded him of *The Great Gatsby*. Back in the glory days, the light stone exterior was partially covered in climbing rose bushes. Now, ivy had taken over, strangling the rose bushes into brown, twisted vines.

"I did a little research on the place today," Kyle said. "The house was built in 1920 by a French count or nobleman—whatever the title is—basically, a rich dude from France named Pierre Arnoult. He lived there until his death in 1960, at which point it was passed to his son, who lived there until 1996."

"That's the Arnoult I knew. Peter was his first name," Jackson's dad said. "He was only here occasionally, as he and his wife owned a vineyard in Napa."

"I remember seeing him around town once in a blue moon," Jackson said. "But he kept to himself. All of us kids were afraid of him." Peter Arnoult had walked with the assistance of a cane and had dark, glittering eyes.

His dad nodded. "His wife, Ana, was friendlier, but she was raised in France and didn't understand much English. Your mom always spoke to her if she needed medical care. Lily wasn't totally fluent, but between the two of them, they communicated well enough to describe the ailment."

"After they died in a plane crash in 1996, Peter's eccentric sister, Stella, moved in. She spent the last twenty years Grey-Gardening it," Kyle said.

Jackson chuckled at Kyle's made up verb, despite the despair that pooled in the pit of his stomach. This once splendid home was in ruins. Walkways were obscured with moss and weeds. Misshapen shrubs hadn't seen pruning for ages. Abandoned flower pots lay vanquished on their sides, with dirty water hosting various species of insects. Spider webs hung from every window pane. Jackson shivered. He hated spiders.

"It's like Sleeping Beauty's castle," Jackson said.

"Except there isn't a princess waiting for a kiss," Kyle said. "Maybe some rats and cockroaches, but that's it."

They got out of the car.

Next to the separate garage, a dilapidated car rusted. They meandered up the stone walkway.

Kyle let them in through the massive front door. The scent of feces and urine besieged them the moment they stepped into the foyer.

"Keep an open mind," Kyle said.

"But a closed nose," Jackson said.

"Did the old lady have a lot of dogs?" His dad raised his eyebrows in horror. "It smells like a third world country in here."

"I'm afraid the answer is yes. The listing agent told me she had several dogs and allowed them to defecate all over the house. Obviously, it would need an entire gutting," Kyle said.

They walked down the hallway until they reached the main room, piled high with boxes and old furniture. Scents of dust and mildew joined the already unpleasant odor. High ceilings with ornate detail, along with a winding staircase to the upstairs, hinted at the home's former opulence.

Kyle led them to the back of the house. An outdated kitchen, obviously remodeled during the seventies given the orange tile and green appliances, looked out to a once stunning backyard. A layer of mud and dead leaves buried the swimming pool.

Still, Jackson could imagine what it could be. He could restore the pool and uncover the stone walkways. A swing could hang from a branch of the old oak that shaded the area to the left of the swimming pool. The lawn could be replanted. A set of lawn furniture and an outdoor kitchen would bring it into this century.

Jackson could imagine it, but he couldn't pay for it. He didn't have the kind of money it would take to buy the place and restore it to its rightful glory.

Kyle looked at his notes. "There are four bedrooms and two baths upstairs. They also need to be gutted and redone." He pointed toward the front of the house. "A home office is that way. And there's a family room off the kitchen." They walked through a skinny door into a room with a fireplace and orange carpet. If possible, the stench worsened. "I would take down the wall here and have the kitchen flow into the family area."

"That would update it for sure," Jackson's dad said.

"Absolutely. Better for family life," Kyle said. "Let's talk outside. The smell's making it hard to think rationally."

They agreed and followed him out to the front of the house. The sun was low in the sky and shot rays of light through the skinny pines at the edge of the meadow.

The moment of truth was upon them. "What's the price?" Jackson asked.

"Remember, there are two acres of prime real estate," Kyle said. "With a view of the ocean from the upstairs rooms."

"Just tell me," Jackson said.

"It's priced just over a million," Kyle said. "Which, honestly, is a steal."

His dad nodded. "For this area, it really is. Why's it priced so low?"

Kyle lifted one side of his mouth in a grimace. "Look at it. Stella's great-niece and nephew are the sole heirs. The niece thinks the place is haunted and refuses to live here. Plus, her realtor told me she needs the cash. The nephew lives in France and wants nothing to do with it."

"I would make an offer in a second if I had the money," Jackson said. "Even if I could secure a loan, I can't raise the twenty percent for a down payment."

"I have an idea," Kyle said. "Just hear me out before you start in with the proud-man speak. What if we go in on it together? I know this sounds weird coming from me, but *if* I want to settle down at some point, I can't imagine a better piece of property. It feels like the country up here." Kyle looked out the window to the yard. "And there's *two* acres, which means I could build a house on the other half of the land when I'm ready."

"When exactly do you plan on settling down?" Jackson asked.

Kyle grinned. "Maybe not settle *all* the way down. But it would be awesome to have a house here to entertain in, at least. Once the resort is up and running, I won't have a reason to be here, and maybe I want one. I can't let you Dogs play poker without me."

Jackson punched his friend on the shoulder. "You're getting soft on us."

"Come on, what do you say? I'll run the loan through my business and my attorney can draw up an agreement between us. It'll be like a loan from me."

"I don't know. Should friends do business together?" his dad asked with a worried expression.

"My attorney will make sure it's iron clad so that we both feel protected. Not to mention, we go way back, Doctor Waller. And, I don't want to sound like a jerk, but this is pennies in the bucket for me. I've made a lot of money with my other investments. Other than wanting an acre of this property, consider this a favor, Jackson —a payback for all the times you paid my rent or bought groceries back when we were in college."

"It's hardly the same," Jackson said. "But I accept."

"You sure? This is a big decision. It'll take a year to make it habitable." Kyle peered at him with his sharp eyes.

"And what about Sharon?" his dad asked. "Shouldn't you consult her?"

He knew his father was right. He *should* consider her feelings, but a feeling of urgency nagged at him. It was now or never. Maggie wanted him here.

"I don't see that as a huge problem," Kyle said. "Even if she doesn't want to live here—this is an investment for both of us. I'll buy you out later, if you want me to. Anyway, if Sharon doesn't fall in love with it after we fix it up, I don't know a thing about women."

Jackson smiled. Kyle knew a thing or two about women. Mostly, how to get them to fall into his bed.

"She'll like that it was built by a count," Jackson said.

"We're not entirely sure he was a count," Kyle said.

"He will be in the story she tells her friends," Jackson said.

CHAPTER FIVE

Maggie

MAGGIE PASSED A construction project on the way out to the cemetery. A resort? That was odd, given Cliffside Bay's loathing for outside visitors. Whoever was building it had the right idea. This town needed a decent place to stay.

The cemetery was a mile north of town down a winding road lined with oaks. Their sweeping branches made a heart tunnel just before the turn into the cemetery.

Her mother rested in their family plot beside Maggie's grandparents and great-grandparents. Someday she would be buried beside her mother. One of the last things she did before she left town was to make sure her father could not be buried in her mother's family plot. *He didn't belong. Let him lie with the Postmistress.*

She parked in the lane closest to her mother's grave site and grabbed one of the bouquets of flowers from the passenger seat. Lily Waller's site was across the cemetery. She would visit it next.

The late afternoon sun filtered through the trees and shed yellow light over the rolling hills. Maggie breathed in the scent of wild sweet peas that grew just beyond the cemetery gates. What did the scent remind her of? It took her a moment to remember— the Arnoult house. The property had acres of wild flowers. In June and July, the sweet peas had bloomed in shades of vibrant pink and purple near the gate where she and Jackson would stand with their hands intertwined and dream of the day when the property would be theirs.

Now, a sparrow sang sweetly from the branch of a sycamore tree. About ten or so feet from the family plot, a sight froze her feet. What was she seeing? Another tombstone. Yes, another gray slab was erected next to her mother's. Maggie's pulse quickened. Her heart now beat between her ears, loud and too fast. Black dots danced before her eyes. She tightened her grip on the flowers. If that bastard had dared to buy his tombstone before he was even dead, she would rip it out with her bare hands and drop it onto his hospital bed. As she drew closer, however, she realized it was not her father's name etched into the stone, but her own.

Maggie Laura Keene
June 27, 1987- August 7, 2005
Our Songbird.

No, this wasn't right. She closed her eyes, sure her heightened emotion had caused her to hallucinate. But no. When she opened her eyes, it was still there. Her birth and death dates? It made no sense. Why would her own name be on a stone? She wasn't dead. For a mad second, she questioned her own existence. Was she a ghost? She pinched the skin of her bare forearms. Had her wanderings the past twelve years been that of a woman stuck between heaven and earth?

No, no. This was a mistake. She was alive. She bled and cried and ate and slept. No one was more alive than she, even on the days when she wished she wasn't.

Who had done this? And why?

The dots before her eyes grew larger and blurred her vision. She put out a hand to steady herself, but there was nothing to grasp. The spots merged into blackness.

Maggie woke with her face in the grass, next to the tombstone. *Her* tombstone. She'd fainted. It was true what they said. When you faint, you fall forward, not backward like in the movies. She sat up, pulling her hair away from her face, and drew her knees up to her chest. *Please, God, tell me what's happening.*

She heard footsteps behind her and whipped around to see a blond man striding toward her.

"Excuse me, but what are you doing?" he asked.

She squinted her eyes at the familiar voice, placing the exact timbre. *Zane Shaw.* It took a second to adjust to his older, narrower face. But his eyes were the same. An aquamarine color, like the Mediterranean Sea. His body was larger now—buff and wide-shouldered. He carried a bouquet of bright pink roses.

"Zane?"

As she said his name, his eyes widened, and his complexion changed hues until it was the color of asparagus soup under his tan. His mouth opened and closed in a way that reminded her of babies when they were hoping for a bite of banana.

"Maggie?"

"It's me." She waved her hand toward the tombstone. "What the hell is this?"

Zane stared at her. His broad chest went up as he seemed to gasp for air. "It can't be."

"I don't understand. I'm not dead." Maggie moved closer to him, surprised she could still form words. Perhaps shock made one calm and logical.

"Is this some kind of sick joke?" he asked.

"Joke? No, the joke's here." She fluttered her hand toward the tombstone. "Who did this?"

"No, Maggie's dead. We saw them lower her ashes into this grave. Who the hell are you?" Zane asked.

"I'm Maggie. I can prove it."

"How?" It came out as more of a growl than a word. Some of the color had returned to his face. Zane, quick to temper, always prepared for a fight.

"You have a scar on your left thigh the shape of a quarter moon from a fish hook when you and Jackson went fishing. You got it the summer between seventh and eighth grade."

His complexion now morphed into the color of uncooked dough. "Oh my God." He peered at her with eyes that could burn holes in a cloth. "I'm seeing a ghost."

"No, you're not. I'm alive. You can pinch me."

"It can't be."

"It's me," she whispered.

"All this time. We thought you were dead. We were at your funeral. Right here."

"Did you see my body?"

"No, your dad said you were mangled in the car accident. He didn't want anyone to see you like that. He had you cremated. That's what he told us, anyway."

"He told everyone I died?" It was him. Roger Keene lied and told everyone she was dead. Why? Why would he do such a thing?

It was her mother's voice in her head that gave her the answer. *To wreck your life. To hurt everyone who loved you.*

"He said it was a car accident," Zane said. "On your way to New York. In Kansas somewhere."

"Kansas? I've never even been to Kansas."

"You had to drive through Kansas to get to New York," he said, speaking like she was a crazed child.

"I did? Yes, that's right. But it's nothing but flat cornfields for miles and miles. No one could die on that highway."

"He said you fell asleep at the wheel. Because of the monotony. I figured, anyway. He never said that part." Zane's eyes were glazed over. He might be the next one to faint.

"I've been in New York all this time. Very much alive."

"It doesn't make sense," Zane said. "There has to be an explanation."

"He did it to hurt us. All of us." Her knees wobbled. She grasped air between her fingers, again looking for that object to hold onto that wasn't there. *I cannot faint again.*

"I don't understand what's happening," Zane whispered.

She noticed the flowers in his hand. They glowed under the dimming sun. "Why are you here?"

"For you. I bring flowers to you at least once a month," he said. "Today's your birthday. So, I came today." He raised his hands and took two steps backward. "You're a ghost. I've lost it. I'm seeing ghosts."

"I'm not a ghost. I'm real. My dad's a liar."

"Your dad. He's sick. Dying." He abruptly stopped talking and fell to his knees. "I don't feel so good."

She knelt next to him and took his hands. "Zane, look at me."

He raised his chin and peered into her eyes. They were wild, like a cornered animal. "I don't know what to do."

"We need a stiff drink," she said.

"Yeah. Okay. We'll go back to the bar and straighten this out. You can tell me who you really are."

When he stood, his legs wobbled. She put out an arm to steady him. "I think I better drive."

He yanked away from her. "No. I'll drive myself. We're getting to the bottom of this the minute we get back to the bar."

* * *

Twenty minutes later, she followed Zane into The Oar. Strangely calm, she took in her surroundings. On the drive from the cemetery everything had become clear to her. The Postmistress had sent back her letters. Maggie had thought they'd abandoned her. They thought she was dead.

Checkered plastic tablecloths had been replaced with crisp white coverings. Refinished wood floors and walls the color of sand had lightened the atmosphere. *Rustic meets sophisticated—a merging of past and present.* She ran her hand over the varnished wood of the bar—same wood, same markings.

About half the tables were occupied. The bar was nearly full.

"What do you want?" Zane asked.

"Vodka on the rocks."

Zane disappeared under the bar and came back up with a bottle of vodka. After he filled two high ball glasses with ice, he pointed toward the back of the restaurant. "Go to my office."

"Your office? Did Hugh retire?"

"He's sick. I run the place now." He gestured toward the back. They passed the door to the kitchen as a waitress came through with a dish in either hand that smelled of garlic and butter.

For the first time, it occurred to her that Zane lived here in Cliffside Bay. She hadn't expected that. "I figured you'd be in L.A.," she said.

"Not for three years now." He held the door and let her pass through. "Sit, please," he said.

She took the chair across from a small desk. Very tidy. Not the mess it was when it was Hugh's office. He could never find a pen under the piles of paper and was always asking to borrow Maggie's. She'd kept one tucked into her bun in those days.

"Your dad? He's sick?" Sweat dribbled between her breasts and her hand shook when she reached out to take the glass he'd set on the desk.

Zane continued to stare at her for a few moments before answering. "Alzheimer's."

"I'm sorry." She took a sip of the drink, careful not to spill, given her nervous hands.

"What year did your mother die?" Zane asked.

"It's really me. Do you think anyone could look this much like me?"

"Answer the question."

"1997."

"You could've seen that on the tombstone. How did she die?" Zane asked.

"My father pushed her down the stairs. He ran out the door with my baby sister in a burlap sack. She was never seen again."

"It can't be." Zane shook his head back and forth, watching her. "How come you never called or wrote?"

"I did. I wrote to all of you. My letters came back—*return to sender*. I thought you all sided with Jackson." The shock must be wearing off; her voice shook when she said Jackson's name out loud.

"What? No. My God, Maggie. No."

"I could never understand why I never heard from anyone. I decided I was disposable. Dispensable. Easily deleted." She paused, turning her eyes away from Zane's stunned gaze. The wall calendar behind him had a photograph of an old car, yellow with big fenders. It was three years old.

"Your calendar's on the wrong year," she said.

"It was my dad's last calendar." He gestured toward the laptop on the desk. "I use the computer."

"The place looks good. You did a great job on the remodel."

"I did most of the work myself," Zane said. "Therapeutic."

He'd excelled in woodshop in high school. She'd forgotten that. She sipped her drink, unsure what to say next. She wanted to know everything. Was he married? Kids? Why had he come home? Was it just because Hugh was sick? But he wasn't ready for "catch up" time. She could practically see his mind trying to reconcile the sight in front of him.

At least thirty seconds ticked by before Zane spoke again. "What reason would your dad have for doing this?"

"I don't know." A buzzing between her ears made it hard to think. "He hated the Wallers."

"Yeah. He did."

"He did it to punish them. Doc pushed the police hard to find the baby's body, not to mention that he made sure I didn't ever live with my dad again. Roger Keene's a vengeful man." For years, when she talked about her father, she called him Roger. Distance from him. That's all she wanted. Until now. Now she had to get the truth before it was too late.

"Well, if that was his intent, then it worked." Zane rubbed at his eyes with the heels of his hands before looking back at her. "Maggie, Jackson's never gotten over your death. Doc agreed to buy him a ticket out there to tell you he didn't mean any of it—that he'd wait for you for as long as it took. He knew he'd made a terrible mistake."

"Then why didn't he come after me? He knew how to reach me."

"Two mornings after you left, your dad told everyone you'd had an accident."

"I wrote to him. Several times. I told him where I was and that if he changed his mind I would wait. I worked it out on the drive from the cemetery. It was Darla. The Postmistress."

"Jesus, Darla. Yes. She sent your letters back."

"It has to be." The post office in Cliffside Bay was small, reflective of only several thousand residents. Darla saw every piece of mail that came in and could have easily sent them back.

"Why didn't you think to email or call?" Zane asked.

"I did. I mean, obviously I could have."

"Then why didn't you?" He continued to stare at her with a mixture of anger and distrust. She wasn't sure if he still thought he was seeing an apparition or that she'd somehow been in on the deception.

Maggie sighed, thinking back to her reasons. "At the time, I didn't have a computer. Cell phones were still flip deals and I didn't have one of those either. I left in a hurry, if you remember right. I didn't go back to the Wallers to pack. I just left that night. After Jackson broke it off." That wasn't totally accurate. She'd stopped at her father's before she left, sobbing and vowing that she would someday be back to get the truth about the baby. It had only taken twelve years.

"You just drove off without saying goodbye to anyone, including me," Zane said. "Did you ever think about how that would feel?"

"I did. Of course, I did. Later, after I was over the shock of what happened with Jackson." She gulped from her drink. "I kind of figured that was part of the reason you sent my letters back. You were angry, so you shut me out."

"Why the hell would you think that? For Christ's sake, we were best friends. You were like my sister."

"I figured you all sided with Jackson."

"Well, that was really stupid."

"I'm sorry." She gulped from her drink, willing herself not to cry. Zane was so angry. She hadn't done this, her father had.

"I'm pissed," Zane said. "Like beyond."

"That's obvious."

"What do you expect?"

"Nothing, I guess. Anger was always your go-to," she said.

"My *go-to*?" His cheeks reddened. A purple vein in his forehead pulsed.

"Whenever faced with anything emotional, you always chose anger instead of fear or sadness." She rattled the ice around her glass. This drink was going down way too fast. She needed to slow down, or she might pass out all over again.

"Well, you always chose to run away, bury your head in the sand, so to speak." He glared at her.

"I guess that explains how we're in the situation we're in." Her bottom lip trembled. She shifted her gaze to the ceiling, unable to withstand his accusatory scrutiny. The crack that looked like an old woman's profile had disappeared, replaced by smooth, eggshell paint.

"So, you just assumed the whole town hated you? It makes no sense. I don't even know what to say. Do you know how much we suffered? How much Jackson suffered? There were times that first year at USC that I wasn't sure he was going to make it. I mean, literally, Maggie. Do you know how many times I found him curled up in a ball on his bed or how many times I found him incoherent on the bathroom floor talking about suicide?"

As much as it hurt to hear this about Jackson, she couldn't help but defend herself. "You can ask my friend Lisa the same thing about me—you…you sanctimonious jerk."

"How in the world did you let this happen?" Zane jerked up from his chair, knocking a stack of receipts on the floor.

She rose to her feet and crossed her arms over her chest. No one, not even Zane Shaw, could talk to her this way. How dare he? "Listen, I didn't let anything *happen*. Jackson broke up with *me*. I had every reason to believe, when my letters were returned, that no one here gave a crap about me. You knew me back then. You remember how fragile I was as a kid. You were a firsthand witness to the kind of damage my dad did to my psyche. Maybe you've forgotten what I lived through? Most kids like me don't end up feeling super lovable or perfectly well-balanced after that. So, excuse me if I jumped to conclusions. Jackson broke up with me with no warning whatsoever. Just threw me away." Maggie sobbed between words. *The ugly cry*, as Pepper called it, but she didn't care. Screw Zane Shaw and his judgment. "My dad did this. Jackson did this. Not me."

"Why are you here, Maggie? Why now?" Zane's voice had risen several decibels.

She pressed her knuckles against her mouth and looked around the room for a box of tissues. *Get it together. Have some pride. Walk away.*

Zane opened a drawer in his desk and handed her a packet of tissues. "Here." His voice was gruff, but almost apologetic.

"Darla called and told me my dad's dying and he wanted to see me. It's the last chance I have to get the truth. I want him to tell me what he did with the baby's body, so that she can rest in peace next to my mother. That's the only reason. I didn't mean to cause any trouble. I let go of you all a long time ago, so you needn't worry that I'm going to mess with precious Jackson's life. Or, yours."

All the energy appeared to rush out of Zane at once. He sank back into his chair. His eyes reddened. "I'm sorry. I don't even know what I'm saying."

"You're in shock, maybe?" She handed him back the packet of tissues.

He pulled several from the packet and covered his face with them. His shoulders heaved once before he looked back up at her. "I know this isn't your fault. Your dad. Jesus, Maggie. All this time."

"I'm sorry, just the same. Your rejection hurt the most of all. I thought we'd always be best friends."

"But I didn't reject you."

"And I'm not dead," she said.

For the first time, Zane smiled at her. "You're not dead. I can't believe it's you." He came around the desk and pulled her into his arms. "You have no idea how much I've missed you."

She swallowed the sob that wanted to burst all over his chest and put her cheek against his muscular forearm. "You got so big."

"My face cleared up too." He let her go but held her at arm's length. "You're prettier than ever."

"No, I'm old." Jackson. She had to know. "Is Jackson married?" Her heart was in her throat, beating fast.

Zane shook his head, no. "But Maggie, he's with someone. They're about to get engaged."

"Oh, well, good for him."

Zane perched on the side of the desk. "It took him a long time to move on—all these years really."

"Well, I expected it. I mean, he's Jackson. Of course, he'd have someone."

"Look, Maggie, this whole town thinks you're dead. But no one's ever forgotten you, most especially Jackson and me. You, this...changes everything. You have to see him. He has to know you're here and alive."

"How does that work exactly? I just walk on over there and knock on the door?"

He stood, ruffling his hair with his hands, brow furrowed. Just then, he looked like the little boy she remembered instead of this muscular man before her. "Maybe it's best if I tell him? I about had a heart attack just now."

She took in a big breath and let it out slowly. "I'd be grateful. It would be nice to see him. I'd like to tell him…I don't know. I guess I'd just like a chance to say goodbye. I hadn't planned on staying tonight after I saw my dad. But this changes everything."

Including how much of a score she had to settle with her father.

"Maggie, you have to stay. At least a couple days. Doc and Miss Rita will want to see you."

"They're alive, then? Not sick?" she asked.

"No, just my dad."

"I don't have any place to stay."

"Stay with me. I have an extra bedroom," said Zane. "I live in my dad's old place above the restaurant."

The reality of what Zane had told her was starting to sink in. It was not that she was not loved, nor had she been rejected. They had not known she was out there, dreaming of them all. Wanting them all. The enormity of what her father had done nauseated her.

"I feel a little sick," she said.

He smiled gently. "Let's go upstairs. I'll have my staff run things the rest of the night. We have a lot to talk about."

She didn't answer as she followed him upstairs. Just follow Zane. Let the rest of it go for now.

CHAPTER SIX

Jackson

JACKSON'S DOORBELL RANG a little after eight that evening. His father had already left for Janet's after they arrived back from looking at the house. Since then, Jackson had busied himself getting ready for the evening.

Steaks were done and resting on the counter. He'd set the table in the dining room with china and a tablecloth.

He opened the door. Sharon stood in the orange glow of sunset. She held out her arms and he scooped her into a hug. "You look beautiful," he said.

"Thanks, love." Dressed in a flowy peach dress and high-heeled sandals that showed off her tanned long legs, she must have turned the head of every man in the airport. With her blond hair and copious eye makeup, she looked more like a Barbie doll than a research doctor. She *was* beautiful, with even features and a wide, full mouth. Smart, too. Smarter than Jackson. She'd graduated at the top of her class. He had as well, but it was more work for him. She excelled at school.

He couldn't do better than Sharon Fox. She was every man's dream.

This was the tape that played in his mind over and over.

He led Sharon into the dining room and held her chair. The candles flickered in the breeze and for a moment he was afraid they might go out, so he closed the windows. He poured her a glass of wine. "Sit and relax. I'm going to get our dinner."

"How lovely, Jackson."

After he set the plates of food on the table, he sat. "Before we eat, there's something I want to ask you." His mind buzzed. He wanted just the right words. This would be a story they told their children. He needed to be eloquent.

He reached inside his sport coat pocket to make sure the ring was still there.

He looked around the dining room. After racking his brain about the most poignant place to ask her, he couldn't come up with anything. They'd been friends in medical school, so their relationship was already established by the time Sharon convinced him that they should start dating. He couldn't think of anything that symbolized them, really. He couldn't even remember where their first "date" was. They just started sleeping together one night three years ago and it kind of stuck. Anyway, it didn't matter. What mattered was the proposal, not the location.

Jackson rose to his feet and pulled the box out of his pocket. He leaned down on one knee. For once, Sharon was speechless.

"I've tried to think of something memorable to say," he said. "But I'm too nervous, so I'll just keep it simple. Sharon Fox, would you be my wife?" He opened the ring box. The oval diamond glittered under the lights.

"Oh my God. Yes. Yes."

He placed the ring on her finger. She stared at it for a moment before wrapping her arms around his neck and kissing him. "The ring's ravishing. You've just made me the happiest girl in the world."

Sharon said words like *ravishing*, which sounded false to him, as if she had gotten bad advice about how to sound sophisticated and smart. *Use pretentious words like dreadful and lovely and absolutely appalling.* She was from Georgia, but any trace of accent and vernacular had been studied away until she sounded almost British, like the modern Madonna. Not the saint, but the singer. How had he never noticed this before?

Jackson stood up too fast. Black spots danced before his eyes. He gripped the back of the chair, afraid he might faint. She said yes. There was no going back.

CHAPTER SEVEN

Maggie

MAGGIE AND ZANE sat on opposite ends of the couch in his apartment above the bar. Fresh wood cabinets and paint gave it an updated look.

"What have you been doing for the past twelve years?" he asked. "Are you on Broadway like you wanted?"

"I've been on Broadway. As a chorus girl. But mostly I've bartended." She clanked the ice around in her glass. "New York was harder than I thought it would be. Much harder." She raised her glass. "I can thank your dad for the fact that I haven't starved the past twelve years. About six months ago, I injured my knee. I had surgery, but I can't dance professionally again."

"Crap. That's awful. I'm so sorry."

"So, I'm at a bit of a crossroads. I knew I had to come home and face my father. That's all I planned to do."

"Not see anyone else?" Zane said.

"That's right. I figured no one would want to see me. I didn't think you'd be living here, either. You always wanted to leave this town."

"And Jackson always wanted to stay," Zane said.

"What made you come back here?" she asked.

Zane unfolded his tale the way men tended to do—the facts told in headlines. He graduated from USC with a business degree, spent eight years in L.A. working as a sales rep for a high-tech firm, and met a girl and got engaged. "Everything seemed like it was going well until Natalie decided to start sleeping with her bridesmaid's husband and call off the wedding. That was three and some years ago. Right around then I started noticing my dad was forgetting things. One night he left the stove on in the restaurant kitchen and almost burned the place down. Shortly thereafter, he was diagnosed. He asked me to come home and help him sell the restaurant and building. The building, especially, is worth a lot of money."

"But you didn't want to sell?" Maggie asked.

"No. This place...this town is my home. I didn't know that until I left. I hated my life in L.A. It wasn't just the wedding that wasn't a wedding. I hated corporate life. Sitting at a desk all day is like my own personal prison. I didn't know that until I did it for eight years. I wanted to come back here and work with my hands. So, that's what I did."

"Are you happier?" she asked.

"Totally. I miss Dad. But I have a set of really close friends that live here—Jackson and a couple other guys from college. We all migrated here eventually. All but one of us, but he'll come back one of these days."

She smiled and held out her glass for him to pour her another splash of vodka. "No special someone, though?"

"Nah. No one of note."

Somehow, she didn't quite believe that. Zane had wavered slightly when he answered. There *was* someone of note. She could still read him like her favorite book.

Zane looked at her over the rim of his glass. "What about you? Is there no one in your life that would keep you in New York?"

"No. Just some really good girlfriends." The vodka had loosened her tongue. The bond and ease she'd always shared with Zane had returned as if no time had passed. Time was no match for true friendship. "My life's been all about my career. And, you know...no one could ever live up to my memory of Jackson." She shrugged and tried to make her voice light, like it was a joke. "It's pitiful, if you think about it. I never got over my high school sweetheart."

"You aren't the only one."

"No, that can't be. It's been twelve years," she said.

"What did you just tell me?"

"He's with someone."

"Sharon is not you."

"Sharon? That's her name?" She'd always hated that name.

"Jackson has always tried to do the right thing," Zane said. "He's finally home and working with his dad. He wants to start a family and build a life with someone. That is not the same thing as being madly in love."

Maggie sat for a moment, taking in all that she'd learned in such a short amount of time. "Do you think he'll want to see me?"

"God, yes. Maggie, this is going to rock his world."

"What if it just messes with his head?"

"It's going to mess with his head," Zane said. "We've mourned a girl for twelve years that's nowhere close to dead. Believe me when I tell you, he's going to question every single thing in his life. For him, nothing and no one has ever been you. Nothing and no one will keep him away from you."

CHAPTER EIGHT

Jackson

THE NEXT MORNING, Jackson woke late. Sharon had left a note on the desk that she was shopping and would be back later. A text from Kyle told him that he'd made an offer on the house and would keep him updated as he learned more.

The house. He'd failed to mention it to Sharon. She was so happy after the proposal that he hadn't wanted to risk making her angry with him. It was Sunday, so he dressed in his running clothes and followed the smell of coffee coming from the kitchen.

Zane and his dad stood at the island in the kitchen, talking quietly. His dad was crying. Something had happened. "What's the matter?" His first thought was Brody. He was at training camp this week. Had he been hurt? Jackson would never admit this to anyone, but he couldn't wait for Brody to retire. Between the concussions and the spinal cord injuries, Jackson worried constantly about his friend. "Is it Brody?"

"No, it's not Brody. Everyone's fine," Zane said. Usually Zane would tease him about being an old lady, but the dark look in his

76

eyes remained. "It's something else. Something I need to tell you."

"Son, you better take a seat."

"You guys are scaring me," Jackson said as he sank onto a stool at the island.

Zane leaned onto the counter with his elbows. "I don't know where to start."

His dad sat on the stool beside Jackson.

"Zane has news that will seem impossible to believe…" His dad trailed off as his voice broke.

"It's about Maggie," Zane said.

Maggie? What about her? "Okay?"

"I went to the cemetery yesterday to leave some flowers on her grave. For her birthday." Zane looked over at Jackson's father as if for help, but his father stared at the countertop. "There was a woman at her grave." Zane's eyes glassed over as he looked once again over at Jackson's father. "And, it turns out it wasn't any woman. It was Maggie."

Jackson blinked. "What?"

"Maggie's not dead. She's alive and well. Her father lied to us. She's been in New York City all this time. Her dad's sick, so she came back to see him—to try and get the truth about what happened to her baby sister. She had no idea that we all thought she was dead. She wrote us letters, but they came back *return to sender*. Darla must have tampered with the mail. Maggie thought we'd all sided with you—that you asked us all to abandon her."

"But why? Why would he do that?" His hands and face were numb. This was a dream. He'd had so many over the years. Dreams of their reunion. This was simply another. "No one would do that. Not even him."

"Maggie thinks it was to punish you and your dad. Or, maybe the whole town. He knew we all hated him and that we'd love to send him to jail for what he did to Maggie's mom and the baby." Zane interlaced his fingers and made a teepee under his chin.

"Why would she think that we'd ever abandon her? It doesn't

make sense." Jackson realized he was crying and grabbed a napkin from a stack on the counter. "This cannot happen. Not in this day and age. Why didn't we ever see anything about her on the internet? She went to New York, right? She's an actress, right? It's impossible to disappear these days."

"She changed her name, legally and otherwise. Other than to her close friends, she became Marlena Kassidy and deleted her former life. Given that Keene was her father's name, she wanted no part of it. And, she wanted to forget you."

"Forget me?"

"Yes," Zane said. "You ripped her heart out, dude. I'm sorry to say it, but your ultimatum and subsequent rejection made her think you hadn't really loved her. Think about how she was, or is, and it makes sense. She was like a skittish kitten or an abused puppy. Remember how long it took after she moved in with you guys to be alone in the same room as your dad? Even with me, one wrong move and she'd run away. Think about how sensitive and vulnerable she was. Her father made sure she believed she was unlovable. When her letters came back, she believed everything he'd ever told her had been the truth."

"This was her punishment as well as ours," his dad said.

"But I don't understand. Surely, we would've seen her on a show or something. I mean, she was going to be a star."

"Her acting career didn't exactly go as planned," Zane said.

"I don't believe it." *I can't believe it.* He pressed his hands together to stop the violent shaking. It did no good.

"She said it was harder than she thought it would be."

"But she didn't feel like she could come home," Jackson said. "Because she thought we didn't want her." The pain in his chest made it hard to breathe.

"That's right."

"Does she hate me?" Jackson asked.

"No, dude. The opposite," Zane said. "She's not like that anyway, but now that she knows the truth about what her father did, she knows none of this was your fault. I told her how you planned to go after her and beg for her forgiveness." Zane looked to the ceiling as his eyes glistened. "I told her how you suffered. How much you still miss her. And, she's missed you all this time."

"Is she married?" He knew the answer. Of course, she would be married. It had been twelve years. A woman like Maggie would've been snatched up the moment she arrived in New York.

"She's not," Zane said. "No one compared to you."

"Jesus. No, this can't be happening. Zane? Dad?" Jackson's entire body shook. A black tunnel swirled and sucked at his consciousness. He placed his hand on the cold countertop. He couldn't pull breath into his chest.

His dad placed his hand between Jackson's shoulder blades. "Just breathe, Son."

"Does she want to see me?" he asked between breaths.

"She does." Zane said.

"Is she the same? Does she look the same? Sound the same?'

"She's more beautiful. Tougher. Stronger. But the same, too," Zane said.

"Oh my God, Dad. Maybe it was her I saw yesterday. By the bench."

His father nodded. "Sounds like it was."

"She's been in New York all this time?" Jackson asked. "Tell me what you said again."

Zane smiled gently. "That's right. She went to NYU. She's lived in Brooklyn and worked on Broadway and bartended."

"All this time?"

"It was harder than she hoped to make it on Broadway. She's been working hard all this time, trying to make it. This is her first trip to the west coast since she left," Zane said.

"But she's going back soon?" Jackson asked.

"She's not sure what she's doing next. She hurt her knee and can't dance any longer. All she wants now is to get the truth out of her dad before he dies."

"He's dying," Jackson said, dull and stupid. Clear thoughts

evaded. Instead, it was an endless spinning and a high-pitched noise between his ears.

"She knows about Sharon. I told her," Zane said.

Sharon. *Sharon.* He hadn't thought of her once. All he could think of was Maggie. "I proposed to her last night," Jackson said.

"What the hell? You did?" Zane asked. "How come you didn't tell me?"

"It was a last-minute decision." He told Zane about how he'd been seeing Maggie everywhere. "I thought I was falling into insanity."

"And proposing was the remedy?" Zane asked.

"I have to see Maggie," Jackson said. Nothing else mattered right now. He would sort out his life after he saw her, after he held her in his arms and told her how sorry he was. "I have to tell her I'm sorry." Tears gushed from his eyes again. "I've wanted to do that for so long."

"She's at my house right now," Zane said. "She wants to see you, but she's scared."

"That's why she sent you here? To tell me?"

"That was my idea. I almost had a heart attack when I saw her."

His dad turned Jackson to face him and looked into his eyes. "You sure you're up for this?"

"Yes, yes. Now, before I have too much time to think about it," Jackson said.

CHAPTER NINE

Maggie

MAGGIE PACED IN front of the window of Zane's apartment, alternating her gaze between the street below and the gentle slope above town where the Waller's house seemed to cling to the hillside. From here, she could see a patch of gray-shingled roof. Zane had been gone too long. Why was it taking this much time? He'd left minutes after they shared coffee and toast, both bleary-eyed from talking half the night.

The sound of heavy footsteps coming up the stairs snatched her from the window. She stumbled into the side table and smacked her shin. Breakfast churned in her stomach. When the front door creaked and opened, she froze, almost blinded with fear and nerves.

Jackson filled the doorway. They stared at each other from across the room. This was Jackson. The adult Jackson. His facial features, delicate when they were young, had hardened into sexy contours. His body was more substantial, thick and muscular.

An invisible hand wrapped around her heart and squeezed until the pain was nearly unbearable.

"Jackson," she whispered. Tears burned her cheeks.

His face contorted into a dozen spasms. "Is it really you?"

She nodded, sobbing now.

He crossed the room with his arms outstretched. She moved toward him through the blurry fog of her tears.

When they reached each other, he grabbed her and pulled her against his firm chest. They trembled as they clung to each other. "I'm so sorry. I'm so, so sorry." He dropped his face into her hair. "I've wanted to tell you for twelve years how sorry I was. I never thought I'd have the chance. There was nothing worse than to think you left the world without knowing how much I loved you —how wrong I was to do what I did."

"We were young and silly," she said.

"I was young and horribly stupid. So careless and selfish. I'm sorry."

"It was so long ago." She brushed the side of his face with her fingertips.

He held her away from him for a moment, searching her face. "It was both a second ago and a lifetime ago."

She lost all sense of time as she stared into his blue eyes and breathed in the scent of his skin. Had his lashes always been so thick and black?

"Here, let's sit," he said.

"Good, yes. I feel like I might faint."

"I'm not feeling too hot myself." When they were seated, he held her hands. "Your eyes are the same." He grazed her cheekbones with the tips of his fingers.

Her stomach dipped like it used to when she rode the surf. "Yours too."

He caressed her cheeks with his thumbs. "Freckles like a starry night."

She resisted the urge to rest her cheek in the palm of his hand.

"That metaphor was always all wrong. Stars aren't the color of nutmeg."

"They should be," he said.

Maggie flushed. Could he see how her heart pounded inside her chest? She traced the tiny lines at the edges of his eyes that made a roadmap to his hairline. "You have crow's feet."

"Medical school."

"You did it. I saw the sign on the office," she said. "Doctor Waller and Doctor Waller."

"It took a long time, but yes. I'm here for good now."

"I've wondered...how you were...if you'd gone to medical school. If you were married and had children." She looked away, willing herself not to blabber and sob. *Strong. Remain strong. Set him free.*

"There was never a day I didn't think of you," he said.

"Oh, Jackson," she whispered.

"There wasn't one day that I didn't miss you like hell. Not one single day."

"For years my prayer was to wake without any memory of you. What a relief it would've been. Like a strong painkiller." She smiled to take the edge off her words, but it didn't matter. From the mournful look in his eyes, she knew he understood it to be an absolute truth.

"I couldn't even look at photographs of us," he said.

"I burned all mine." She swallowed as a dull knife twisted in her stomach.

They both looked away. Suffering between two people was palpable. Pain molecules hovered in a charged mass between them. At any moment, the mass could unleash and spill agony all over Zane's clean floor.

"There were a lot of good times," he said. "They were almost all good when we were together."

"Until we weren't."

They sat in silence for a few seconds until he took her hand and traced the lines in her palm. "I had a prayer too. I prayed that I would wake up and discover it had all been a nightmare. You were still here by my side. But some prayers couldn't be answered. Until today." He ran his hands up her bare arms. "You're here. You're really here."

"Zane told me you're involved with someone."

He flinched. "That's right. She's a doctor I met in medical school. A research doctor."

Maggie conjured every acting class she'd ever had. "She must be smart."

"She is." He looked down at his hands. "She's a fine person, but...it's not like us. She could never be you. I could never feel about her like I did you."

"Jackson, don't."

"No, I have to say it. I let you leave here once without knowing what was in my heart. I lived with that for twelve years. But now, I have this second chance to tell you what's in my heart. I don't want you leaving here without knowing that I never let you go, not your memory, not the place in my heart that was just for you. I've never stopped loving you. When your dad came over to the house to tell us about your accident and that you'd died, there was a part of me that didn't believe it. I always thought, given how close we were, that I'd feel you leave the earth."

She just shook her head, unable to think of anything to say.

"I told my dad and Zane, but they thought I was crazy. Which, you know, seemed reasonable. At the time."

Maggie wiped angry tears from her cheeks with the backs of her hands. "When my letter came back, I should've come back and confronted you."

"I pushed you away. What else were you supposed to think?" he asked.

The guilt and regret in his eyes almost broke her resolve to stay strong. She had to find the right words to set him free. "The past is past, Jackson. I'm glad we had a chance to say what we needed to say before I have to go."

"Do you have to go? Right away?"

"You have a good life and I'm a disruption. I should've stayed away."

"No. That's wrong. We have a second chance. I want to know everything that's happened between then and now. Every detail."

"How do we do that?" she asked. "You have a life. I have a life. *Separate* lives."

"They don't have to be."

"But you're involved with someone." Maggie's voice caught. So much for all the acting lessons.

He rose from the couch and went to the window. "Would you believe it if I told you I was having doubts? Even before you came back from the dead."

A giggle escaped before she could clamp her mouth shut. "I didn't come back from the dead."

He grimaced, obviously trying not to laugh. "It's not funny."

"What else are we going to do but laugh? I mean, this is one heck of a high school reunion."

He joined her back on the couch. "This is *not* the way it was supposed to turn out. Your dad interfered with fate."

"We were eighteen years old. Our aspirations made it impossible for us to be together. You were right to break up with me."

"You're forgetting the other part. Before I got all irrational and insecure, the plan was to meet back here no matter how it all turned out for you. Either you'd be a huge star who could call the shots, or you'd have given it your best try and been ready to come home."

"As much of a pipe dream as that was, we believed it, didn't we?" she asked. "Talk about naïve. Remember how we used to stand outside the gates of the Arnoult place and talk about how many kids we wanted and what we would name them?"

"I remember. I believed it, too. Every bit. It would've happened if your dad hadn't interfered."

She stared into his eyes. "Do you really believe that?"

"I came here to say I was sorry and to ask your forgiveness. But it's not enough. From the moment I walked into this room today it morphed into something else. We're meant to be together. I know it with every fiber of my being. Everything about you is familiar to me, like the prints of my own fingers. Love like ours doesn't just fade away over time. Others maybe, but not us."

"Too much time has passed."

"I disagree," he said.

"I can't stay here, Jackson."

"Because of New York? The dream?" A bitter edge slipped into his tone. Who could blame him? Her ambition had cost them everything.

"No, not because of New York," she said. "I'm leaving there."

"Zane told me about your knee."

She lifted her skirt to show him the scar. "This is my replacement knee that was supposed to save everything, but it didn't. It's over for me."

"I'm sorry." He brushed the skinny pink scar with his thumb. "I know how much it must hurt to let your dreams go."

"Sometimes it doesn't seem real. Like my injury and surgery and recovery were a bad dream." She stalled, searching for the right words, even as she wished she could keep them hidden. How could she tell him of her failures when her decision to leave had cost them this great love? "I wish I could tell you that our sacrifices had been worth it, but that would be a lie. I gave you up for nothing. All I've ever been is a chorus girl and a bartender and a waitress. I'm broke and broken."

She told him of the endless auditions, of her constant money worries. "You think, always, maybe tomorrow will be the day. But tomorrow never comes. There's always someone with a better voice or a better dancer, and, recently, younger. By quite a bit." Her voice cracked; she'd never been able to move the margin of truth even a fourth of an inch in his presence.

"I wanted it for you. Even if it didn't seem like that by how I acted during the months before you left. I've always been so proud of you. I never had any doubt that you were meant to be a star."

"You were wrong to believe. I failed. I'm a failure."

"No. That's not how it is. You tried something that required great courage. You were brave, Bird. Braver than almost every other person walking the planet. Do you know how many people wouldn't have even had the courage to try? And, with no one by your side. No one to tell you to keep going." Jackson's voice broke. "I should have been that person for you. I'm the failure." He fell silent as he played with a tattered section of his shorts. "Fear makes us irrational and reckless. It's stronger than anything else. I was afraid you might never come back. So, I sabotaged us. I hate myself for it."

"Please, stop. You need to forgive yourself. I forgive you. I can't forgive my father, but you and me? We didn't have a chance to make up and figure things out because of him. Nothing you did or didn't do will change that fact."

"I have to know," he said. "Did you ever stop loving me?"

"It doesn't matter now," she whispered. *No, and I never will.*

"Stay. Give me the chance to make it up to you. Give me the chance to prove that we belong together."

"What about Sharon?"

"Maggie, it's you. It's always been you. Please, don't walk away without giving us a chance to see if what we had is still there."

"It's not fair of me to show up and turn everything upside down," she said.

"I don't care." He captured a lock of her hair between his thumb and finger. "I can't let you go a second time."

"I can't think what to do," she said. "My head's spinning."

"I bought the Arnoult house yesterday."

What? *Impossible.* "It was for sale?"

"Yes. It's a disaster, but I'm going to fix it up." He paused for a moment. The muscles of his neck moved as he swallowed. "When I was there yesterday, I thought it was a sign from God that it came up for sale on your birthday. I imagined you sent it to me from heaven—that I should move forward with Sharon—move on with my life without you. But that wasn't it. I was meant to buy it for *us*."

"For us?"

He took her hands. "I don't understand what's happening exactly. All I know is that I've never stopped loving you. And I won't."

"Jackson, this is wrong."

"Do you have someone else? Do you love anyone else?"

"No. God, no."

"Why? Tell me why someone like you doesn't have someone."

"Because I've never loved anyone but you." So much for staying strong. "I've never gotten over you."

"Then, what're we doing?" he asked. "We have to give this a chance. I can't let you go. Not again."

"We don't even know each other anymore. I've changed. I'm hard and bitter."

"No, you haven't. Not in here." He tapped his chest.

"You've changed. You're a doctor like you planned. I'm nothing."

"For twelve years, I've wished I could have the chance to tell you how sorry I was that I messed it all up between us. I bargained with God a thousand times that I'd give up anything, even my career, if I could beg for your forgiveness. I never thought I'd get a chance. I got my chance and your forgiveness. But I can see it's not enough. I want more. I want you. I'm going to fight like hell to convince you that you and I belong together. Please, say you'll stay and give me enough time to prove that I'm right."

"I'm supposed to be figuring out what Plan B is," she said. "I need to figure out what I'm doing with the rest of my life."

"What if your Plan B is me? What if everything you've ever wanted is right back where you started?"

She placed a finger in a blond curl that hung over his left ear. "That would technically mean this is Plan C. I mean, if Plan A was New York and you, then Plan B would be just New York, making you and Cliffside Bay Plan C."

He grabbed her hand and placed it against his chest. "I'll be whatever plan you want. I'll be C all the way through Z, if you'll let me."

"This is insanity. People don't do this."

"Most people aren't dead for twelve years and suddenly come back to life," Jackson said.

She giggled. "I wasn't dead."

He smiled as a tear ran down his cheek. "It's not funny."

"And stars aren't the color of nutmeg."

"They should be," he said.

"What if you're wrong? What if you ruin what you have only to discover that you don't love me—that I'm just a fantasy you were never able to let go of? I want you to have a good life, Jackson. That's all I've ever wanted."

"You were my life. I want that again. I know what I know. Most people aren't us. Most people aren't still in love with the girl they loved when they were eighteen years old. But I am. God's granted us a second chance, Maggie Keene. It would be further tempting fate to deny it."

"I never could say no to you," she said.

"I'm counting on that." He grinned, then sobered in the next second. "I have a few things I need to settle with Sharon."

"A few things?" A shot of jealousy as hot as lava erupted from her stomach and scorched the back of her throat.

"Yes." He splayed his hands over his knees and rocked slightly back and forth. *He's thinking of what to say. How much to say.*

"Yes?"

He lifted his chin and gazed into her eyes. "I'll tell her the truth. I'm in love with someone else. But right now I want to talk to you. I want to know everything about your life. Don't leave out any details."

"You first," she said.

"Fine. So, I went to USC as planned..." he said.

Four hours later, her mouth was dry, but her heart felt fuller than it had in a long time. Jackson glanced at his watch. "I have to go."

"Go? To her?"

"I have to talk to her. But I'll be back. Will you be here?"

"Yes," she whispered. *Always.*

CHAPTER TEN

Jackson

JACKSON FOUND SHARON on his father's patio under the shade of the awning. She lounged on a chaise and flipped through the pages of a magazine. *Please don't be a bridal magazine.*

She looked up as he approached. "Where have you been? I've been waiting for you for hours. It's nearly time for cocktails."

He looked out to the view of the sea, gathering courage. Sailboats with brightly colored masts dotted the endless blue. Farther out, a cruise liner hovered, its movement invisible. On numb legs, he sat on the other chaise. How could he do this? What did one say? *Guess what? The love of my life isn't really dead.*

The invigorating scent of the lemons in the potted tree hung in the air. However, the taste inside his mouth was of their sour juice. "We need to talk." He folded his hands like a tent under his chin. No, this was wrong. He moved them to his lap.

She sighed and set aside her magazine. "If this is about when I'm moving up here, I don't want to talk about it. Not on such a stunning day."

91

Irritated with a suddenness that surprised him given his guilt and his soon to be delivered confession, he gestured toward the kitchen. "It's not about that. I'll open some wine." He tugged at the collar of his shirt. "Let's talk in the kitchen. I'm too warm out here."

"Yes, fine." She tossed her mane of blond hair behind her shoulders and rose from the chaise. Her high-heeled sandals clicked across the wooden deck.

Once inside, she sat at the island's counter while he poured them both a glass of white wine his dad had open in the refrigerator. He set the glass in front of her, but instead of sitting, he moved to the other side of the island. "I'm not sure where to begin."

"What's going on? You look dreadful."

"I'll just say it outright." He took in a deep breath. *Outright?* Any way he said it would sound like a joke. *Maggie's alive,* cue the devious background movie. "The thing is—something's come up. Something unexpected."

"For Christ's sake, what's the matter with you? Are you sick?"

"No, I've had a shock, that's all."

She sipped from her glass of wine. "Out with it."

"You remember Maggie."

She let out a long sigh. "Yes, Jackson, I'm quite aware of who she is. If you recall, she's the reason I asked you to go to therapy."

"Right, yes. I know." He swallowed. "It was a rhetorical question."

Sharon set her glass down. "What the hell's going on?"

"Maggie's back. I mean, she's not dead. She's alive. Her father lied all those years ago—faked her death, and now she's here in town. Zane saw her at the cemetery. Her father's dying, so he called her home. To make amends. As if he could."

She opened her mouth, then closed it just as quickly. Her eyes were wide, like toothpicks pried them open. "Have you lost your mind?"

"No. I spent the afternoon with her. She's very much alive. Roger Keene lied to the whole town. We had a memorial for her and everything. There was no reason to suspect that anything was amiss."

"It's preposterous."

"I know." He flashed to the memorial. Roger Keene had put an urn and a photo of Maggie when she was little up in front of the church. How could he live with himself knowing there were no ashes in the urn? And then, to bury it in the family plot? *Not now. Focus on Sharon.*

"I've heard of people faking their own deaths for insurance purposes, but nothing like this. Why would he do that?" Sharon picked up her glass. Her hands shook so violently the wine splashed like a lake in an angry storm.

How could he do this to her? After her loyalty to him? What had his mother always told him when she knew he would rather lie than tell her the truth of what he'd done? *The truth. The truth shall set you free.* If only it were as simple as confessing to stealing beer from the refrigerator like he had in high school.

"Her dad didn't want us to be together," he said. "Or, maybe it was to punish me. He hated my family."

"Why?"

"It's complicated." He pressed his fingers into his forehead. "Too hard to explain or go into right now."

"Try."

"It's not relevant," he said. "I'm sorry."

"I'm your fiancée. Everything about you is relevant. Or, it should be."

Sharing Maggie's story with Sharon seemed wrong, like a betrayal. "I don't want to go into it right now."

"Well, anyway, it's nice that she's not dead, but it doesn't have much to do with us." The literal meaning of her words didn't match the way they were said. *She's doubting herself.* Her usual self-confidence had wavered. Somehow that made him feel even worse. It was awful to watch someone so self-assured become diminished right before his eyes.

Her blue eyes were still as round as saucers. He was certain she hadn't blinked for at least a minute. "I mean, you've been reassuring me for months the past was past. Only the future matters. The future with me. You don't know her any longer. You two were children when you saw each other last."

There was no way to move forward without sounding like the coldest man on the planet. He would say it as truthfully as he could. Get it all out there. No sugarcoating. People accused him of being too nice all the time. He couldn't be nice now. He must be clear.

"It changes everything. I've loved Maggie my entire life. I've mourned her and missed her every day since she left here. She's alive. Alive and well. I can't ignore the feelings that have rushed back to me. I have to explore those feelings and see if there's anything worth salvaging between us. It's not fair to you to pretend otherwise. I can't marry you. It would be wrong to do so when I have feelings for someone else. You know you deserve better."

"For all that's holy, you were eighteen years old." Had her Georgian accent come back? "Do you really think if she'd been alive and well all this time—or should I say that you'd *known* she was alive and well all this time—that you'd be together? No one marries their high school sweetheart."

"That's not true. People do. People like Maggie and me." He hadn't meant to say the last part. There was no reason to hurt her more than he already was.

It seemed as if Sharon hadn't heard him, for she continued without taking a breath. "She left you and went to New York. *She* made that choice years ago. That's still true. Have you forgotten that? She chose her ambition over you."

"It's more complicated than that. I made her choose. I was wrong. Not her."

Sharon rose from the stool and pushed against the island like she wanted to flip it on its side. "You're unbelievable. Don't you see that's what you've done with me too? You've made me choose you over my work. And yet, here you are, getting it all. Everything you want, like we should just all fall into place when you snap your fingers."

"What are you talking about? That's not how I am at all," he said.

"Are you blind? You refuse to give up this ridiculous notion of taking over your father's practice. News flash—it is not 1950. As much as you'd like to make it so, it isn't. And, if you recall, I've acquiesced. I—unlike Maggie—have agreed to give up my work, which, by the way, is actually important, and move here to Podunk to be the obedient wife to a small-town doctor."

"You agreed to it. You said you supported it. Has that changed?" Turning the argument back on her was pure instinct. But what did it matter now, except to alleviate his own guilt? *Be better. Rise above. I'm the one hurting her. She has the right to lash out.*

"I was right. You've never gotten over Maggie. And now, voilà, she's alive."

He clasped and unclasped his hands, unsure what to do. "I don't know what you want me to say."

"I want you to tell me you're sorry for putting me through this. You've been in love with a ghost this entire time. You never loved me. What was I? An item to tick off on your list? Become a doctor. Move back to daddy. Marry a pretty blond. Have two kids. Oh, but wait, the woman I really love is miraculously alive, so raincheck on the blond."

"That's not fair." It *was* fair. Everything she said was true. He *had* loved a ghost.

"What's not fair is that you're just tossing me aside like I meant nothing to you." She held up her hand. The diamond sparkled. "You gave me a ring. You don't get to change everything because your little friend came back to town."

"It's not unreasonable, when thrown this kind of curve ball, to need a little time to think."

"I've always known Maggie was a threat to us. I just didn't know she was this much of one. You know you're not doing her or you any favors by trying to conjure the past into the present. You were children. God, you're so transparent. I can't pretend that I don't see in your eyes that you've already decided. You're a fool."

"I'm sorry, but I need time to sort through my feelings." Zane's voice seemed to whisper in his ear. *Liar. You already know.*

"You need *time*. Isn't that the mantra of our relationship. For six years I waited for you to figure out how good we were together. All that time, I waited. For what? This? To hear after we *finally* get engaged that the love of your life is suddenly alive. In what universe is that all right to do to the woman who loves you? You are mine. I earned you."

His mouth went dry. *I earned you.* Like a piece of furniture or a car or a house? Sharon had her agenda and she wanted everyone to get into line. But they weren't cells on a microscope that one tampered with to get the result she wanted.

"I'm sorry. I truly am," he said. "But this is my life and I get to decide how to live it."

Sharon twisted her ring around and around her finger. Tears fell from her eyes. Streaks of mascara ran down her cheeks. "I was willing to move here and become a boring housewife. For you. I was willing to do it for *you* and now you're repaying me like this."

"I'm sorry," he said again. How stupid his words sounded, even to his own ears. But he *was* sorry. She had no idea of the doubts that had plagued him even before Maggie reappeared. He had to tell her the truth, as harsh as it was. "I hate hurting you. But I've had doubts long before this. I haven't felt certain we were compatible. You deserve someone who loves you…" He trailed off, uncertain how to finish.

"The way you love Maggie?"

"Yes." As much as it made him horrible, it was the truth.

"Then why did you propose? Why did you make me think I'd finally won?"

"Won?"

"The war with a ghost," she said.

The war with a ghost? Perhaps Sharon didn't love him as she imagined she did. Was he more attractive because he was essentially unavailable?

"You're willing to just throw all that away in the hopes that the girl you had a crush on when you were a kid is the one you're supposed to be with? It's ridiculous. We have a life together. We have *had* a life together for six years."

"It's not like that. She wasn't a crush. I loved her. We were in love. If her father hadn't tampered with things, we would be married by now."

"You're an idiot. You're delusional and insane. You should run, not walk, to your therapist and tell her how you've just sabotaged the best thing that ever happened to you."

Sharon was not even close to the best thing that had ever happened to him. He could see that clearly now.

"I'm sorry." How many times had he said that phrase in one day? He rubbed his temples and willed himself not to vomit.

"You'll regret this. And when you realize what you've lost, don't come running back to me." She yanked the engagement ring from her finger and threw it across the kitchen. It landed in the sink with a clink. "You can take your minuscule diamond and stick it up your delusional behind." Again, the Georgian accent reared to life.

"I'm truly sorry," he said.

She was already at the door. "You will be. I'll make sure of that."

He dropped his face into his hands and cursed under his breath. She wasn't going to make this easy.

CHAPTER ELEVEN

Maggie

MAGGIE SAT AT the table in Zane's kitchen and opened a small box of photographs Zane had left for her. He was already downstairs at work. Doc was on his way over, but she had a few moments to herself.

The first of the bunch was of the three of them at high school graduation. She studied it carefully. Jackson's face was drawn. Dark circles under his eyes hinted at grief. His mother had died just a month before. She looked at herself standing next to him. How thin she'd been, even for a dancer. Her cheeks hollow. Her eyes too big for her face. Her arms like a skeleton.

Oh, Lily. You left us too soon.

The next photograph was of her mother and Maggie at about age five. How had this one gotten in here? She traced the outline of her mother's face with the tips of her fingers. *I look so much like her now.*

Strange to think that her mother was younger than Maggie was now when this photograph was taken. *She was dead five years later. I've lived longer already than my mom did.*

She set the photograph aside and went to the window. From here, she could see her father's house. Her *mother's* house. It belonged to them. For all these years, he'd lived in it. Since the day he killed her.

Don't remember. Don't think of it. You've already gone over it in your mind a thousand times. It was no use. The last few days of her mother's life rushed back to her in painful clarity.

She was ten years old and it was bedtime, five days before Christmas. Mama sat on the side of the narrow twin bed and brushed Maggie's bangs back from her forehead. "I have something important to tell you. I'm divorcing your dad. He won't be able to hurt me any longer." The pinched look had disappeared from Mama's face. It was because her father was away—gone, hopefully for good. He'd been away for almost a year, working on an oil rig in Texas. They'd been at peace without him. Just the two of them. No shouting or pushing. No black eyes or bruises that her mother hid with long sleeves.

"I don't want him to come home," Maggie whispered. "Will he? Will he come and find us again?"

"I've filed papers and the lawyer sent them to him in Texas. He won't be able to come back into this house ever again. This was my mama's house and her mama's house before that. Someday this will be your house. And honey, I have something else to tell you. It won't make sense to you because you're so young, but I love another man. It's wrong because I'm married, but we love each other. I'm going to have a baby. His baby."

"What about Dad? He won't let you go. He'll come back and hurt you."

"Not this time. He won't be back for another week, but when he comes, the locks will be changed. It'll just be us." She laid her hand on her stomach. Maggie had noticed it was rounder than it used to be. She didn't know it was because of a baby.

"Doctor Waller says it will be a girl," Mama said.

"A baby sister?"

"That's right. And, we're going to be so very happy. But you can't tell anyone about the baby or the divorce. Not Jackson or Zane, you promise?"

She nodded. "But why?"

"Not until your father knows. Then, you can tell them all about it. But for now, it needs to be our secret."

The next night, Maggie arrived home around seven after spending the day with the Wallers. They'd had cookies and hot cocoa and trimmed the tree. When she came into the house, all the lights were off, like her mother was gone. She was never gone at night. Then, she heard a strange sound. At first, she thought it was a hurt animal. But no, it was her mother's scream. She ran up the stairs. Her mother was in the bathtub, her face as pale as the white tile. "Get Jackson's daddy," she whispered. "The baby's coming, and fast. Too early. Hurry."

Maggie ran all the way to the Waller's, stopping only once at the steepest part of their driveway. When she reached the back patio, she ran inside. No one locked doors this early. She screamed for Lily. Only Jackson was there. Doc was with a patient. Lily had gone to take cookies to Miss Rita.

She gripped Jackson's arms. "You have to come with me. I'm scared. Mama's having a baby."

He looked at her like she spoke a foreign language, but he followed her out the door.

They ran down his long driveway and then the few blocks to her house. She gasped when they arrived in their driveway. "That's my Dad's truck."

She looked up at the window of her mother's bedroom. Shadows danced behind the curtain. A tall shadow and a shorter one. "Jackson, we have to save her."

They rushed through the kitchen door as a scream pierced the dark. *Mama.*

Another scream, this time primal, like an animal trapped between steel claws. "Mama," she shouted, running toward the stairs with Jackson behind her. Too late. Mama tumbled down the steps, rolling over and over until she reached the floor. Her head made a sickening sound as it smacked the last step. At the top of the stairs her father wobbled. *Drunk.* He held something in his arms. A bulge, like a piece of firewood, covered in a burlap sack.

"Get the doctor," he shouted down to them with slurred words. "Your mother's fallen."

Maggie ran to her mother's side, cradling her head. A gash leaked blood, sticky and hot on Maggie's skin. Her mother didn't move. "Mama, wake up. Jackson, run home and get Doc."

But he was already gone. She heard the backdoor slam shut. He would find his dad. Doc would make everything all right. He would fix Mama. "Mama, wake up."

Her father lunged past her, with the parcel in his hands, to the front of the house. The front door creaked open and a shadow ran past the front window. Where was he going? Outside, his truck roared to life. Tires squealed.

"Mama, please wake up."

Time shrunk and wavered after that. Maggie stayed glued to Mama. Jackson was the fastest runner in class. He would get there soon. He would know what to do. He would find Doc and Lily.

Finally, they burst into the room. Lily screamed the moment she saw them on the floor.

"Where's your father?" Lily asked.

"He ran away. Something was in his hands. Something in a sack."

Lily knelt next to them. "Oh, Mae. No." She cried as she picked up Mama's hand and pushed her thumb into her wrist. "No, no. Mae. Not this. Not now." She looked at Maggie. "Sweetie, did he push her?"

"When we came inside the house, I heard her scream. He was up at the top of the stairs, but I didn't see exactly what happened. Just all of the sudden, Mama was falling. She hit her head."

Lily pressed into her mother's belly. It was still rounded like the night before, but softer. "Did she have the baby?"

"I don't know." Maggie sobbed. "She told me the baby was coming and to run for Doc. When Jackson and I came back, my dad was here."

"Where's the baby? Maggie, is the baby here?" Lily's voice had risen several octaves. She pressed her bloody hands against her thighs.

It wasn't until then that Maggie understood the bulge had been the baby. "He took her. She was in a bag. The kind potatoes come in, I think. He ran out the door."

Lily stood, brushing her hair back from her face, leaving bloody streaks on her cheeks. "Jackson, take Maggie home and lock the door."

"I can't leave her. What if she wakes up?" Maggie sobbed harder. "Please don't make me leave her."

"You two run as fast as you can to our house and lock the door. Don't answer it for anyone but your dad or me. Jackson, do you understand?"

Now, a knock on Zane's door pulled her from the memory. *Doc.* Her heart settled in her throat as she crossed the room and yanked open the door. A sob escaped as she fell into Doc's arms.

* * *

Maggie and Doc sat across from each other in Zane's living room. They'd already talked for an hour. Doc asked most of the questions. Maggie did most of the talking. She'd filled him in on the past twelve years, concluding with the news about her knee. "So, no more dancing. Which leaves me at a crossroads."

"Crossroads can be good," Doc said. His brown hair had morphed to an attractive salt and pepper. Despite some wrinkles, his dark eyes were still sharp. *Jackson has his mouth. I'd forgotten that.* "Just don't stay in the cross too long."

She must have given him a quizzical look, because he continued. "Nothing good comes from indecision or a state of deep freeze. Your new path will become obvious if you're open to finding one. Take it from me, openness is key. It took me about thirteen years to figure that one out."

"Zane told me about Janet Mullen," Maggie said.

The corners of Doc's mouth lifted into a smile, taking years from his face. "Yes. Janet Mullen. She's quite special. I didn't think love would come twice in one lifetime." His eyes twinkled. "Can you believe an old guy like me gets another shot at love?"

"She's a lucky woman. You're the best man I ever knew, other than your son."

Doc sobered. "Zane told me what you thought all these years. It breaks my heart to think you thought we'd abandoned you. You were like my daughter."

"It was the returned letters that did it," Maggie said.

"Darla will pay, if it's the last thing I do."

"I have to go see him, but I don't want to. He scares me. After all this time. Which both infuriates and motivates me."

"He's in bad shape. He can't hurt you ever again," Doc said. "But still, I can't imagine what he wants with you."

"Darla said he wants to make amends. Whatever that means. Apparently, he's found God."

"How convenient for him."

"I want him to tell me the truth about the baby," she said. "And then he can rot in hell where he belongs."

"Sweetheart, no one wants that more than I, but this is Roger Keene we're talking about. He's stuck to his lie for twenty years. From the beginning, he told the police that your mother fell and that there was no baby when he arrived. I'm not sure impending death will prompt the truth."

"I have to try," Maggie said.

"Yes. You do."

"I came here for that purpose. I wasn't prepared for what I found. You know, all of you...wanting to see me and stuff."

"We missed you. More than you can imagine."

"I can imagine," she said.

"Losing you almost killed Jackson," he said. "All these years, he's never let go of your memory. So don't think for a moment he's not going to fight to get you back. This is Jackson we're talking about."

She smiled. "He said as much."

"He was never one to play games."

"But what about Sharon?"

"He's breaking the engagement."

"Engagement?" A roar like waves in a storm buzzed between her ears. Jackson was engaged? He hadn't told her. Why hadn't he told her?

Doc's eyes glinted in the light. "He finally proposed, Maggie, only last night. He'd hesitated for months and months. His heart wasn't in it, but he wouldn't admit to it. He kept seeing you everywhere. Not the real you, but women with red hair. He honestly thought he was going crazy. Asking Sharon was his last-ditch effort."

"To finally move on," Maggie said. "To prove he wasn't insane."

"That's right."

"Poor Jackson." She could imagine exactly how he had come to the decision he did. Many times, she'd ached to do something, anything, to forget him. To finally move away from memories and into life. If she had been an impulsive person, she might have slept with every man in New York. She'd known, however, that nothing would help her get over Jackson but time. She could make every bad choice and wake up feeling worse, not better.

"It's not right—not fair to Sharon that I just appear out of thin air," she said. Last night? He proposed last night? A wave of nausea rolled through her as an awful thought occurred to her. He'd slept with Sharon last night. He'd made love to her on the night of her engagement because that's what people do.

"Sweetheart, he's suffered over the years and just this once—right now, as a matter of fact—he's doing something for himself," Doc said. "He's giving you guys a chance. You can't punish him for it."

"But what if he's making a mistake? We've changed. We're no longer kids."

"Is that what you really think?" Doc asked. "That everything you once felt is no longer there?"

She stared back at the man who raised her, who knew her like he'd been her real father. She could not lie to him or herself. "I've loved Jackson all my life. When I saw him today, it was as if no time had passed. But that's not the case. A lot of time *has* passed and we're adults now with complications we didn't have when we were teenagers. He has a relationship with someone else. I'm broke and broken." She gestured toward her knee. "I have no idea who I am anymore or what I'm supposed to do with the rest of my life. Who knows if we can work through all of those complications and become 'us' again?"

Doc crossed one leg over the other and hooked his hands over one knee. "I've lived on this earth a lot longer than you. I've loved two women. Amazing women. In both cases, there were a lot of complications, especially with Lily because we were young and poor. Lily was the daughter of a southern preacher, who did not approve of a wild California kid with years of medical school ahead of him. But we got married anyway, betting everything on each other. We got pregnant at the absolute worst time. I was still in medical school and Lily was supporting us on her teacher's salary. But Jackson arrived and nothing, not money, or fear, or anything, would have changed how we felt about him. We were so grateful he was ours.

"I had debt up to my eyeballs from medical school, but we moved here and bought the practice anyway. When the practice started bringing in more money that I had to pay out, I thought we had it made. We wanted more children. Lily had three miscarriages right in a row. Those were hard times, even though we had the perfect boy. Then, there was your mom's death and the rage and sorrow that came with it, but there was you—so small and fragile and broken. You needed us to be strong. We clung to each other for strength. And that was enough to get us through every bump and turn.

"When she was sick, and we knew she was dying, we held even tighter to that love. We celebrated it, knowing that soon we would have to part. I swear, we sucked every last drop of happiness out of those last days together. Because at the end, sweetheart, the only thing that matters is love. The rest is just noise the devil puts in our way to distract us from what we're put on this earth to do—love each other."

Maggie's eyes filled as she swallowed the lump in her throat.

"Please, sweetheart, after what you and Jackson have both endured, don't waste this second chance. Cling to each other and vow to get through whatever hardships come your way *together*. If you're offered a chance for love, you better take it."

* * *

Maggie walked along the main street. The scents of eucalyptus trees and sea air and fresh baked goods tickled her nose. The smells of home. At Doctor Waller's office, she paused, and traced Jackson's name with her index finger. Next door, little girls in pink leotards did pliés on the dance floor of Miss Rita's studio. Their instructor, a young woman dressed in black, demonstrated proper form.

According to Zane, Rita was going strong, still teaching and living by herself in the apartment above the studio. Maggie glanced up to the windows of Miss Rita's apartment, but the shades were drawn. After she saw her father, she would see Miss Rita. Zane had promised to call her and tell her of Maggie's return.

She continued down the street until she reached her family's home and stopped outside the rickety wooden gate. As much as she'd rather walk past the house and to the beach, she must gather courage and go inside the house.

Over the years, Maggie had developed a coping mechanism for auditions that served her well in many situations. She centered herself with three deep breaths. With each breath in and out, she expunged any thoughts of current worries or fears until she was focused only on the task at hand. Auditions were comprised of either dancing in a group and hoping to stand out enough to be kept for a callback or singing sixteen or so bars of a song. Both seemed easy compared to confronting her father.

Jackson's face slipped into her consciousness, despite her first breath in and out. She could not keep the thought of him out of her mind. Their reunion, so brief, yet powerful, had crept into the molecules of her body. *Jackson. Jackson changes everything.* He always had.

She took in a second breath and peered into the yard at the tangled weeds. Her three breaths would not work today. Instead, she spoke kindly to herself. *Just go inside. Be brave. You can do it.* Shaking, she went through the gate and around to the back. An overgrown hedge narrowed the pathway. She squeezed by a particularly bushy section and into the back yard. It too was in shambles, with patchy grass and a weather worn patio, only a hint of its former attractiveness remained. Mildew covered her mother's stone bird bath. Would a brave bird drink from the black water? Yet, amid the overgrown yard, a clump of orange poppies sprouted toward the sun with vibrant optimism.

Maggie knocked on the back door. A moment later, the door opened, not by Darla, as she would have thought, but a beautiful young woman wearing scrubs. Her eyes were the color of melted dark chocolate and brown hair hung in a long braid down her back. "May I help you?" She had a husky voice with hints of an east coast accent. A large diamond ring on her left hand sparkled in the sunlight.

"I'm Maggie Keene. I'm here to see my father."

An expression like a startled deer crossed her pretty face before she stepped outside to the patio and closed the door. She extended her hand. "It's nice to meet you, Maggie. I'm Kara Eaton."

Right, this was Kara. Zane had told her all about her. She was nurse practitioner who worked for Jackson and his dad. She would soon marry Brody Mullen—one of the other *Dogs* Zane had mentioned. All these Dogs rattled the brain.

"Zane called us this morning to tell us about…the situation," Kara said.

"The situation. That's one way to say it," Maggie said with a smile. "Are you here looking after my dad?"

"I'm on call this weekend, and his wife left a message early this morning that he was having trouble breathing, so I came to check on him."

"What's wrong with him exactly?"

"The question is more, what's *not* wrong with him? Basically, his organs are shutting down."

"How long does he have?" *How long do I have to get the truth?*

"Weeks at most."

"Weeks. I can work with that," Maggie said.

Kara raised an eyebrow but didn't ask for clarification.

"Did Zane tell you why I came home?" Maggie asked. "The whole sordid story?"

"He did. It's only natural you want to get the truth before he dies."

"You have any good drugs that would make him talk?" Maggie smiled.

"The pain medication he's on might do just that," Kara said.

Maggie gestured toward the house. "Better go ahead and get this over with."

"You want me to go with you?" Kara asked. "Darla's out right now. I told her I'd wait until she got back from the store before I left him alone."

"No, I'll be fine."

She followed Kara into the small kitchen. It had been remodeled since she was last here, with new appliances and a new floor. The tiles had been black and white checkers. Now, they were a tan linoleum. *Ugly.* The Postmistress didn't have good taste.

The house smelled like damp wool. "Your father's in the living room," Kara said. "He hasn't been able to get up the stairs in a while. I'll be here in the kitchen if you need anything."

The sound of the oxygen machine greeted her even before she entered the room. Her father lay in a hospital bed with his eyes closed. With lead in her sandals, she trudged to his side and stared down at his weathered face. Sallow and wrinkled, he was not recognizable as the young army sergeant he had been when he'd first met her mother.

His eyes fluttered open. He mouthed her name and looked up at her with rheumy, sunken eyes. "You came." His raspy voice conjured an image of a long raindrop splattering on hot concrete.

"Yes." Maggie's body and mind had gone numb. Where was the anger that had propelled her across the country?

"You look pretty, kid."

She flinched. His kind words were a hard slap across her cheeks. "Why did you want me to come? After all the trouble you took to make sure everyone thought I was dead, why did you want me back here?"

"I wanted you to know the truth," he said.

"About what? There's quite the list to choose from."

His watery eyes looked up at her. *He wonders what I know.*

"I went out to the cemetery and saw my own tombstone," she said.

His right hand shuddered and convulsed into a fist. "That, that was for you."

"How in God's name was it for me?"

"You had to get away from here. That Waller boy would've kept you small."

The tips of her fingers tingled back to life. How she would love to wrap them around his scrawny neck and choke him until he agreed to tell her the truth. "Jackson Waller never made anyone feel small in his life. That's your particular poison."

"You had to go—had to get out. This town was no friend to the women in your family. I wanted better for you."

"That's not the reason. You've never thought of anyone but yourself."

"You would've wasted your talent on that spoiled brat."

"I know you had Darla tamper with my letters. A federal offense, you know."

"Leave Darla out of this," he said.

"I won't. She'll pay for this. Think about that as your legacy. You'll be gone, but she'll be punished."

"It was the right thing to do," he said.

"No. You ruined any chance of my happiness when you told such a wicked lie."

"You would've given up everything for that miscreant. You were like your mother—could never resist the idea of romance."

"Trust me, you squelched all sense of romance the first time you almost killed her."

"She was no angel, Maggie. I need you to understand that."

"She's an angel now. Thanks to you."

"I didn't kill her," he said. "She slipped."

Maggie went to the window and opened the shade, knowing it would hurt his eyes. That's what she wanted. To hurt him like he'd hurt her mother and the baby. The little sister that would be a young woman now. Someone for Maggie to love. A family.

Remember the goal. Get what you came for. Maggie turned back to him and purposely softened her voice. "You're dying, so there's no chance you'll go to jail. I just want to know what you did with my sister's body. Please, as a gift to me, let me bury her next to Mama. That will mean something to God. You'll die with a clean slate."

"I've already made my peace with Jesus."

"I see. How convenient."

"What do you want, Maggie?" His slimy eyes narrowed. A hint of the formidable man he once was glared up at her. "Why did you come here?"

But she was no longer afraid of him. She had the power now.

"I came here to get a full confession. I want you to admit you pushed Mama. I want you to admit you killed the baby in a rage and then hid the body somewhere. I want you to tell me where she is. Who knows, maybe it'll get you points with the God you so conveniently believe in now."

He turned his face to the other wall. "There was no baby when I got there. She said it was born dead. I have no idea what your crazy mother did with it."

"I saw the baby in your arms. You ran out to your truck with her. What did you do to her? Don't spare any details. I want to know everything."

"That's not how it happened."

"I remember every moment of that night." Maggie closed her eyes, so she wouldn't have to look at his twisted, ugly face.

Her father's grasping hand reached out to her, bringing her back to the present. She darted from his reach.

"She told me she'd given birth to another man's baby," he said. "It was born dead. She got rid of the body, so I would never know that she'd cheated on me. She didn't know I was coming home that night. When I found her all bloody, it was obvious what had happened. We fought, and she slipped. It was an accident. Please, let me die in peace knowing you believe me."

"You were drunk. Enraged, like you'd get right before you beat the crap out of her. You think I didn't see it hundreds of times?"

"She cheated on me while I was away providing for my family and then tried to hide the evidence. That's the kind of woman your mother was. Who's to say she didn't kill the baby herself?"

"No. No, she would never have done that. She didn't care if you knew about the baby or the man she loved. She just wanted to get away from you. The night before you killed her, she told me everything. She said it was a second chance for us to be happy."

He sat up slightly and gestured toward the water glass on a makeshift table made of cement blocks. "Please, can you give me some water?"

She crossed her arms, staring down at him. "Admit to me you pushed her."

"I admit we had words."

"Words? Is that what you call beating the crap out of her? Words?"

"She sent me papers in Texas. Had me *served*, like a dog. Like I was nothing. You best understand the truth little girl—how she treated me—how she ruined *my* life—before I die. *I'm* the victim, not her. They took you, Maggie. They stole you."

"Who did?"

"The Wallers. I lost my little girl to them because they were rich and I was poor. They spread rumors that I killed your slut mother's baby and ostracized me from this whole town. That's the *true* story here."

She staggered away from the bed. It was always about him. He'd brought her here to convince her of *his* innocence, *his* victimization. A lying narcissist. He would never change, not even in the face of death.

"So that's why you told everyone I was dead? As revenge?" At least she would get him to admit that.

"They deserved to hurt like they'd hurt me. I knew your death would do it."

"You're a sick and twisted psychopath. You'll burn in hell." Maggie stepped away and covered her mouth with her hand, afraid she might be sick. A photograph on the mantel of a younger Darla and her father standing next to his old Ford truck caught her attention. For a second, she couldn't place what was wrong with it, but then the truth assaulted her like a bucket of ice water thrown in her face. He'd sold the truck shortly after Mama died. But he hadn't known Darla then. Or, had he? She picked it up and examined it closely. The photo showed the same old, faded blue truck that had been in the driveway that night.

This meant Darla was with him then. He must have met her in Texas and brought her home with him. Perhaps she helped him. A likely scenario unfolded. Divorce papers served prompted their return. They wanted money or revenge? A *plan* brought them here. They killed both the baby and Mama. It had to be. But how to prove it? She needed to talk to Jackson and his father—ask them what they remembered of that night.

Doctor Waller pressed the local police to investigate, but they'd found no traces of blood in his truck or anywhere else. There was no body, so no charges were brought. If Darla were there—she could have taken the baby and hidden her remains. That's how he got rid of the baby so quickly. He'd had a helper. The baby had been given to Darla to dispose of. She'd done it, too.

Darla knew what had happened that night. Thanks to the postal service being under federal law, Maggie had the leverage to get it out of her.

She set the photograph aside and moved back to the hospital bed. His sick eyes burned with a feverish hatred. He knew she knew.

"Darla came back from Texas with you." Not a question. A statement of fact.

"What does it matter?" His voice had weakened since she'd arrived. He would be dead in a matter of days. One didn't have to be a nurse to see that.

"This is your chance to tell me the truth," Maggie said. "Or I'll get it out of Darla."

"The truth is this and only this. Your mother was a whore." He gasped for breath. One of the machines beeped.

If Kara hadn't come in at that moment, Maggie might have placed her hands around his throat and finished him off herself. Fortunately, that wasn't the case.

Maggie didn't stick around to see Kara do the work of keeping him alive. *Screw you, old man. You'll meet the devil soon enough.*

* * *

The sun was low on the horizon when Maggie knocked on the Waller's back door. The scent of lemons from the potted tree soothed her nerves, but not enough to stop the trembling in her arms and legs.

Doc opened the door and ushered her inside. The layout of the kitchen was as she remembered, other than the countertops and cabinets had changed. The cabinets were now white with silver knobs. The countertops were black with subtle sparkles of blue. "You remodeled."

"Just last year," Doc said. "You're shaking."

"I've just come from my dad."

"Come into my study. I'll pour you a drink."

"Yes. Thanks. Is Jackson here?"

"I think he's upstairs showering. I just got home myself," Doc said. "I had a few errands to run."

As if on command, Jackson appeared in the doorway between the kitchen and living room. Damp hair and flushed cheeks substantiated the shower theory. He wore shorts and a t-shirt, which displayed his trim stomach and wide shoulders to great advantage. Despite her rage, she shivered with desire. When was the last time she'd wanted a man? And this was Jackson. Not any man, but her love. Her *one*.

Jackson crossed the room and took her into his arms. "Are you all right?"

"Yes. I've just come from my father's," she said.

"I'm about to fix us all a drink," Doc said.

"I could use one," Jackson said.

No one commented on why, even though they all knew. Maggie followed the men to Doc's study. She almost cried at the familiar scent of leather and scotch of the study. "Oh, Doc, it smells the same."

"Does it?" Doc grinned. "Lily used to say she couldn't smell leather and bourbon without thinking of me."

"I was just thinking the same thing," Maggie said. Above her, a ceiling fan turned lazily. She shrugged out of the light sweater she'd worn to her father's, as the room was warm and drowsy. *I'm calm here. Safe.* This is the way it had always been. She and Jackson had come to this room when Lily had told them to run home that night.

Jackson patted the back of one of the leather chairs arranged with its twin by the tall window. "Sit here, Mags." He lifted the wooden shades and opened a window. The softness of twilight washed the room in dusty orange. Filmy white curtains fluttered in the breeze.

Doc poured them all a scotch and took the opposite chair. Jackson perched on an ottoman, his tan, muscular legs crossed at the ankles.

"I did it. I went to see him," she said.

"I'm afraid to ask," Jackson said.

"Did you get anything out of him?" Doc asked.

"Even with his supposed redemption from Jesus, he wouldn't tell me the truth." Maggie took a drink and let it burn down the back of her throat.

"I knew it." Doc clicked his tongue against the roof of his mouth.

"He's sticking to the ridiculous story that my mother disposed of the baby's body. He suggested Mama had killed the baby to keep the fact of her cheating from him."

"You've got to be kidding," Jackson said.

"He did admit that faking my death was to hurt you and Jackson. He feels he's the victim because you stole me from him."

"We did steal you from him. There was no way in hell Lily and I would ever have let you go back into that house."

"How *did* you get him to agree?" Maggie asked.

"I told him you'd be staying with us from then on or I would kill him."

"Dad, really?" Jackson asked.

"Really. I had a revolver I'd inherited from my dad. He was a marine, you know, and I pulled it out of a drawer and went to his house and shoved it in his face."

"I can't imagine you doing that," Maggie said. Gentle Doctor Waller shoving a gun in her father's face. The image, although surprising, gave her a rush of satisfaction.

"It's not something I'm terribly proud of, but I had to protect you," Doc said.

"But you could've gone to jail. What good would that have done?" Maggie asked.

"I knew it would never come to that. Bullies are innately scared. I figured he'd back down if he thought I was serious. Which, he did. He never said one word about wanting you back. He got to keep your mother's house. After what he did, that was bad enough." Doc raked a hand through his hair. "The moment Zane told us you were alive, I knew exactly why he did it. I can't help but feel partially responsible. Maybe I shouldn't have tried so hard to prove his guilt and he wouldn't have felt compelled to take you from us."

"Doc, this was no one's fault but my father's," Maggie said. "He insists that Mama slipped."

Doc nodded. "I think it's possible that your mother *did* slip. She'd just given birth and had lost a lot of blood. But, regardless, he beat her and chased her to the end of the hallway. Whether she slipped or not, he killed her. As far as the baby goes, I don't know what he did exactly. He's always stuck to the same story. He came home and found Mae covered in blood, having obviously given birth, but there was no baby."

Maggie glanced over at Jackson. His expression was impassive, but she knew differently. He was remembering the horror of that night.

"When Jackson and I came into the house, my mother screamed. Not like earlier when I heard her in labor. This was like someone ripping her heart out—a cry of mental anguish, not physical. I believe that's the moment she discovered what he'd done to the baby. And, I know what I saw. He had something wrapped in a burlap sack in his arms when he came down the stairs and ran out the front door. That was my sister's body in the sack."

"I agree," Doc said. "However, there was no trace of the baby's blood or DNA anywhere other than in the bathroom of your house. Not in his truck. Not in the driveway or sidewalk. I had the authorities dig up every inch of your backyard. They couldn't find anything. We even had trained dogs comb the streets and beach. Nothing. Without a body, it was hard to prove your dad had anything to do with it."

"Do you have any idea who my mother's lover was?"

He shook his head no. "Honestly, I have no idea. It might have been anyone."

"I don't understand why he never came forward." Maggie said.

"Maybe he didn't know? Lily always assumed it was someone she met away from here because otherwise he would've known she was pregnant. Or, maybe he was married too? Or, maybe he didn't want to get involved in the investigation?"

"The night before she died, she told me she loved the father of the baby and we were going to be a new kind of family, but that it had to wait until her divorce was final. She may have thought she would get the divorce first and then tell him. Unless, she thought he was something special or serious and he was a jerk. Mama didn't have the best taste in men."

"I don't know. Lily said Mae was so happy that year your dad was in Texas. We both knew she was pregnant, since I was her doctor, but she never said anything to either of us about it being another man's baby. We suspected it, obviously, given the timing. I don't suppose there's any way we'll ever find out."

"There might be. I saw a photograph on my father's mantel." She explained her theory about Darla. "I have something to bargain with now. Either she tells me what she knows, or I go to the police about her mail tampering. It's a federal offense, which means federal prison."

Doc's face scrunched up for a moment. "She was there. Shoot, I never thought of that. I thought at the time that maybe he had help, but there were no leads to prove that to be true."

"They pretended that she moved to town after my mother's death. But the photograph proves otherwise," Maggie said.

"When did she start working at the post office?" Jackson asked.

"I don't remember," Doc said. "I didn't realize she was with your dad until quite a while after Mae died. Why?"

"No reason," Jackson said. "All I know is that Maggie has a way to get the truth out of her."

"I have to take it," Maggie said.

"She'll bite," Doc said. "There's no way she's risking federal prison."

CHAPTER TWELVE

Jackson

LATER THAT EVENING, Jackson and Maggie walked barefoot across warm sand as the sun slowly lowered over the horizon. Groups peppered the beach, preparing cookouts and picnics. The air smelled of grilled hotdogs, sunscreen, and the sea. Tireless children still played near the shore with buckets and shovels.

They headed south, hugging the shoreline and leaping from an occasional far-reaching wave. Maggie hadn't said much since they left the house. "You all right?" He reached to take her hand, but she pulled away.

"When were you planning on telling me you were engaged?"

"Oh. That."

"You should've told me," she said. "It's more than just being *involved* with someone."

"I'm sorry. You're right. You *know* why I didn't tell you," Jackson said. "Are you mad?"

"I'm not mad. But it makes me feel even more guilty."

"Which is why I didn't tell you."

"I'm aware of why you didn't tell me." She covered her mouth with her hand, trying not to laugh. A nervous laugh escaped anyway. "It's not funny. I'm not laughing because it's funny."

"I'm aware of that." He grimaced. "More than aware."

"What did you tell her?"

"I told her I couldn't in good conscience marry her when I have feelings for someone else."

Maggie didn't say anything, just stared up at him with eyes cast in shadow.

"I have no business marrying her when I'm in love with you," he said. "And I told her that."

"Jackson, I'm afraid."

"Of what?"

"That you've made a mistake," she said. "That you'll regret it."

"I've lived with regret for twelve years. *This* decision will not lead to regret. Whatever it takes to win you back, I will do. No more regrets."

"But we don't have any idea what's going to happen," she said. "My life's in complete chaos. I can't live here with Zane indefinitely. I need a job and money and a plan. You had a plan with someone else."

"And I blew it up. I'm not letting you go without fighting this time. You can count on it."

"There's no work for me here."

"What about Hollywood?" He hated to ask, but for her sake, he must. Whatever her answer, he was prepared to fight for her. He would leave Cliffside Bay and move to L.A. if he had to. "There's opportunities there, right? You don't have to be a dancer in television or film."

"That's true," she said.

"Maybe your agent in New York could hook you up with the right people."

"That's not really how it works. Regardless, I'm not sure Hollywood's the answer for me. I'm tired. An acting life is like an endless interview process." She brushed her fingers on his forearm. "Let's stop and watch the sunset." They found a large piece of driftwood big enough for two and sat. Orange rays of sun glistened in her hair and on the water. What he would give to have a lifetime of sunsets.

"I'll go with you wherever you want," he said.

"You can't do that."

"I can."

"But your dad and the practice—you can't just bail on them," she said.

"Then stay here. Just long enough to decide if you want to be with me," he said.

She poked the stick into the sand. Her shoulders rose and fell. "I wish I'd come home triumphant."

"Would you agree to stay then? If you'd accomplished what you'd wanted?" he asked.

"I think so. I love it here. I've been so homesick. You have no idea."

"I do. I felt that way the entire time I was gone," he said.

"See, right there. You can't leave. Not after all your hard work."

He picked up her hand and placed it in his lap. "Let me be clear. I'll give up anything to be with you."

"I want to stay. I just don't know if I should."

"What gives you joy?" he asked.

"Dancing. Music." She leaned her head against his shoulder, like she used to when they were kids. "Can I tell you a secret?"

"Please," he said.

"I've been writing songs. Pop songs."

"Why's that a secret?"

"Because I'm too scared to sing them for anyone. Only Lisa knows. She thinks they're good, but she loves me, so who knows."

It took him a second to remember who Lisa was—the roommate and best friend. So much about her life that he had missed. *But you have her back. Focus on that.*

"Would you play one for me?" he asked.

"Maybe." She laughed when he turned to look at her. "Not

here. I need my guitar." She picked up a stick and drew a circle in the sand. "I have an idea of something I might try—I haven't told anyone, but I'm thinking maybe I could…write songs and sell them. Does that sound ridiculous?"

"Why would it sound ridiculous?" he asked.

"Because it's almost impossible."

"*Almost* impossible, which means it is possible." Jackson squeezed her hand. "And I don't have to hear your songs to know they're great. I remember the ones you wrote in high school. They were fantastic then."

"*You're* ridiculous," she said, her voice soft as velvet. "I *do* have a few connections from college that might be able to help. And I have about twenty-five songs written with the music transcribed. I'd need a demo tape and a bunch of other stuff that I can't pay for. Seriously, it's a long shot."

"But you have me and Zane and my dad. We'll help you. You're not alone," he said.

She shifted to look him in the eye. "Am I crazy to think I could resume a life here?"

"You know what I think."

"I've not hoped for anything in a long time. Not since I blew out my knee. It scares the heck out of me to let go and want *this*." She gestured toward the ocean before turning back to him. "And music. And you."

"I'll never let you down again." He dropped to the sand and knelt before her. "I know we have a lot of time to make up and I know it can't happen overnight, but I'd like permission to court you."

"Court me?" She laughed. "That makes you sound a hundred years old."

He smiled as he took both her hands. "What I mean is, I'd like to win you back the right way—remind you of the reasons we were so madly in love. Remind you that we're soulmates." The skirt of her sundress shifted in the breeze, revealing the scar on her left knee. He placed his hand over the scar. "There's a second act for you, Maggie. I know there is. Whatever you're meant to do next will reveal itself. You have my word. I'll never ask you to give up your dream again."

"What if it's just our memories fueling these feelings?" she asked. "What if we discover that we're not soulmates? What then?"

"The only way to find out is to spend time together. You're here for a few weeks at least. Give me that time to remind you of what it feels like to be an 'us.' I know, like I've never known anything in my life, that everything we once felt is still part of our story. We will be an *us*, once again. Wherever our love and your next dream lead us, I'm ready. If not—if your fears prove to be true—that we don't belong together—then we'll part knowing the truth. At least then we can finally move on with our lives."

She ran her fingers along his cheekbones, as if reading braille. "I give you permission to court me. Even though I think we've both gone crazy."

"There's another way to test my theory," he said.

"What's that?"

"Let me kiss you."

He felt her shiver.

"*May* I kiss you?" he asked.

"You don't have to ask," she whispered. "You've never had to ask."

With his hands in her hair, he lowered his head and brushed the spot just below her ear with his lips. She drew in a sharp breath. "You smell…like every good thing," he said.

"You do too." Her fingers dug into his shoulder blades. The tension in her body was like a coiled spring. What would set her free to love him?

He traveled the length of her jawline, leaving soft kisses along the way until he reached her mouth. "The prettiest girl in the world." He touched his lips to hers and kissed her as soft as the sea breeze, hoping she would respond. She did, opening her tender mouth to him—a gift that only she could give. When he deepened his touch, she pressed her torso against him and wrapped her arms around his neck like someone who had found something they'd lost and would never let go of again.

They remained intertwined, kissing like the teenagers they once were, as the very last of the golden light disappeared from their small section of the ever-spinning world. Somewhere else the sun rose, and lovers kissed good morning. In another place, they danced under a black, starry sky. But here on this patch of sand and under this sky that transformed above them into an inky purple, a sliver of moon rose like a smile. The first audacious stars appeared. And he kissed the only woman he'd ever loved.

A shift inside him happened as fast as the speed of sound. Twelve years ago, the news of her death had shattered his heart. Now, her kisses pieced together the broken bits.

His Bird had returned to him.

This, right here, right now, I will remember for the rest of my life.

And it seemed to him, there amongst the smiling moon and the first brave stars, that the meaning of life was found in the moments where love stretched and breathed like a living creature. It was in these brief snatches of time that one's whole life made perfect sense. Love given and received gave our toiled years meaning. Love told the story of our life.

Because at the end, when all that remained were the memories captured in paintings hung on walls, or photographs in a box, or merely flashes of moving pictures behind our eyes, it would be a moment such as this that whispered our life's story. *This is your glory, your meaning, your purpose.*

"I'll never give up on us," he said when they finally came up to inhale the briny sea air.

"Us." She buried her face in his neck. "My favorite word."

CHAPTER THIRTEEN

Maggie

THE NEXT DAY, Maggie watched from just inside the front door of Miss Rita's studio as little girls in pink tights and leotards formed two lines in front of the full mirror. Miss Rita was as slim and straight as a pencil. Dressed in a black leotard and tights, she called out commands in time to piano music. "First position. Plié. That's it." Clusters of mothers huddled in corners. A few rocked baby carriers with their feet. Several toddlers sat against the wall looking at a book and eating graham crackers.

Maggie breathed in the familiar scent of hairspray, leather dance shoes, and Miss Rita's perfume.

White streaks ran through Miss Rita's tight bun. Fine lines were imprinted onto her gaunt face. When Maggie took her first class at three years old, Miss Rita was in her early thirties. *Not much older than I am now.* This studio had been her work for over thirty years. After a short career with a professional ballet company, Miss Rita had moved here with her husband Alec. They'd never had children of their own, having to settle for the countless little girls and a few boys who had danced over this very floor.

As Maggie watched the little girls, she traveled back through the years, remembering her own time here. She'd gripped her mother's hand that first day, frightened to join the group of girls gathered in the middle of the floor. Miss Rita had reached out her hand and Maggie was swept away from her mother to the magical place of dance—emotion and expression through movement.

It wasn't until she went to live with the Wallers after her mother's death that she discovered she had a beautiful singing voice. Lily Waller had loved music. There was always something playing on her stereo—everything from pop music to show tunes. Lily had insisted she take lessons from the local teacher, Miss Hillary. Miss Hillary insisted she learn an instrument. There was a guitar at the Wallers—a birthday present for Jackson who had shown no interest or aptitude. It sat in the corner of his bedroom for a year before Maggie presented it as an option to Miss Hillary.

Could I play a guitar?

That'll do just fine. For now.

Miss Hillary had smelled of patchouli and wore thick black glasses. She dressed in long skirts and blouses with no bra. She stuffed carrots and tomatoes into her juicer for meals. Despite the lack of protein, the woman was a taskmaster. Every week Maggie was given new chords and exercises. Calluses developed on her fingertips. Like dance, it was hard work, but, unlike school, which often bored her, music filled the empty spaces left by her mother's death.

She knew now that self-expression through dance and music healed her—allowed her to live in the world without her mother. Without it, she shuddered to think what she might have become. An empty shell of a person who simply goes through the motions of life with shuttered eyes? *That* she could not have done. Even knowing the outcome. She would not dance again. But she had. She'd danced and danced and danced.

And she could still open her mouth and strum her guitar and sing from the sweet nectar of her soul.

Despite all the heartache and disappointment her chosen path had provided—it was hers and hers alone. She had not let anyone, or anything, deter her. Right here in this very room, she had discovered her passions and had never let them go out of fear. This she would choose to be proud of. She hadn't just *talked*, she had *done*. She had worked and hoped and tried again. Even the torn knee and the nights she sang in bars where every customer was either smashed or talking or looking at their phones were part of her journey. *The story of me.*

Now, Miss Rita dismissed class. The room reverberated with little girls' voices as they ran to their mothers.

Maggie crossed the dance floor to her old teacher. Miss Rita put her thin arms around Maggie and held her close. "Oh, how can it be that you're here? It was almost impossible to believe when Zane told me, but here you are right in front of me." She drew away and placed her hands upon Maggie's shoulders. "My goodness, you're beautiful."

"I'm ten pounds heavier than I used to be." Maggie hadn't planned to confess, but somehow that was what came out of her mouth. "They told me I needed more meat on my bones." That had been one of the first bits of feedback at auditions. *Gain a few. You look like a skeleton. It hurts me to look at you.*

For ballet, she had been just right, but not in the new world she'd plunged into. Lisa had been jealous. All she ever heard was to drop five pounds, even though she was perfectly proportioned with muscles and sexy curves. In show business, it seemed one could never win. Too short. Too tall. Too skinny. Too fat.

"You glow," Miss Rita said. "Perfection."

Maggie blushed, pleased. "Thank you. You look well, too."

"A few more wrinkles, but age can't touch me in here." Miss Rita tapped her bony chest. "Come along, let's take a stroll along the walkway. Moving is necessary if we're to catch up on the last twelve years."

The studio had emptied by the time they stepped through the front door to the sidewalk. Maggie donned her sunglasses while Miss Rita locked the door. When she looked back to Maggie, Miss Rita looked her up and down before voicing her approval of Maggie's long-sleeved linen shirt and cropped cotton leggings. She wagged a long finger at her. "However, we must stop into Violet's and get you a hat. You've taken care of your skin. I'm glad to see it, but this sun will ruin you."

"You told me to always wear my sunscreen." Maggie's makeup had sunscreen in it. Almost always, when she put it on in the mornings, she had remembered Miss Rita's advice. Until a few days ago, those memories were accompanied with a flash of pain. But now, here they were. Together again.

"Good girl." Miss Rita slipped her arm into Maggie's as they crossed the street to the shop called "Violet's Treasures."

"She has everything you can imagine in here," Miss Rita said. "And they're all made from something recycled. Wallets made from tires and such."

"We had one in Brooklyn too," Maggie said. "Too expensive for me, but it's a neat concept."

"Well, I'm buying you a hat as a welcome home gift."

"What happened to the liquor store?" Maggie asked.

"Mr. Cooper sold it. He owns a few apartment buildings and spends his time on the beach with one of those machines that look for metal."

"A metal detector? Do they still make those?" Maggie asked.

"Unfortunately, yes. It's a terrible waste of a life. To think he spends his energy looking for lost watches in the sand."

Maggie smiled as they walked inside the shop. It looked nothing like the old liquor store. Attractive products ranging from wallets to phone cases to beach chairs were displayed on shelves and tables. Clothing items hung on racks. Jewelry sparkled in a glass case. The young woman behind a glass counter, with hair the color of honey and skin tanned a golden brown, was hunched over a stack of receipts. She didn't look up until Miss Rita called out to her.

"Good afternoon, Violet," Miss Rita said.

Violet jumped. "I'm sorry. I didn't hear you come in." A worry crease had furrowed her brow, but Maggie suspected she was in her mid-twenties. Violet, as if she knew Maggie's thoughts, slid a finger across her forehead and put on a smile that seemed a touch too bright.

"We've come for a sunhat," Miss Rita said.

Violet came from around the counter to stand near them. "I have some pretty ones over here." She led them to the other end of the shop where various types of hats were displayed on a rack. "This one here is made from an old pair of jeans." Violet held it up for them to see. It was indeed a sunhat, but it looked more like a bottom in a pair of jeans. Maggie shuffled her feet, unsure how to express politely that she didn't care for it.

Violet seemed to pick up on her ambivalence because she reached under the display case and pulled one out made of a feminine pink and green floral cotton print.

"Yes, that's better." Maggie pulled it low over her head. The green matched her eyes. *Not bad. For a redhead.*

"Perfection," Miss Rita said.

They followed Violet up to the counter. After she rung them up, Violet smiled shyly at Maggie. "Do you remember me at all? From school? I was two years below you and Zane and Jackson. Violet Ellis?"

Maggie searched her memory. Yes, there it was. *Violet Ellis. Cheerleader. No siblings.* Her parents had owned a boat and Maggie and Jackson had gone to a party on it once when Violet's parents were out of town. Violet hadn't meant for the party to become so large. Zane and Jackson had to make everyone leave.

"I remember you," Maggie said. "It took me a moment. Your parents had a boat."

"You were on it once." Violet tossed her shiny hair behind one shoulder and beamed at Maggie. She'd been pretty back in school, but she was beautiful now, with toned muscles and that bronzed skin that looked like a piece of toffee.

"I'd forgotten that party until just now," Maggie said. "Zane and Jackson had to toss a couple of the guys into the water to get them to leave."

"Yes, that's the one," Violet said, blushing. "The entire night traumatized me. I never did another rebellious thing for the rest of high school. And, my parents totally found out when they got home. One of the other boat owners ratted me out. Having a party on the docks wasn't my brightest idea ever."

Maggie laughed. "No, probably not."

"I was grounded for two months." Violet crossed her arms over her chest and shook her head as if she couldn't believe what she saw. "It doesn't feel real to see you. I'm sorry for what your dad did. It's awful. You were very missed."

"Thank you. It's awkward to come home and discover your own tombstone, to say the least."

"For Jackson's sake, I'm glad you made it back finally. It would be nice to see him happy again." Violet clamped her hand over her mouth. "I'm sorry. I said too much."

"It's all right," Maggie said.

"I know it's not my place to say anything," Violet said. "Jackson's such a good man. We've wanted someone special for him. And Sharon, well, she's...not you."

Maggie inwardly cringed. What could she say? *Sharon's been kicked to the curb because I wasn't dead after all?* The facts made both Jackson and her look awful. Maybe they were. How could they ever maneuver through this and keep their sense of integrity?

After they said goodbye to Violet, Maggie and Miss Rita walked arm-in-arm down Main Street toward the beach. Miss Rita asked Maggie to tell her about the years in New York. However, they didn't get far before being stopped by a woman about Miss Rita's age. Maggie had no idea who she was, but the woman knew her. "Maggie, I just heard the news. Such a terrible thing. We're glad to have you back."

Maggie mumbled a thank you and they moved along. Minutes later, it happened again. She suspected the whole town had heard the story. Cliffside Bay seemed to have invented the telephone tree. *Everyone* knew. And *no one* appeared embarrassed to express their outrage or ask personal questions, including: had she seen Jackson yet?

It took them a good thirty minutes to reach the beach. They headed left on the cement pathway that ran above the beach. Wide enough for two lanes, walkers and runners were to stay to the right, anything with wheels to the left.

"Well, that was embarrassing," Maggie said.

"The people of Cliffside Bay never have learned to mind their own business," Miss Rita said. "It's as maddening as ever. However, the busybody ladies have finally stopped asking me when I'm going to have a baby. I guess when you're over fifty, they figure it's too late."

"Did you want one?" Maggie asked.

"I would've been happy if it had happened, but it never did, so I just decided it wasn't meant to be. I've always been one to ride the current, not fight it. I suppose it's due to the bohemian years I spent in France." Miss Rita laughed her sultry laugh. "I surprised myself when I settled down with Alec and moved to this little town after all the excitement of Paris. But love will do things to a person's brain. But, oh, the fun I had back in the day. Paris rained men. So many men."

"Miss Rita? Really?"

"Have I shocked you?"

"A little."

"I had many, many suitors, my girl. Yes, indeed. But I merely flirted and turned them all away. First, in the name of art. Later, for the love of one man— one I loved enough to move to the only provincial town on the coast of California."

"Is it provincial? I never thought that when I lived here," Maggie said.

"That's because you've never lived in Paris. Americans are so conservative and they don't even know it. But what about New York? Were there men?"

"No, not so many. A few."

"Yes?"

"Actually, none. None is more accurate," Maggie said.

"But why?" Miss Rita asked. "New York didn't rain men?"

"There's men, yes. But, like you, I chose art over dalliances. It seemed to me that all that ever came from men were tears. For my friends, anyway. And, I'd been hurt. Jackson, you know."

"Yes. I remember quite well what a distraction he was. He and Zane were determined to ruin your dance career on that surf board. Not to mention your skin."

Maggie laughed. "We had such fun back then."

"Those boys." Miss Rita shook her head in obvious disapproval. "I suppose Jackson still has his same magical influence over your heart?"

"It seems so, yes."

"You can't possibly stay here. Not now. Not after all you've accomplished."

"About that," Maggie said. "It's not exactly as I imagined it would be. Success has been somewhat elusive."

"Elusive?"

"I've landed a lot of chorus girl roles over the years. Always the chorus girl never the girl, if you know what I mean. In between gigs, there were a lot of bartending and waitressing jobs."

"Well, that's to be expected. The life of a 'song and dance' girl isn't paved in flat stone."

Flat stone? Miss Rita had a knack for coming up with obscure metaphors.

"It's been a slog. A long, hard slog. I have good friends, but other than them, I don't have much to show for twelve years of hard work," Maggie said. "Not much of anything to leave behind."

"Leave behind? You mean you're not returning?"

"Despite your fears, it wasn't surfing, but I blew out my knee last year. I won't dance again. I *can't* dance again." Maggie's voice caught. Why now? Hadn't she cried all the tears there were to cry? Perhaps it was the presence of Miss Rita, her first teacher, who had wanted so much for Maggie and who'd believed in her more than anyone before or since. "I'm trying to figure out Plan B. When Darla called, it was the catalyst to begin the process of finding my new life."

"I see," Miss Rita said.

Maggie stole a glance at Miss Rita's profile. Was her mentor disappointed? She couldn't be sure, but a nagging sense of failure hovered at the fringes of Maggie's consciousness. How many times had she dreamt of sending Miss Rita a program with her listed as the star of the show? Not that it would have mattered. They all thought she was dead. No one would have gotten a letter even if she'd sent it.

"I gave it my best try. Every single day," Maggie said.

"Well, then, you can rest easy knowing you tried your best. That's all one can expect in this life, I'm afraid."

"Are you disappointed in me?" Maggie asked.

"Absolutely not. I'm disappointed *for* you, but not in you," Miss Rita said. "You risked everything for your dream. You worked hard, and you never gave up. So, no, I'm quite the opposite of disappointed. I'm bursting with pride. It's easy to give up, or to never start in the first place. You did neither."

They walked in silence for a few seconds. Overhead, the seagulls called to one another. The sound of waves as they crashed to shore soothed Maggie's frazzled nerves. "I missed this beach," Maggie said.

"Are you thinking of staying?" Miss Rita asked.

"I'm not sure."

"For Jackson?"

"Maybe," Maggie said.

"Maybe?"

"The feelings are still there. Our connection was as deep and strong as they get. I can't ignore that."

"You were very young." Miss Rita's pace slowed as they

reached the end of the cement walkway. The cliffside steepened here, making it impossible for human feet. Below, the sandy stretch of beach ended, dwarfed by hillside. They turned back to go the other way.

"I always got the feeling you didn't like Jackson," Maggie said. "Why was that?"

"It wasn't that I disliked him. He's a fine man, as is his father. But you were extraordinarily talented. Too many times in my life I've seen women give up their dreams to be with a man. Or, once they're married his wishes or dreams become the priority and she's an afterthought. The woman's plans are forgotten, even when they're the one with the talent or intelligence. For generations, we've traded our dreams for the men we're with. I didn't want that for you."

"Is that what happened to you?"

"Heavens no. I've always done exactly as I pleased. Alec accepted that about me a long time ago. It just so happened that my dreams morphed right around the time he appeared. I had done what I wanted, which was to dance in the ballet. I traveled the world. And then, when I reached an age where I could no longer perform, I decided to come home to California. I found this little town when I was out exploring one day. Something inside me told me this was *the* place. I opened my studio and started a new life. I'd lived here a month when I went over to Hugh's bar— Zane's bar now—for a bite to eat and Alec was sitting at the counter, drowning his sorrows in a martini."

"What was he sorry over?"

"A woman. It's always a woman. Unless it's their jobs or the lack of a job. Men are much more fragile than we are. Anyway, I sat down next to him and ordered a glass of wine and he started telling me all about it. It was no problem to distract him from her." Miss Rita smiled wickedly. "I had my Paris training, after all. And voilà. We've been together ever since."

"You've been happy?" Maggie asked.

"Not every moment, but yes. He has annoying qualities, as do

I. But we work it out. Someone once told me it wasn't the grand gestures that make a marriage work, but the daily kindnesses. We've always been good at the small stuff. But enough about me. Tell me, dearest, what's it like to be home after all this time?"

"It's not what I thought, obviously. I had no idea anyone missed me or wanted me home." She shared with Miss Rita the returned letters and how she'd interpreted them as rejection. "I thought everyone sided with Jackson—that you all thought I was selfish to leave."

"You poor girl," Miss Rita said.

They were at the other end of the walkway now. At the bench, they sat. Umbrellas of all shades and sizes dotted the beach. Children dug in the sand. Boogie boarders screamed as they rode a wave into shore.

"Have you ever thought about why you believed the lie so easily?" Miss Rita asked.

"What lie?"

"The one you told yourself when the letters came back unopened."

"That wasn't a lie. That really happened."

"It was Darla's lie. The question is why you so readily accepted that people who'd loved you your whole life would suddenly not want anything to do with you. Many people, when not receiving an answer to their letters might have emailed. Or called. Instead, you chose to believe that we'd all abandoned you. That we'd chosen Jackson over you. Which, is ridiculous."

"I guess I haven't thought of it that way." They sat in silence for a few minutes.

"You were the most talented student I've ever had. Also, the hardest working. We were close. How could you think I'd abandon you?"

"Because I always felt like the charity case around here. My drunk and dangerous father was a known murderer—my mother was dead—so the town had no choice but to take care of me. When the letters came back unopened, it confirmed my suspicions. No one wants me. I imagined you were all relieved that I wasn't here any longer."

"That, my dear, is a pretty big leap."

Maggie flushed with embarrassment and pulled her hat lower on her forehead. "It seems foolish now, but at the time, I was disoriented and hurt. I decided then and there that I would never think of this place or any of you ever again. It worked, too, for the most part. I was busy in college with friends and new experiences. When I graduated, I thrust myself into my new life. Auditions and classes and waitressing jobs consumed most of my energy."

"You were wrong about everything. You were the beloved daughter of this town, especially to Doc and me. We loved you as if you were our own flesh and blood." Miss Rita's hand shook as she took Maggie's into her lap. "My girl, how I grieved for you."

Maggie's vision blurred with tears. "I missed you too."

"Perhaps this summoning from your father was a sign to come home."

"Maybe."

"I'm retiring," Miss Rita said. "At the end of the year. It's either sell the studio or shut it down."

"Retire?" Maggie couldn't imagine town without Miss Rita's studio. "What would you do?"

"Spend more time in my garden. Worry less about the annual recital. It's become rather tiresome over the years. I'm worn out. There's a young woman who works for me, Christina, who's interested in buying the studio from me. But she's not sure she can handle it alone, both the financial burden of the loan and running it. She has small children and a husband who travels."

"Does she have the money?" Maggie asked.

"She has enough for a down payment and I imagine she could get approval for a small business loan. The business is lucrative. All little girls want to take ballet. Plus, we have adult classes now. Zumba, for one. And Violet teaches yoga. There's potential for more, with the right vision. I'm old and set in my ways. Christina had to fight me tooth and nail to get Zumba in there. She has a good sense of what people like, especially adults."

"That's great. What's the problem then?"

"Like I said, Christina's not sure she could handle running it on her own. Although, perhaps she could partner with someone. Like you, for example." Miss Rita's sly glance and smile made Maggie laugh again.

"I know nothing about running a business."

"You know how to dance. You were always so good with the little ones when you were in high school. You could teach a musical theatre course for the older kids. They want one, but Christina doesn't have the background for it."

"All my savings went to this." Maggie pointed to her knee. "There's no way I could get the money together."

"Well, think about it, won't you?"

"Sure. I'll think about it."

This was a lie. Maggie didn't want to run a dance studio if she couldn't dance. It would be salt in her wounded knee every single day. No, the studio wasn't it. The problem was—what was it? And where was it?

And would Jackson be there?

* * *

By the time Maggie left Miss Rita back at the studio, it was a little after five, so she headed into the bar to see Zane. Jackson had texted that he would meet her there after work. He wanted her to meet some more of his friends. Like a silly schoolgirl, she shivered with pleasure at the thought of meeting the people who had been such a huge part of Jackson's life. Could she be part of all this? Did she want to?

The Oar was quiet, occupied with only a few scattered tables. People were still at the beach, but she suspected it would fill later with hungry and thirsty patrons. Zane had the windows open and the outside tables and umbrellas set up for the evening. A soft breeze and ceiling fans provided cool air as she walked through the bar area to the counter.

Zane looked up as she slid onto a stool. "Hey. Nice hat," he said.

She pulled it from her head and set it on the counter. "Thanks. I bought it at Violet's little shop that used to be the liquor store." She ran her fingers through her hair, then twisted the entire mass into a bun and fixed it with a pin from her bag. "Speaking of which, where does everyone buy booze now?"

"The market. Or here. *Preferably* here."

"Does Old Man Cooper really use one of those metal detectors on the beach?"

Zane chuckled as he wiped under the beer spout. "Not every day, but frequently."

"Violet seems nice," Maggie said. "It took me a moment to remember her. Then, we had a somewhat awkward exchange."

"Yeah?" Zane asked. "Not surprising."

"She told me how unhappy Jackson's been and that Sharon was no me."

"Yes, ma'am," Zane said. "She's not shy with her opinions."

"I was stopped like five times. Pretty much everyone finds a way to ask if I've seen Jackson yet, which I find excruciating."

"Why?"

"Because," she said.

"Because it makes you look like the bad guy and you hate that?"

"Yes. Exactly," Maggie said, laughing.

"I'll tell you what Brody told Jackson. Sometimes it can be about what you want and not about everyone else. Plus, who cares what other people think?"

"Me?'

"Listen, Mags, life sucks pretty much all of the time. If you have a chance at love, you better grab it up. Your responsibility is to yourself, not bitchy Sharon."

"Zane! That's unkind."

"What? It's true."

"If the lectures over, can I have wine, please?" She smiled to soften her words, but she needn't have bothered. Zane was clearly not troubled by her scolding if his grin was any indication. How could it seem as if no time had passed? Was this the test of true friendship? Years could batter hearts and bodies, but not our intimate connections with others. She had a sudden image of the three of them in their golden years, white-haired and shrunken, but still making one another laugh.

Zane poured a glass of chardonnay for her and then hustled around the bar, setting up for the evening.

"Is Violet married? I didn't think to ask," Maggie said.

"No, but she has a little boy," Zane said. "Dakota. He's a cute little bugger. Poor kid broke his arm the other day and Jackson had to put a cast on it."

"Where's his father?"

"No one knows," Zane said. "Violet's super close with Honor. The rest of us don't know her that well."

"Honor is Brody's assistant, right?"

"Yes." Zane seemed to be avoiding her eyes.

"What's Honor like?" Maggie asked. "Is she sweet like Kara?"

"She's okay." He hesitated before continuing. "Violet and Kyle hate each other. I mean, *hate*."

"Wait, is she the one who pickets in front of his resort?" Maggie asked, just putting two and two together.

"That's the one."

"You guys are like Melrose Place around here."

"Hardly."

"Why don't you like Honor?" she asked.

"I like her fine. What gives you that impression?"

"I've known you a long time," Maggie said.

"How was your walk with Miss Rita?"

"Changing the subject for the second time in thirty seconds. Duly noted."

"I forgot what a pain you can be," Zane said.

"Fine. You don't want to talk about Honor." She rubbed her hands together in a mock gesture of evil. "I'll get it out of you later."

Zane held a glass up to the light, obviously ignoring her.

"Miss Rita's as feisty as ever," she said.

"Yep. When I went to her house to tell her about you, she gave me the full stink eye. She's never forgiven me for teaching you how to surf."

"She admitted as much today," Maggie said.

Zane's gaze moved from her to the door. Or, rather, to the blond bombshell that just walked through the door.

"Who's that?" Maggie asked.

"*That's* Honor Sullivan," Zane said.

The infamous Honor Sullivan. Cue the dramatic background music.

Honor waved as she glided across the floor. Her voluminous shiny blond hair bounced around her shoulders like she was filming a television commercial for hair products. She wore shorts that barely covered her rear, a tight tank top and high sandals, leaving little of her hourglass figure to the imagination.

Maggie glanced at Zane. His face had gone from relaxed to tense.

"Hey, Zane." Honor Sullivan had a surprisingly sweet, high-pitched voice, almost like a child's.

"Maggie Keene, meet Honor Sullivan," Zane said. No wonder Zane had a thing for her. She was a beauty with a heart shaped face and butterscotch skin. Her big brown eyes exuded intelligence. The rest of her exuded sensuality.

For the first time since she entered the bar, Honor took her eyes from Zane and looked over at Maggie. "Oh my God, you're Maggie. The dead girl that isn't dead."

Maggie smiled and held out her hand. "That's me. Still not dead."

"It's a miracle." Honor ignored Maggie's hand and pulled her into a tight embrace. Spicy perfume wafted from Honor's golden, freckle-free skin. Lucky girl. She didn't have to wear a sunhat and long sleeves.

For a woman no taller than most middle school boys, Honor's grip was strong. *A force. Like a tornado.*

"It's so awesome to meet you. Jackson's the nicest guy in the whole world and he's talked about you so much over the years that I feel like I know you." Honor fluttered her petite hands. Perfectly pink manicured nails shone under the light. "You're the prettiest. Your hair and eyes. What's going on with your mouth? It reminds me of a flower. Wow. Jackson told me you were beautiful, and he did *not* lie. No wonder you're an actress."

A hugger who loves superlatives. Maggie couldn't help but like her immediately. Honor reminded her a little of Pepper. She almost laughed thinking about Honor and Pepper in the same room. Now that would be a recipe for trouble. The best kind.

Maggie stole a quick glance at Zane. A muscle in his cheek flexed. Was he gritting his teeth?

"I haven't seen you in a while," Zane said. "Where you been?"

"I've been out of town for work," Honor said.

"I saw your car drive through town this morning. You just get back?" What should have sounded like a friendly question, didn't. In fact, it sounded downright accusatory.

Honor flashed Zane a saucy smile. "Are you stalking me?"

He shrugged and picked up a towel. "Hardly. Just figured you were pulling one of your disappearance acts from some guy's house."

Maggie could feel the heat rising from Honor's body. "Not cool, dude."

"Just calling it as I see it," Zane said.

Why was he acting like such a horse's rear? Maggie wanted to reprimand him and send him to bed with no supper.

"Do you want something to drink?" Zane asked.

"Sure. White wine, please." Honor's voice shook slightly.

Zane had hurt her. Maybe Honor wasn't as tough as she looked.

"Mind if I join you, Maggie?" Honor asked.

You better believe it. I need to get to the bottom of this. "Please. I'd love it."

As Zane poured Honor a glass of wine, one of his bartenders arrived, providing a convenient exit.

"I've got work to do in the office," Zane said. "Enjoy your drinks, ladies."

"We will. Now that you're gone," Honor said under her breath.

"I heard that," Zane said as he disappeared around the door.

"Awkward," Honor said. "Sorry about that."

"It's fine. No need to apologize."

Honor let out a long sigh. "We have a difficult relationship."

Maggie wanted to know every detail, but it wasn't her place to ask a woman she'd known for five minutes.

Turns out, she didn't need to ask questions. Honor was as effusive with her inner thoughts as she was with her hugs. "We slept together a while back and ever since then it's been weird between us. It might have something to do with the fact that I left him in the middle of the night while he was asleep. It's kind of my thing."

"Thus, the dig."

"Yep."

"He likes you. A lot. I can tell," Maggie said. "Even if he's acting like a jerk. Well, *especially* if he's acting like a jerk."

Honor waved her hand, like she was shooing away a fly. "Never mind all that. It's deadly dull. We're idiots who'll never get our act together to admit we like each other. It's ridiculous. We're both children, which is only part of the issue. But anyway, I want to talk about you. So, this whole thing's beyond weird, right? I mean, you're dead, but not. Brody told me Zane found you at your own tombstone. What the hell? That is messed up."

"Yeah. Not something one expects when coming back to town to see your dying father." Maggie played with her napkin, embarrassed. How could she live here? She would forever be known as the *dead girl who wasn't dead*.

Honor continued to peer at her. "The famous Maggie. Such a total trip. Hugh, Zane's dad, used to talk about you sometimes. I worked for him while I put myself through college. On slow nights, he told me funny stories about when you and Zane were kids. He was the greatest. *Is* the greatest, I mean."

"Hugh? I agree. I'm sorry he's not well." If only he were, she could ask him questions about her mother.

"Zane told me all about how you and Jackson were so in love and that he wanted a love like that for himself. He didn't think Jackson should propose to Sharon who, by the way, is the *worst*."

"Why don't you like her?" *Sharon.* Still a bitter taste in her mouth. This group of friends knew everything about one another. Like her and Lisa and Pepper.

Honor's brown eyes seemed to dance with mischief. "I don't like Sharon because she's controlling and manipulative. And, I didn't think she'd ever move here, no matter what she told Jackson. Which, I am right about and have been from the beginning. None of that has anything to do with you."

"What do you mean?" Maggie asked.

"I mean, they were never going to get married unless Jackson agreed to move back to L.A. Which he never would. He's wanted to take over his dad's practice forever."

"Yes, that's true."

"Right. Duh, I know you know that. My point is, if you're feeling guilty about breaking them up—don't. You were the catalyst, but it would've happened anyway."

"That's what Zane thinks too."

"Is your love story as epic as everyone says?"

"Jackson and me? Epic?"

"Yeah, epic."

"I don't know what epic means exactly. I loved him with all my heart. But we were young when I left. Things are more complicated now." Why did she keep using that word? Things *weren't* complicated. She loved him just like she always had.

"Things are complicated only when we make them that way. When we break stuff down to two fundamental questions—all becomes clear. What do you want? What are you prepared to do to get it? If I were a betting girl, which I'm not—money should never be so carelessly treated—I would bet on you two being meant to be. Freaking epic." She paused only long enough to drink from her glass. "I'm not the most romantic girl in the world, but even I can see that this is a love story for the ages. I mean, seriously, after all these years, the two of you together again. If that's not meant to be, I don't know what is."

Just then, Kara appeared, carrying a bouquet of flowers. "Hi ladies." She handed Honor the flowers and kissed her on the cheek. "Happy Birthday, beautiful."

Maggie might need to reconsider friendship with these two. They were both way too pretty to hang around with, just like Pepper and Lisa. Kara's long brown hair was fixed in waves today. She wore a sleeveless cotton sundress that showed off her muscular arms.

"It's your birthday?" Maggie asked. How come Zane hadn't said anything? Did he not know or was he just being rude to Honor?

"Guilty," Honor said. "Zane obviously didn't remember."

"Maybe he doesn't know," Kara said. "You could tell him."

Honor rolled her eyes. "Kara's a fan of sharing your 'feelings' with the other person." She made quote signs in the air.

"If you'd done that already, Zane would know you're crazy about him, and perhaps things would be a little further along," Kara said, as she sat on the stool next to Honor. "Just an idea."

Honor smiled as she turned to Maggie. "It might just be that he *drives* me crazy but that I'm not crazy about *him*."

Kara pretended to bang her forehead against the counter. "You know that's not true."

"Maggie, you've known him forever," Honor said. "What's the secret to Zane's heart?"

Maggie thought for a moment. Could she answer with assurance? The Zane she remembered from their youth was sweet and thoughtful, although not one to share his innermost feelings unless pressed. Pushed, more like it. He was quick to anger, too. A temper. A bad temper. She'd leave that part out. "He's not completely forthcoming about his feelings."

"Most men aren't," Kara said.

"Jackson is," Honor said.

"He is." Maggie laughed. "Zane used to say he was like a girl that way, which is rude."

"But kind of true," Honor said.

"I don't remember him ever being serious with anyone," Maggie said. "All the girls had crushes on him in high school. I mean, not surprising. Look at him."

"I had the biggest crush on him when I first moved here." Honor spoke softly with an occasional glance at the door to the kitchen. "The first summer I worked here, Zane came home from college to help his dad out between semesters. He didn't even know I was alive then. Later, after his wedding was called off, he came home for good and I started crushing on him all over again. He's so...dreamy. It's not just that he's smokin' hot. I dig his personality. He's manly combined with that laid-back surfer vibe. Plus, he's smart. Really smart. And scrappy, like me. I admire the way he runs this business. He's made it even more awesome than it already was when Hugh ran things." Honor swirled her wine around the glass and looked mournful for a moment. "But I blew it. He won't even talk to me, unless it's to chastise me for something I've either done or not done."

Zane. Passing up this woman? What was wrong with him? "If you want, I can talk to him. I have ways of getting stuff out of him."

"Like what would you say?" Honor asked.

"What would you want me to say?" Maggie asked.

"Maybe that I'm not all bad and I wouldn't mind another chance."

"I could do that." Maggie smiled at the other women. A surge of contentment jolted through her. They could be her friends, like Lisa and Pepper back in New York. The love of her life, friends—so much potential for joy here in this town that was quickly becoming her home again.

"I don't know, though," Honor said. "I grew up in foster care, so you know, there were some bad men who did some bad things. So, I have issues. Zane deserved better than what I did. He deserves better."

Maggie's heart thudded heavy in her chest. She knew what Honor meant by bad men. God only knew what Honor had gone through. "It's understandable to have issues. Maybe give yourself a break? No one's perfect."

"Maybe. Hugh was the first man I ever met who was nice to me without wanting anything," Honor said. "I'll always love him for that."

"I worked here at the bar all through high school," Maggie said. "Hugh was a huge influence in my life too."

Honor's eyes misted. "I go to see him every week, if you'd ever like to tag along. He won't know you, unless he's having a rare good day."

"I'd really like that," Maggie said.

The exercise band on Kara's wrist buzzed. "It's a text from Brody," Kara said. "He's on his way. Maggie, you're staying for dinner, right?"

"Jackson already invited me. However, he didn't tell me it was Honor's birthday."

"Men often leave the most important stuff out." Honor finished the rest of her wine and gestured for the bartender to bring another. "Please stay, Maggie. It's going to be a super fun night."

"Thanks. I will." The back of Maggie's throat ached, touched by her new friends' kindness and acceptance.

"What're your plans for the future?" Kara asked. "If you don't mind my asking."

"I'm not totally sure," Maggie said.

Kara gazed at her with watchful eyes. "We're hoping Jackson doesn't get hurt all over again."

"I've been in love with Jackson since I was six years old,"

Maggie said. "The last thing I'd ever do is hurt him. All these years, I've never loved anyone else."

To Maggie's surprise, both Honor and Kara's eyes glistened with tears.

"Wow, dude. See, that's epic." Honor held up her bare arms for them to see. "Goosebumps."

"I didn't believe in soulmates until I met Brody," Kara said. "I keep thinking about all the years you guys had to be apart. It feels so unfair."

"My dad's a vengeful man," Maggie said.

Honor tapped the counter with her fingertips. "But maybe you needed that time apart to do the things you needed to do. You had to go to New York and chase your dream. If you hadn't, who knows who you would be now."

"I suppose," Maggie said.

"Maybe you guys weren't ready yet and now you are," Honor said. "Seasons and all that."

Kara stared at Honor. "You're getting sentimental and philosophical in your old age."

Honor flushed. "Well, you know...you and Brody are like so... inspiring. Or, disgusting, depending on how you look at it."

Kara wrapped her arm around Honor's shoulders. "Let's go with inspiring."

Honor swirled wine around and around her glass. "Do you guys ever feel like you were brought to a place and to certain people for a reason? Like there's more than just coincidence?"

"All the time," Kara said. "Look at me—coming here and getting a job with Brody. What are the odds that I'd find the love of my life in a place I'd never even heard of before I decided to move west?"

Kara went on to explain to Maggie that she'd relocated to Cliffside Bay from Philadelphia after a bad breakup. "It was meant for me to come here at the exact time I did. The first night I arrived, I came in this bar and sat in the very same spot you're sitting now. Zane was so kind to me and suggested an agency to talk with about a job. Next thing I knew, I was working for Brody."

"And they fell in love in like two seconds," Honor said. "It was awesome."

Kara nodded in obvious agreement. "It sounds so obvious to me now, but I had to learn to let go of the past so that I could embrace the future. You can't let your dad's hatred ruin your chance for a new beginning."

"And, a second chance," Honor said. "This town gave me one." She told Maggie how she'd inherited a house from a great-aunt. "Apparently, she could leave me a house, but not take me in when I needed a family. Whatever. At least she brought me here where I belong."

Kara raised her glass. "To second acts."

"To epic love stories," Honor said.

"To new friendships in an old town," Maggie said.

The ladies clinked glasses as Zane reappeared. He ran his hands through his hair and grinned at Maggie. "Don't be mad, but I just told our band to take the night off."

"Why would that make me mad?" Maggie asked.

"Because that means you have to play tonight," Zane said.

"What? No. I can't. Not tonight," Maggie said.

"But I have to have music on my birthday." Honor smiled with a wicked gleam in her eyes.

Zane's forehead furrowed as he looked at Honor. "It's your birthday? I totally forgot."

"No big deal," Honor said.

He flushed and rubbed his forehead. Maggie knew that expression. He felt bad that he'd forgotten. *He cares about this girl.*

"Come on, Mags. You have to do it." Zane put his hands together like a prayer. "Please."

Maggie shook her head. "No. The crowd expects a rock band. Not a singer with an acoustic guitar."

"I have a piano too," Zane said, pointing to the other end of the restaurant.

"I'm not a good fit," Maggie said.

"You have more of a coffee house sound, am I right?" Kara asked.

"Right," Maggie said. "Not what a summer crowd in a bar wants."

"Who's to say?" Honor asked. "I happen to love that kind of music."

"You do?" Zane asked. "I would've figured you for a metal band."

"Really? Do I look like a sixty-year-old chasing her youth?" Honor asked.

"The youth part, maybe," Zane said.

"Don't be rude." Maggie slapped his hand.

Zane smirked as he rubbed his hand. "I'm just kidding."

"It's fine. I refuse to rise to the bait on my birthday," Honor said.

Kara turned to Maggie. "Come on. You have to do it. Jackson and Zane told us how good you are."

"Please, Maggie," Honor said. "It'll be a treat on my birthday."

Maggie looked from one woman to the other. "If I'm terrible you only have yourselves to blame."

"We'll take that risk," Zane said. "Any day of the week."

CHAPTER FOURTEEN

Jackson

JACKSON WATCHED AS Maggie and Zane set up the stage for her performance. A guitar hung from a strap around Maggie's neck. She strummed a few cords before tuning one of the strings. Zane's bartender adjusted the sound coming from the speakers.

Maggie had run upstairs to change clothes after Honor's birthday dinner, coming down in a black cotton dress that clung to her slender figure, paired with wedge sandals. Her hair hung loosely around her shoulders and she'd made up her eyes and lips. For the first time since her return, he saw a glimpse of the glamorous girl who lived in the most sophisticated city in the world.

Was Cliffside Bay too small for her now? Could she be happy here?

Brody and Kara sat across from him. Honor was at the head of the table. Kyle had brought a birthday tiara, which Honor wore like it was made for her.

Kyle came back from the bar with several pitchers of beer and took the seat next to him.

"I'm actually nervous for her," Jackson said.

"She'll be fantastic," Kyle said as he poured beers.

Honor rose from her seat and came around the table to stand next to Jackson. She squeezed his shoulders. "I'm happy for you."

"Thanks, kid." Jackson smiled up at her.

"Listen, you *cannot* blow this." Honor scooted around the chair to peer into his eyes and speak in her best *know it all* voice. "I mean, this is *so* meant to be. Just like Kara and Brody. You've got to go big or go home. This is epic stuff we're talking about. Not *modern guy plays it cool.* You've got to *Brody it up* and pull out the romantic gesture of the century."

"I'll take that into consideration," Jackson said. No one could lay it all out there like Honor Sullivan.

"Holy God, every guy in this place looks like they want to eat you for dinner, birthday girl. Have a seat next to me, so I can protect you," Kyle said with a brotherly tug on her arm. "All the men have suddenly turned into the Big Bad Wolf and you're Red Riding Hood. Could it be because your bottom's barely hidden? Girl, seriously, how am I supposed to stop a bar fight with you in those shorts?"

One time, Violet had said Honor possessed the body of a pole dancer, the face of America's sweetheart, and the brain of Warren Buffet, which had made them all laugh because it was true. Don't judge a book by its pretty cover. The girl under that adorable outside was as clever as they came.

If only Zane would get over himself and admit that he was madly in love with her—if only Honor would get over herself and admit that she was madly in love with him—all would be well. Sadly, they were in a marathon game of chicken.

He would not do that with Maggie. Never again would he make that mistake. Pride didn't keep you warm at night.

"Oh, man," Kyle said, staring into his phone. "I just got a text. They accepted our offer. We're proud owners of Grey Gardens."

Jackson took in a deep breath. "No way."

"Yes way. Now we just have to fix that dump up," Kyle said. "I have a feeling you might need it for a certain redhead."

"Kyle!" Kara said.

"What?" Kyle jumped.

"You'll jinx it," Kara said.

"No way," Brody said. "It's meant to be. Nothing's an accident." He gestured upward. "The big guy's got a plan." He and Kara looked into each other's eyes and smiled. "You just never know when a miracle's about to happen."

"You two are nauseating," Kyle said, grinning.

"Seriously," Honor said. "But Brody's totally right. Meant to be."

"I think she's ready to start," Kara said as she gestured toward the stage.

Maggie scooted onto a bar stool set in the middle of the stage area and smiled out at the crowded restaurant. Zane grabbed the microphone from the stand. Like obedient school children, the crowd hushed.

"Evening, everyone. Thanks for coming out tonight. We love having local bands play here, but this particular singer has a very special place in our hearts." Zane halted and stared at the floor, obviously composing himself, before looking back up to the crowd. "This is Maggie Keene, visiting from New York City. Our hometown star has returned to share her talent with us tonight. Please give her a warm welcome. We'd like her to stay for a while." Zane put the microphone back on the stand. Maggie smiled up at him and mouthed a word of thanks.

The sound of clapping hands and a few whistles filled the room.

Maggie adjusted the guitar on her lap. "Hey there. Glad to be here. Thanks for sharing your night with us. So, I might as well get this out in the open for the locals in the audience tonight. You've most likely heard the gossip. Surprise, I'm not dead."

Cheers and more clapping.

"For anyone new to town, I'll quickly fill you in. I came home and found my own tombstone. Awkward, right? Especially when you've been alive and well in New York City for the past twelve years. For any of you who hated me in high school, sorry, but I'm back."

The audience laughed.

"No one could ever hate you, Maggie," said someone from the back.

"Welcome home, Maggie," said another—female this time.

Jackson gazed at her in amazement. When had she become so funny? She was loose and easy up there, with no traces of the shy girl she once was. His Maggie had blossomed into a true performer. How could the idiots in New York not see that she was a star?

"You guys are too kind. Anyway, enough about that. I'm going to start with a classic James Taylor song, "Carolina in My Mind." Years ago, I lost someone who took me in and loved me like her own when she didn't have to. This was her favorite."

The crowd went silent as Maggie's crystalline voice floated into the room, pure and sweet. Behind him, someone gasped as she held a long note. Jackson's throat ached. His mom's favorite song about her home state.

"Goosebumps," Honor whispered.

Maggie's formal training was obvious by the roundness of her vowels and the resonate, effortless quality of her voice. Yet, her interpretation of this classic folk song was perfect in its simplicity and approachability. She had been talented when they were young, but her craft had risen to a higher level, obviously honed over years of work. All traces of her former breathiness had disappeared.

If needed, he knew she could belt out a show tune in a musical, but he suspected she preferred this music. At least she had when they were young. From what he could hear now, she still did.

For the next few hours, she sang a variety of new and old popular music, rock ballads, and folk songs. The crowd appeared to love her, if their loud applause was any indication. Couples danced, including Brody and Kara.

Zane joined them at the table after the first few songs. Jackson caught him stealing glances at Honor. She appeared oblivious. He suspected she wasn't.

At the end of the first set, Maggie met Jackson's gaze. *Do one of your songs*, he mouthed to her.

She smiled and shook her head.

"Do it," he whispered.

"So, there's a certain someone in the audience who I admitted a little secret to earlier," Maggie said into the microphone. "And now he's coercing me into sharing it with you all too."

"Out with it." Honor stood and held her beer up as if to toast.

Maggie smiled. "I've written a few songs, nothing special, really. But I'll sing one now, and then I'll take a little break."

She picked a few notes on the guitar before leaning close to the microphone to sing the opening lines.

We danced under the purple sky...

* * *

It was after midnight when Jackson walked Maggie up the stairs to Zane's apartment. They'd said goodbye to the birthday girl and the rest of the gang and left Zane behind to finish a few tasks in the bar. Maggie flipped the light on as they entered the living room.

"You blew everyone away tonight," he said. "When did you get so funny?"

"Was I funny?"

"At times, yes. You just seemed so natural up there."

She shrugged as if it were nothing. "I feed off the crowd, especially ones like this. I sing at a bar in my neighborhood sometimes, and the audience is not nearly so encouraging. Mostly they're drunk."

"We don't get your kind of talent that often," he said. "People appreciate it here."

"Maybe I was always destined to be a big fish in a small pond and not a real star."

"You will always be a star to me." He caressed her neck with his thumb. "And, the most beautiful woman in the world."

She tilted her face to look up at him. "You always made me feel like a star."

"You are. You just are. And, your original song was beautiful. I knew they would be." He fixed his gaze on her small, pink mouth. "I don't care what those idiots in New York told you. You're as talented as anyone out there. You proved that tonight." He placed his hands in her hair. The strands slipped like silk through his fingers.

She trembled as his arms wrapped around her waist. "Are we foolish?"

"Foolish?"

"To think we can start again?" she asked.

"Foolish would be to think we couldn't," he said. "When we were young, do you remember how Miss Rita and some of our teachers at high school used to tell us that it was ridiculous to think we would stay together through college—that people just didn't do that?"

"I remember."

"And do you remember how it sometimes caused us to fight?"

"Yes," she said.

"Until one of us reminded the other that we weren't like other people."

"We were Jackson and Maggie," she said.

"The moment I forgot that is when I messed up. I let those ideas get in my head. I started to believe they were right. You'd go to New York and fall in love with some big actor or something instead of remembering. We were Maggie and Jackson."

"We belonged together."

"Soulmates," he said. "We've known it since we were six years old."

"When you beat the crap out of Tyler."

He pulled her close to him and breathed in the scent of her hair. "We're the lucky ones, Maggie. To have this thing between us that's not understandable to other people. It's us."

"I have something to tell you. It's a little embarrassing."

"Go ahead. I won't tease you," he said.

"I haven't been with anyone since you."

"You mean, that way?"

"Yes."

His heart pounded harder. "I can't say I'm sorry to hear that, but I'm surprised. Was there a reason?"

"Other than no one compared to you? No."

"Bird, you've always been my sweetheart, and you always will be." He leaned closer, breathing in her scent. When his lips met hers, she sighed and pressed herself against him. He kissed her gently at first, until she opened her mouth to let him capture her bottom lip between his. The world fell away, and it was only this moment, this woman. His one and only. She'd come back to him at last.

CHAPTER FIFTEEN

Maggie

MAGGIE WOKE THE next morning and rolled over to see Jackson in a similar spot as when they'd fallen asleep, curled on his side with a throw blanket clutched close to his chin. She took in every detail of his face. If she didn't see him with her own two eyes, she would have thought she'd dreamt the entire past two days.

They'd talked long into the night until they'd both fallen asleep in their clothes from sheer exhaustion.

Now, he stirred and opened his eyes. "Maggie, it's like a dream. Only it's real, right?"

"It's real. Now get up, sleepyhead. I smell bacon."

"Wait. I have something I want to tell you."

She snuggled closer to him, kissing his neck. "What is it?"

"None of that, or you'll get me off track," he said.

She scooted away slightly so she could look into his eyes. "What is it?"

"I want to take you out to the house later today," he said.

"I'd like that, but first I have to talk to Darla. I've put it off long enough." Jackson Waller had a way of distracting a girl.

"I have to get to work," he said. "But I'll pick you up around six and take you out to the Arnoult place."

"Don't you mean the Jackson Waller place?"

He groaned. "I really hope I haven't made a huge mistake."

"Following your dreams is never a mistake," Maggie said.

"Do you mean that? Despite what happened in New York City?" he asked.

She played with the collar of his t-shirt. "You know, I do. I've been thinking about all that since I got back here. We can't know what roads will lead where. All we can do is trust our instincts and be as brave as possible."

* * *

After Jackson left, Maggie knew it was time to call Darla. Her hands shook as she located Darla's number in her phone. She could do this. *Be tough. I have the cards.*

The phone rang several times before Darla answered. "What do you want?"

"I need to talk to you," Maggie said.

"I'm busy."

"Make time. I'm coming over in five minutes," Maggie said.

"Not the house. Your father's sleeping. Meet me at the little park in the middle of town."

"Five minutes."

"Yes, okay."

Minutes later, Maggie sat on the bench near the statue of one of the founding fathers of Cliffside Bay, Jacob Meeker. Why were there never any statues of founding mothers?

Darla was as she remembered. Short and stocky with a fluff of frizzy brown hair. Eyes like a trapped ferret's, suspicious and nervous. She plopped onto the bench like her legs were about to collapse. She wore a cotton dress in need of an iron and sports sandals that did nothing to hide jagged toenails.

"Your visit upset your father. It took me hours to get him calmed down." Darla smelled of stale cigarette smoke.

"I plan on upsetting him more before I leave," Maggie said. "After what you two did, I'm not too worried about whether he's agitated by my visits."

"I told him it was a mistake to contact you. But he said God told him to, in a dream, of all things." She rolled her eyes. "A hell of a time to get religion."

"It happens when faced with your own mortality," Maggie said. "Let me get straight to the point. I plan on going to the authorities about what you did. Last time I checked, tampering with mail was a federal offense."

Darla picked at her left thumbnail. "You'd have to prove it."

"Shouldn't be too hard to get a coworker to squeal," Maggie said. "Especially if Brody Mullen asks them to." Where had that come from? Name dropping was so tacky. Somehow, though, she knew Brody Mullen would be happy to help.

Darla crossed her arms, staring at Maggie with her ferret eyes. "Can't you see we did it for you? Your father wanted you to have a chance. That Waller boy was trouble."

"Jackson's a doctor with the moral code of a priest. How was he trouble?"

"Your father knew you'd give up your dream to be with him."

"What did he care?" Maggie asked. "He hadn't been a father to me. Ever."

"He cared."

"He wanted revenge."

"Maybe he believed in you," Darla said. "Ever think of that?"

"If he did, it was because he hoped to get money out of the deal."

Darla shrugged and opened her mouth to speak, then shut it again. By the pinched expression on her face, Maggie knew she'd pinpointed the reason for his "belief" in her talent.

"Whatever I say won't change your mind about him," Darla said. "Those Waller people poisoned you against him."

"He killed my mother and my baby sister. How's that for poison?"

"He had nothing to do with the baby."

"Do you really believe that, or is lying just second nature to you?"

"What do you want? Because I need to get back to your father."

"How about you give me what I want in exchange for me keeping my little mail fraud theory to myself," Maggie said.

"I'm listening."

"I want to know the truth about what happened the night my mother died."

"Why would you think I would know?" Darla said.

Maggie turned to get a closer look at her father's wife. Whiskers sprouted under Darla's chin, sticking up like the first growth of a Chia Pet. "I think you know because I believe you helped him."

"I didn't even know him then."

"You're lying. You want to know how I know?"

"Not particularly."

"The photograph on the mantel of you and my dad in front of the old Ford? Yeah, he sold that truck after my mother died. You were with him in Texas, weren't you? You guys met there and when my mother sent the divorce papers, they enraged him. He wanted revenge and the payout from the insurance policy he took out on her. So, he decided to come home and kill her and make it look like an accident." Maggie was bluffing about the insurance policy. She didn't know if he had one out on her or not, but it wouldn't surprise her, and it was certainly worth fishing. "Maybe you helped him come up with the plan to kill her for the insurance money. Two little lovebirds hatching their plan for a little nest?"

"She didn't have insurance money." Darla scoffed and turned away, but not before Maggie saw the tremor of her upper lip. *I'm right. There was a policy.*

"She did. You know why? Because she was afraid he was going to kill her in one of his drunken rages and she wanted there to be money to take care of me if he succeeded." This invention of a story was second nature. *Thank you, improvisation classes.* "Here's the thing. I don't know if you helped him or not, and frankly, I don't care. You'll rot in hell someday right alongside him. As much as I'd love to see you in jail, I care more about the truth. You tell me everything you know, and I'll leave you alone."

"How do I know I can trust you?"

"You don't," Maggie said. "It's a risk. But it's guaranteed that I *will* go to the police the minute I leave here if you don't start talking."

"What do you know?" Darla asked.

"Let's state the facts. She was pregnant with another man's baby. A man she loved and planned to be with. When I left her that night she was about to give birth. When I returned, he was there. I heard her scream. I saw them fighting in the stairway and he pushed her. She fell and died. He carried a burlap sack, which held an infant. He ran out the door and met you. Did he come up with the plan of what to do with the body or did you? Was it spontaneous or planned? Tell me, what did you two do with the baby? Where did you dump the body?"

"You're right. He gave her to me, fully believing she was dead. He asked me to get rid of her."

"Why? Why did you care about getting rid of her?"

Darla's face crumpled. "Because he thought he'd killed her. It was an accident. When he ripped her from your mother's arms, the baby dropped on the floor and stopped moving."

"Then he stuffed her in the burlap bag and asked you to get rid of his dirty work?"

"That's right," Darla said.

"Is that what my parents were fighting about? She saw him kill the baby and was running away from him?"

"She screamed and scratched him before she ran down the hallway."

161

"Tell me the truth. He pushed her, didn't he? Please, I want the truth." Maggie hated the sound of her own begging, but she couldn't let go now when she was so close.

"Yes."

Maggie wept as relief flooded through her. Finally, the truth.

Darla's face seemed set in stone, her mouth barely moving as she continued her story. "He wanted me to take the baby's body up to that lookout point and toss her over. You know the one."

Maggie nodded, barely breathing.

"But as I was driving there, I heard a noise from the bag.

"A noise?"

"Yes. A cry, like a kitten."

Oh, my God.

"I pulled to the side of the road and tore open the bag. The little mite started screaming her head off."

Please don't say it. Please don't tell me you killed her.

"I was shaken up, as you can imagine, so it took me a few minutes to figure out what to do. Then, I remembered this thing from the movies about fire houses."

"Yes?" Maggie's mind was whirling so fast she thought she might faint.

"So, that's what I did. I drove into San Francisco and I dropped her off at a fire station."

"A fire station?"

Oh, God. Could her sister be alive? "Which one?"

"I couldn't honestly tell you. It was twenty years ago. I was upset."

"Does my dad know?"

"No, he still thinks he killed her and that I carried out the original plan and that by luck, the body never washed to shore."

"Why didn't you ever tell him?"

"I was afraid. You know how he is when you don't do what he wants," Darla said.

"Did you guys plan all this when you were in Texas? To murder my mom and the baby?"

"No, it wasn't like that. We didn't have a plan other than to take what was rightfully his," Darla said.

"What was that exactly?"

"There was money hidden under a floorboard. Money your mother didn't know about. But when he got there that night, he found her upstairs. She'd just given birth to the baby. He'd been drinking heavily since Arizona. He lost it. Snatched the baby from her arms and tossed it to the ground." Darla's right eye twitched in an erratic rhythm.

"Wait. Which was it? Did he drop her on accident or throw her to the ground?"

Darla whispered. "He threw her."

Finally. Answers.

"He killed an innocent baby just to hurt my mother?"

"And to hurt the baby's father. Your mother's lover. He couldn't stand that she'd found someone else—shared her bed with someone else."

"Isn't that what he did with you?"

Darla looked away. "He didn't see it as the same."

Maggie shook her head, trying to think. Her dad knew who her lover was. "How did he know?"

"Roger had a friend here in town who saw them together. He put two and two together."

"Who was it?" It had to be someone in town. Maybe even someone she knew.

"Hugh Shaw. Your mother was running around with Hugh Shaw."

Zane's father? Sweet Hugh who had always treated her like a daughter? Hugh, quiet and reserved, had been her mother's lover? She had a sudden image of him at her mother's funeral, stooped over, crying into his hands.

"Did he know about the baby?" Maggie asked.

"I don't know."

"Oh my God." *Zane.* She had to tell Zane. *We have a sister somewhere.*

"Darla, can you please try and remember the fire station? If I know that, then I might be able to find her. Please, I'm begging you."

"It was fire station thirty-eight."

"I thought you said you didn't remember?"

"It just came to me."

Liar. "Jesus, Darla. How can you be with him? He's a murderer. He tried to murder an innocent baby."

"He was a looker back then." Darla shrugged and wiped a lone tear from her left eye. "I loved him from the first moment I set eyes on him. And, look at me. I'm not much. I'm ugly. I know that."

"For your sake, I hope he dies soon so you can be free."

"Don't wish that. He's all I've got."

"You're his prisoner."

"He's mine and I'm his. All we got is each other in this stupid world. When he's gone, I won't be anybody's anything. Like before."

Maggie stood on shaky legs. "I'll keep my promise to you, Darla. I won't go to the police about your part in all this, but I will tell my dad I know the truth about what he did. He can't hurt you now."

"He's suffered. That's the thing you don't see. He's paid for everything. The guilt has eaten him away until he's nothing."

"So, his revenge on the Wallers and on my mother's lover weren't enough to satisfy him after all?"

"No. If anything the guilt slowly killed him."

"I think it was booze, not guilt."

"You don't know him like I do," Darla said. "He had such passion for life. He cared too much about everything."

"I never thought I'd say this, after what you've done to my life, but I pity you. Please, get help. Thank you for the truth."

Maggie was halfway to Zane's before she remembered to turn off the record button on her phone.

* * *

Maggie found Zane in the kitchen sipping coffee. He'd already been out for his early morning surf and had showered and dressed for work.

"Hey, beautiful," Zane said. "Want coffee?"

"No, I've already had some."

He patted the chair next to him. "Come talk to me. You look strange. What happened?"

"You could always read me so well," she said.

"You're not much of a puzzle. Even for the denser of the world such as myself. Your thoughts and feelings pretty much play out on your face."

Maggie took a seat at the table. "You remember how you felt when you had to tell Jackson and Doc that I was alive?"

"Yeah. Surreal. Terrified. Excited too."

"Well, that's the kind of story I have for you."

"I'm not following."

"I met with Darla this morning and told her I'd refrain from calling the police if she told me the truth."

"Did it work?"

"Yes, it worked. She sang like the fat lady."

Zane smiled. "That's not the saying. It's either 'sang like a canary' or 'it's not over until the fat lady sings.' "

"Right. Right. That's what I meant. Anyway, this is where it gets a little crazy." Her voice cracked. She set her hands on the table and took in a deep breath. "My dad thought he killed the baby when he tossed her to the floor. After he pushed my mom, he ran out the door with the baby in a burlap sack. I saw that part with my own eyes. Darla told me today that he instructed her to get rid of the body."

"So, he did kill her, like we've thought all along," Zane said.

"Not exactly." Her voice shook, but she continued. "While Darla was driving out to the cliff to toss the sack over, she heard a faint cry. The baby was still alive. He hadn't killed her after all. Darla took her to a fire station and left her there. You know, one of those 'safe haven' type of places. Station number thirty-eight in San Francisco."

"What? What the hell? Jesus, okay." Zane pushed into the top of the table with his hands, like he was trying to steady it during an earthquake. "You're saying she could be alive? Like twenty years old, right?"

"That's right. But there's more. My mother's boyfriend—the likely father of her baby—was your dad."

He blinked and cocked his head to the side as if he hadn't heard her correctly. "What's that now?"

"My mother and your father were having an affair. I don't know if he knew about the baby or not, but I'm assuming he did. She told me right before she died that as soon as her divorce was final we were going to have a new kind of family with the man she loved."

Zane stared at her without blinking. "What are you saying?"

"I think our parents were in love. And we have a sister out there somewhere. That is, if she survived whatever injuries my dad did to her that night."

"I can't believe this," Zane said. "It makes no sense."

"Do you remember ever seeing them together? We were ten the year my dad was in Texas."

He shook his head as if to say no, and then appeared to remember a detail. "There were voices coming from the living room one time in the middle of the night. My dad's voice and a woman's. I went to investigate, but it was just my dad. When I asked him if he was talking to someone, he said it must have been the television. However, I thought he was lying. It just popped into my mind. I hadn't thought of it in years."

"It could've been my mom. It probably was my mom."

"I had no idea. He never dated that I knew of. His life was the bar and me. Or, so I thought."

"Should we try and find her?" Maggie asked.

"I don't know. Maybe she doesn't want to be found. Or, maybe she didn't make it. She was tossed on the floor. You shouldn't get your hopes up."

"You're probably right," Maggie said. *Like heck. She's made of tougher stock than that. We're looking for her.*

She looked out the window as a flock of sparrows flew by the window and landed in the large oak. Logically speaking, Zane *was* right. Getting ones hopes up was never a good idea. She'd learned that lesson many times over the years. But still, the moment Maggie learned it was possible that her sister might be alive, an intense yearning stretched into every crevice of her body. If she was alive, she was the only family Maggie had left. Zane, too, for that matter. His dad didn't know him, and his mother had left when he was a baby. That said, maybe he didn't feel the need for family like she did. He had the Dogs. From what she'd observed last night, they were like family.

After a few minutes, she turned back to Zane. "Have you ever tried to find your mom?"

His eyes widened with surprise. "That's a random question."

"Have you?"

"Nah. Why would I? There's nothing to say to her. She left her own infant to follow a rock band. I have zero memories. It's not like she was ever a mother to me. We share DNA, that's all. Anyway, whatever. My dad was more than enough."

Liar.

"Did you ever miss her?" Maggie asked. "Like when we were growing up?"

"Sure. Sometimes."

"When?"

Zane scratched behind his ear. "I don't know. There were times when it would've been nice to have a mother. Not someone like my birth mother, but one like Lily Waller. My dad was the best, don't get me wrong. But I think I'd be a better man if I'd had a woman around to teach me to be gentler, less aggressive and judgmental."

"What do you mean by gentler?"

"Are you asking me these questions to avoid the situation at hand?" he asked.

"No, actually. I'm asking because I want to know. When I was away, I thought a lot about how I could've been a better friend to you. A friend who inspired loyalty."

"Let's put a pin in that for a second," he said. "To answer your question, I wonder if I'd been easier to talk to and more interested in her feelings, if things might've ended differently with Natalie. The guy she left me for is the exact opposite of me. He's got long hair that he puts in one of those man-buns and wears clothes made out of hemp and works as an environmental lawyer. He's the approachable type that women love."

"You're approachable."

"Not like him. He's a Buddhist, I think. Is it Buddhism? I think so. Anyway, he was always talking about how everything was connected to everything else and that's why one shouldn't kill a spider."

"But one can run off with someone else's fiancée?"

Zane laughed. "That must not be as important in the karmatic order of things. Spiders first, humans second."

"Is karmatic a real word?" she asked.

"Who knows? We'd have to ask Jackson. Anyway, what I'm trying to say is that I could've been a lot better boyfriend. If I had to do it over again, I'd change some things."

"Like?"

"Listen more and instruct less. Deny my initial instinct to 'fix' things instead of just being there. Encouraging her more, instead of being such a realist pig. Some of the things I said to her make me cringe. I could have amped up the romance, too. Another thing that having a mother might've given me. All I learned from watching my dad was how to work my tail off."

"Maybe that's why Natalie came into your life. You had to learn these lessons to be ready when the right woman comes along. Because, trust me, compared to my girlfriends' men over the years, your list of grievances is minor."

"I'm not really interested in having a relationship," he said. "It's probably best if I keep to myself instead of having my heart wrecked again."

"Are you lying to me?" she asked. "I'm pretty sure you're lying."

"Why would you say that?"

"I'm not stupid. I saw how you react to Honor."

"Honor Sullivan." An expression of annoyance muddied his face. "You have no idea how much trouble she is."

"You used to like trouble," she said.

"When I was young and stupid, yes." They were quiet for a few seconds.

"How come you never talked about your mom?"

"Boys don't do that."

The flock of sparrows lifted from the oak and soared as one entity toward the sea. "We have to at least look for her."

Zane fidgeted in his chair . "I know."

"They say it's better to risk a broken heart than never love at all. Or try."

"People who say crap like that are people who've never had their heart broken," Zane said.

"Then, we're fine. We've already had ours broken a thousand times, so we have nothing to lose."

"What do we do?" Zane asked.

"I have no idea. How do you look for people?"

Zane snapped his fingers. "I have an idea. Brody's housekeeper who's like his second mom gave a child up for adoption when she was only sixteen. She hired a private detective to find him."

"Did it work?"

"Yes, and pretty fast. But, it might cost a lot of money."

"Maybe we can do it ourselves? There's this thing called the internet," she said.

"We have the number of the fire station and a date of birth, right?"

"Correct. She was born December 21, 1997."

"What if we started with searching public records?" Zane asked.

"Or, a call to the fire station? Maybe someone there remembers."

"Let's just put the date and fire station number into Google and see what we find," Zane said.

"Good idea." She put her hand on his arm. "But wait, are you sure we want to do this?"

"Let's do it before we lose our nerve. My computer's on the coffee table."

Zane gestured for her to follow him into the living room. She paced in front of the window as he opened his laptop. "I'll search for 'baby left at fire station' with that date."

"Good. Yeah. Go." Maggie's stomach catapulted like one of those hammer rides at the fair that Jackson and Zane used to make her go on with them.

"Oh, God," Zane said.

She turned away from the window to look at her friend.

"It's an article about fire station thirty-eight finding a baby girl on the morning of December 22, 1997. This is her. It has to be."

Maggie joined him on the couch. Accompanying the article was a picture of a firefighter holding a tiny bundle in his arms and grinning at the camera. According to the article, the baby was taken to the local hospital and was in perfect health. The firefighter who found her was quoted as saying, "She was perfectly calm. Calmer than me."

"It's her," Maggie said. "Right there in his arms."

"The article says there were over a hundred couples who wanted to adopt her."

"How do we know who got her?" Maggie asked. "If it was an open adoption, it shouldn't be too hard. I guess. I've heard it's a lengthy process in situations like this. She could've gone to foster care first."

"Wait. I have another idea." He typed additional words into the search engine: adoption of baby found at fire station thirty-eight.

An article popped up right away. A photograph of a couple holding a fat baby and the caption "Childless Couple's Christmas Miracle."

"This is them. It has to be. I can't look." Zane popped up and immediately began pacing. "You have to read it first."

Maggie read through the article before summarizing for Zane. "It says Micky and Rhona Woods had been trying to adopt a baby for years and had almost given up hope. They'd decided to try foster care instead and were already approved in the program when they saw the local news program about the baby left at the fire station. They rushed down to the hospital, along with a lot of other hopeful couples. Ultimately, because they were already approved in the system, the baby went home with them, but it was another year before they could legally adopt her. They had to make sure they couldn't find the biological parents first, along with a bunch of other red tape. Rhona, the mom, says there were many moments of heartbreak—wondering if they would be able to adopt her or if her biological mother would suddenly appear. Two days before Christmas, when the baby was already a year old, they made it official."

"Their Christmas miracle took a whole year. It must've been brutal, waiting to make it legally binding but having no control."

"It's awful to think about." *Loving someone so much and knowing she could be yanked from them at any moment. Talk about brave.* "I don't get it, though. If they were looking for her real parents, how come your dad never came forward? And why wouldn't the police have thought to look for her?"

Zane looked up from the screen. "I guess they just assumed she was dead and never thought to look for anything *but* a body. I mean, no offense, but the local cops aren't really used to dealing with murders. As far as my dad goes, he must've assumed she was dead."

They put the names of the adoptive parents into the search engine. It didn't take long to find their profiles on Facebook, along with an article about their participation in getting the Safe Haven

Law passed after the adoption of their baby girl, Sophie Grace, who had been left at fire station thirty-eight. The law allowed people to leave babies at fire houses with no risk of arrest or punishment. "It's her. It has to be her," she said.

"Seems like it," Zane said. Even Zane couldn't hide the hopeful tone in his voice. *He wants this as much as I do.*

"They named her Sophie Grace. I love that name," Maggie said. "I wonder what she looks like?"

"Maybe it's not right for us to bother them."

"What about *her*, though? Wouldn't she want to know about us? That she has two half-siblings."

"I would want to know." Zane looked away as his face contorted like he had a sudden pain.

"What is it?" Maggie asked.

"You remember what her parents said about how excruciating it was not knowing if they could keep her forever."

"Yes?" Where was he going with this?

"It made me wonder what kind of woman leaves her baby when he's only six months old?"

Like his mother left him.

"I'm not sure," she said.

"I get it if people decide they can't be married to someone. But how could she leave me?"

"Sometimes people's demons make it impossible to love and care for someone."

"Even their baby?" Zane asked.

"I guess so."

"I had my dad. Can't forget that."

"He was the greatest," Maggie said.

"Anyway, enough about me. What's our next step here?"

"Do we reach out to her, or the parents?" Maggie asked.

"Her, I think." Zane picked up his phone from the table. "Let's see if she's on Instagram."

"All young people are on there, right?" Maggie asked. "Not just entertainers?"

He raised an eyebrow, teasing her. "Yes, us regular folks use social media too."

She poked him in the ribs with her elbow. "Don't be mean."

Zane typed in her name. Several women with the same name came up, but only one from California, and only one with eyes the color of the Mediterranean Sea. "Zane, those are your eyes."

"My dad's eyes," Zane said.

Maggie stared at her photograph, looking for her mother or herself in the young woman's face, but could only see Zane and his father looking back at her. "She's pretty, just like you," she said.

"And, she's from the Bay Area. Look." He pointed to her profile photograph. "That's the Golden Gate Bridge in the background."

"Um, yeah, and it says it in her profile description too," Maggie said.

Sophie Grace Woods. San Francisco. UC Berkley graduate. Marathon runner. Dog lover.

"She sounds like a super star," Maggie said.

"Totally."

They sat there looking at one another for a few minutes, stunned and unsure what to do. A knock on the door startled them from their reverie.

It was Jackson, dressed in shorts and a t-shirt. "You two look like the cat that ate the canary. What happened? Did you get anything out of Darla?"

"You could say that," Maggie said.

"We have some news," Zane said. "You better sit down for this."

CHAPTER SIXTEEN

Jackson

JACKSON SPRAWLED ON Zane's couch as Maggie told him of Darla's confession and their subsequent discovery. When she was finished, he stared at her for a moment before he spoke. "I guess this explains why my dad never found the body. There wasn't one."

Zane paced between the couch and window with his hands clasped behind his back. Maggie stared at Jackson with feverish energy, her face bleached of color. "Bird, sit down by me. You don't look so good," Jackson said.

She did so, letting him take her hand. Her palm felt clammy inside his warm, dry hand.

The baby had lived. A sister. Zane's dad and Maggie's mom? He'd had no idea and he was certain his parents hadn't either. "Do you want to try and contact Sophie?" Jackson asked.

"We, we don't know exactly," Maggie said.

"It's a lot to take in. Maybe take your time to decide," Jackson said.

"Do you want to see her photograph?" Maggie asked.

"We found her on Instagram," Zane said, handing Jackson his cell phone.

Jackson first looked at her profile photograph. His pulse quickened. *Holy God.* "Her eyes."

"That's what we thought too." Maggie trembled next to him.

Sophie's feed was filled with photographs typical of a young woman: selfies with friends, a latte with a heart drawn in steamed milk, her arms wrapped around a golden Labrador, and her in front of a ride at Disneyland. She *appeared* harmless and normal, but pictures could deceive. Who was this girl, exactly? A stranger to them. Maggie had been through so much trauma and change in the past few days. Zane's heart was as tender as it had always been. What if Sophie Grace Woods rejected them?

Or, worse. She could play them. Not everyone had integrity or good intentions. She might claim that she was owed half the bar, for example.

Zane wagged his finger at Jackson. "Stop it. This is nothing to worry about."

"We're not even sure what we're going to do yet," Maggie said.

"We're going to think it through carefully," Zane said.

"You're both such liars," Jackson shook his head as involuntary muscles stretched his face into a smile. Maggie had always been a *leaper*, whereas he was a *looker*. A long looker, analyzing each piece of data before making a move.

Zane was somewhere in the middle. Usually.

"What harm could come from contacting her?" Maggie asked. "Worse case, she tells us she's not interested in expanding her family, so to speak."

Jackson scrutinized Maggie, expecting her to continue with something along the lines of, *but she won't.* Instead, she pressed her fingers to her lips and stared back at him with sparkling eyes.

"Whatever happens will be fine," Maggie said.

What sounded like a benign comment, wasn't. He would bet his life Maggie didn't believe for one second that the girl

175

wouldn't want to meet them. She'd always been romantic and overly optimistic, as well as too generous with her love. Not everyone had good intent. Not everyone yearned for family like Maggie.

This Sophie had a family of her own. Right, what about her parents? If they were alive, which it looked like they were if the photo Sophie labeled as "My Amazing Family" was any indication. Maybe the "Amazing Family" didn't want anything or anyone to wreck what looked to be a perfect unit.

"Remember when you convinced us that sneaking out of the house to go to that Foo Fighters concert was a bad idea?" Zane asked.

"Sure," Jackson said. "But that's hardly the same thing as calling up an unsuspecting young woman and telling her that, surprise, she has two new siblings."

Maggie put her hands on her hips and glared at him. "Jackson Waller, I'm surprised at you. Where's your sense of destiny?"

He sighed and threw his hands up in the air. "You two were always impossible to reason with."

"We love you for worrying about us." Maggie moved closer to him and rested the side of her face on his shoulder. He placed his chin on the top of her head. How could hair smell this good?

"Even though you sound like somebody's grandmother half the time," Zane said.

"Someone has to be the voice of reason," Jackson said. "Do you think I like it, always being the mature one? It's not nearly as much fun as it looks."

"I'm still mad about missing that concert," Zane said. "For the record, that grievance is still on the table."

"You should be thanking me for the extra brain cells you still have," Jackson said.

"True. I didn't have any extras to spare," Zane said.

Maggie tossed a throw pillow at him. "You had plenty to spare."

"Had?" Zane tossed the pillow back at her.

"You're not as bright as you used to be," Maggie said. "Especially when it comes to your love life."

"Why do I tell you stuff?" Zane asked.

Maggie blew him a kiss. "I have my ways of getting stuff out of you. It's futile to resist."

Zane once again began to pace, this time between the coffee table and the bookshelf. "Jackson's right, though. You have to be prepared for the worst. We have to prepare for the worst."

Maggie nodded. "I've been auditioning for the last twelve years. I think I know a thing or two about disappointment."

Jackson squeezed her wrist. What he would give to wave a magic wand and give her everything she wished for. Even if it meant leaving him. He would follow her if he had to. Maggie deserved to be happy. Whatever he could do to make that happen, he would do.

"We *have* to call her," Maggie said. "I have to let her know, at the very least, that we're out here and would love to meet her if she wants to."

"She'll want to know about her birth parents," Zane said. "Even if she doesn't want a relationship with us. Most people would want that, anyway."

Jackson's stomach clenched as he realized the pain in Zane's comment. His mother had left when he was an infant. Zane didn't remember anything about her. Now his father didn't recognize him. Possibly, Zane yearned for more family as much as Maggie.

"She deserves to know the truth," Jackson said. "I just don't want you two hurt. You've already been through enough."

"Nothing can hurt me now. I have you two back in my life," Maggie said.

Jackson kissed the top of her head. "I say give it a week to let it sink in. Do not call her this afternoon, for example. You're both in shock."

"Fine," Maggie said. "You're absolutely right. We're all still adjusting to the fact that I'm not dead." She giggled. "I'm sorry. I know it's not funny."

"You always laugh at inappropriate times," Jackson said. "Do you remember that time in Mr. Wilson's geometry class when Melissa Camp slipped and hit her head on the side of the table?"

"That was awful of me," Maggie said. "It's a nervous reaction when I'm scared. I still feel bad about that."

"She didn't know," Jackson said.

"Because she was knocked unconscious," Maggie said, giggling again. "See? What's wrong with me? I'm a bad person."

Zane kicked the side of the coffee table as his neck flushed with heat. "This situation is not funny, Maggie. At all. Your dad robbed us of twelve years."

She stood and took Zane's hands, halting his erratic pacing. "I know. But if we're bitter, he wins. We can't let him ruin any more of our years."

Zane perched on the arm of a chair. A tight grimace spoiled his handsome features. "You know I can never let go of a grudge."

"This one's hard to let go of," Jackson said. "I keep wondering what my mom would say if she knew what he'd done."

"I wish we could ask her," Zane said. "Or my dad."

Maggie wandered over to the hutch and moved a vase about two inches to the left. What would their parents say to them? What would they have them do now? "Lily told me once that God presented hardships for us to grow into the people we're meant to be."

Jackson's chest tightened. His mother had said similar sentiments to him more than once. What good had cancer given her? Cancer took her during the prime of her life. He rested his neck on the back of the couch and fixed his gaze on the ceiling, fighting the angry lump at the back of his throat.

In the bright afternoon light, tiny brushstrokes were visible in the paint. An image of his mother played like a movie on the ceiling. She watered plants on their deck and listened to his story about something that had happened at school and laughed. Her blond curls bounced and looked like corn silk under the sunlight.

He blinked to shake the melancholy and moved his focus to Maggie.

She moved to the window and looked out toward the direction of the ocean. "My biggest mistake was seeing the world through my dad's eyes. He set it up for me to believe the worst in the people I loved." She turned from the window to look at them. Her voice deepened to a throaty tone as she spoke. "I let myself embrace the anger and abandonment I felt, instead of looking into my heart and thinking about how out of character it was for any of you to delete me from your lives. Do you see that's what my father wanted? He wanted me to be bitter and suspicious and full of hate. It worked. But I can't live that way for one more day. I believe that most people are good—and most certainly you two are. I'm not going to waste one more second on anger."

Jackson stole a glance at Zane just as his friend wiped under his eyes. "Mags, you're more highly evolved than I," Zane said. "No surprise there. It's hard to let go and forgive, but you're right, it only gives him more of what he wants if we let anger fuel us." He glanced at the clock. "Shoot, it's late. I need to get downstairs and open the restaurant."

"And I need to get back to work," Jackson said.

"I'll come down and help you get ready for the lunch crowd," Maggie said.

As the three of them headed down Zane's stairs, she returned to the subject of Sophie. "We should wait a week or so before we call Sophie. That way we can come up with our script."

"Script?" Zane asked.

"Yes. We need to write down what we want to say, so we don't blow it with a clumsy exchange. It's always good to know your lines before you call a long-lost sister," Maggie said.

"This isn't an audition," Jackson said, teasing. "Even if it feels like one."

"I know, but I still like to be prepared," Maggie said.

"I'll let you do the talking," Zane said.

"That's probably best," Jackson said.

* * *

That evening, Jackson stood next to Maggie by the empty swimming pool at the Arnoult house. They'd completed their tour, which had reinforced Jackson's fears. What had he done? The place was chaos incarnate. A fire hazard. A health code violation. It smelled horrific. Seriously, what had he been thinking? This was a perfect example of why one did not make decisions in the span of an evening.

But this house—this house was the stuff of dreams. This *place* had represented all his dreams. His desire to buy it had overwhelmed all sense of lucidity.

This house had represented Maggie. Being here had made her seem real and close. Had he thought it would bring her back to him somehow?

Had it?

Was he insane?

No. Maggie was real. Right now, she strolled with Kyle toward the large sycamore with her sun hat dangling from her hand.

Hot, Jackson wiped his forehead with the back of his hand as he followed them toward the shade of the sycamore. From the shade, he surveyed the yard. The pool would need an entire resurfacing. Grass would have to be reseeded. Flower beds weeded and replanted. It could shine again with a facelift or two.

Kyle, dressed in a stylish tan cotton suit, took off his jacket and folded it over his arm. How did he always look so cool and put together?

"Maggie, what do you think?" Kyle asked.

Jackson glanced over at her, expecting to see the horror he felt reflected on her face. Instead, she bounced on her feet like an excited child. "It's magnificent."

"Really?" Kyle said. "Because I can tell Jackson's about to have a heart attack."

She grinned. "Imagination, Jackson. You have to use your imagination."

"You know I was never good at that," Jackson said.

She slipped her hand into his. "No worries. I have enough for both of us."

Kyle took his phone from his pocket. "Let's talk dates. I can have a crew out here by the middle of next week. We'll start with getting rid of everything inside and then strip walls and remove flooring. I'll have you meet with my decorator. She can walk you through floors and paint colors."

"Don't forget the kitchen," Jackson said. "We'll need new appliances."

Kyle laughed. "Don't worry, bud. I've done this before."

* * *

After Kyle left, Jackson spread a blanket under the sycamore tree. He set up a low, portable picnic table he'd borrowed from his dad as Maggie had grabbed a cooler with their dinner from the back of Jackson's truck. While he opened a bottle of cold white wine, she arranged bread, cheese, and salami onto plates. He poured them each a glass and leaned against the back of the tree, watching Maggie's graceful hands spread a piece of bread with goat cheese.

"Tell me about your friends in New York, Bird."

She chirped away for a few minutes about Lisa and Pepper with stories of their antics in college and afterward. There were tales of auditions and parties and shifts at the bar where they worked. "Lisa was a cocktail waitress, but I worked as a bartender. I lied and told the owner I'd been to bartending school. He never checked because I knew how to make drinks well by then. Thanks to Hugh." She popped a piece of salami into her mouth and chewed. *She makes eating salami look like a work of art.*

"Hugh taught you that in high school?" Jackson asked. Maggie had been underage when she worked for him.

"Don't look so scandalized," she said. "He taught Zane and me how to make drinks during off hours. Not for actual customers, but as practice for when we went to college. He said you could always find work if you knew how to tend bar."

"He never told me that," Jackson said.

"You worked for your dad. No bar shifts for you. What did Zane used to say? You were born with a silver spoon in your cheek."

"Not cheek. Mouth," he said. She could butcher a saying like no one else.

"Mouth. I knew that."

He chuckled. "Zane and the silver spoon thing used to get on my nerves."

"He was just jealous," she said. "Mostly because you had such a great mom. I don't think either of us realized how much it hurt him that his mother left them."

"Zane's tough to read. Even for me."

"He always has been. He keeps his cards close to his sleeve."

"Close to his chest." Jackson laughed. "God, you're adorable."

"I'm like the opposite of a savant when it comes to sayings." Maggie swatted away a fly before it landed on the slab of cheese. "Seriously, what's wrong with me?"

"Nothing. Not one thing. You're perfect."

"No I'm not, but I love that you say so," she said.

She leaned over close to him and planted a kiss on his cheek. He grabbed her face between his hands and kissed her soundly on the mouth.

"Stop that now," she said. "The ghost of Aunt Stella might be watching."

He shuddered and picked up his glass of wine. "You don't really think its haunted, do you?"

"No, of course not. There's no such thing." She sipped her wine and wrinkled her brow, clearly thinking of something else.

"Penny for your thoughts?" he asked.

She tilted her head and gazed at him with soft eyes. "Your mother used to say that."

"Yeah, I remember."

"Penny, not a nickel." Maggie grinned. "Is that correct?"

"Yes."

"I was thinking the only ghosts around here are the two of us." She pointed toward the driveway. "If I close my eyes, I can see the two of us just outside the gate when we were about twelve years old. Bicycles overturned in the grass—noses pressed against the emblem of the eagle—talking about how many kids we would have and that we'd have pool parties and dance under the light of the moon with all our friends." Her voice had become wistful and husky as she spoke.

His eyes stung, but he smiled and made a joke to hide how her words made his chest ache with hope and regret all intermingled like the various wildflowers in the field. "It was you who said we'd dance. Not me. You remember my two left feet."

She touched the tips of her fingers against his lips and looked into his eyes. "But you would, for me?"

"I'd do anything in the world for you, Bird. Anything. Even dance."

"You promised to dance with me at our prom, do you remember?" she asked.

"I would've too. If we'd been able to go. If you'd let me take you."

"I couldn't. Not that day." Maggie's eyes filled with tears.

"My mom wanted us to go. She told me to make sure I took you, no matter how sick she was."

"I couldn't. Not when we lost her that same day. The prom suddenly seemed stupid. The dress and the corsage and everything—none of it mattered if your mom wasn't there to take our photograph." Maggie's swiped her cheeks with a napkin. "So many things would've have happened differently if your mom hadn't have died. When I think of it...of all the loss..." She trailed off.

He pulled her close against his side with his arm around her waist. "Bird, it's over now. You've come back to me. We have time still. Lots and lots of time."

"Have you danced with anyone else?" Maggie's voice trembled. "I know you slept with Sharon, but if you danced with her—I might not be able to stand it."

He spoke into her hair. "No. Not anyone else. I couldn't. I wouldn't. Not after I lost you. You were the only one I ever made that promise to."

"Do you remember what you promised me?" she asked. "Do you remember exactly?"

"Yes. I promised you I'd dance with you at prom and our wedding and any other time you wanted."

"Did you mean it?"

"Every word."

She nestled her face into his chest. "How is it that this feels so right? After all these years, it's just the same."

"Because we're us," he said. "Simple as that."

They sat in silence for a few minutes. The early evening air was still and fragrant with the scent of sweet peas. He imagined he heard the buzz of bees as they flickered from flower to flower, sucking sweet nectar.

"Do you really think this is a good idea?" He gestured toward the house.

"Why wouldn't it be?" she asked.

"Because I won't be able to live here without you," he said.

She played with a small hole in the thigh of his jeans. "What if I said you didn't have to?"

"Bird?" Did she mean it?

"What if I said that the ghosts—the ones at the gate—whispered to me that I belong here? With you."

"I would say—I believe they're right."

"What if I said I don't want to live without you by my side for one more day?" she asked.

"You know what I'd say back?" he asked.

"What?"

"I would say I don't want to spend one more day without you by my side," he said.

From the branches above, a bird squawked an ugly song, loud and jarring. Maggie jumped. Jackson laughed. "So much for our romantic moment."

"What's wrong with that bird?" Maggie asked.

"He sings like I dance."

"Then he must have a partner who loves him very much," she said. "Who doesn't care how he sounds, only that he sings for her."

CHAPTER SEVENTEEN

Maggie

THE NEXT MORNING, Maggie sat across from Zane in his living room as he opened his laptop. They'd promised each other they would wait a week to contact Sophie, but there was no way that was going to happen. Curiosity may have killed the cat, but they didn't care. Today was the day. They were writing to Sophie.

"You do it from your Facebook account," he said. "It's less likely to seem creepy coming from another woman."

"Good point." Because they were not "friends," Maggie couldn't be sure she would see it, but they thought it was worth trying before they attempted to locate either an email address or phone number. Maggie was glad to see that Sophie didn't have too much information out there for the public to see. There were a lot of creeps who loved to prey on young women.

Dear Sophie,

This will sound strange. There's no way around that. I'm writing because I think you're my sister. My mother, Margaret (Mae) Keene, gave birth to a baby girl on December 21, 1997. That same night, my mother died, and the baby was taken without permission and dropped at Fire Station 38 in San Francisco. The woman who dropped the baby at the fire station was not part of our family but was directed by my father to do so. He and my mother were estranged at the time. She had an affair and became pregnant. I believe you are that baby.

Until recently, I believed my mother's baby had died that night and the body disposed of. Police could never find any evidence of foul play, although it was quite clear my mother had given birth hours before she died. Without a body, it was impossible to bring charges against my father, who I and others believed was responsible for the baby's death as well as my mother's.

My father and I had not spoken for many years. Several days ago, I came to see him, knowing that he has only weeks to live. My intent was to find out the truth. I have done so. You are the baby I thought died that night. You were taken from Cliffside Bay to a fire station in San Francisco. I'd like to meet and at least talk. I would be happy to do DNA tests to see if my hunch is correct. I also believe you have a brother—the son of the man my mother had the affair with, i.e., the man I believe to be your father. He is still alive but has Alzheimer's. If my assumptions are correct, he never knew about you. I don't want anything from you, other than to meet you and have the chance to tell you about your mother. Your half-brother, Zane Shaw, would like to meet you as well.

Please email me at SongandDancegirl@bmail.com or call 555-239-1678 if you'd like to talk further.

With hope,

Maggie Keene

When she finished, she asked Zane to read it to see if he wanted to add anything.

"No, it looks good. Let's do it," Zane said.

She hit send.

They stared at each other. "What now?" Maggie asked.

"We wait."

"I've always been terrible at that," she said.

"Me too." Zane reclined in one of his lounge chairs and put his feet on the coffee table.

"How about we talk about something else? Something to take our minds off the wait?" Maggie asked.

He raised an eyebrow and crossed his arms over his chest. "Like what?"

"How about Honor Sullivan?"

He let out a long breath. "What about her?"

"How come you're not asking her to go steady?" Maggie asked.

"No one has said 'go steady' since 1960."

"I just said it. I'm going steady with Jackson."

He rested his cheek in his hand and smiled. "I'm glad. It's meant to be between you two. I always knew it, even when I was in love with you back in the day."

Her mouth dropped open. "What did you just say?"

"I was madly in love with you for a decade, but I knew your heart belonged to Jackson, so I suffered in silence."

"You were *not* in love with me."

"I was."

"How come you never said anything?" Maggie asked. "I always thought I was like your sister."

"I'm a good actor too."

She couldn't think of what to say next. Did Jackson know?

He grinned. "Don't look so horrified. I lived through it."

"Did it hurt?"

"At the time, a little. But unrequited love is also a pretty safe route. You know, the long-suffering best friend in love with Jackson's girl—makes it easy to stay on the sidelines, so to speak. It also gave me all kinds of excuses for dating other young ladies as a distraction."

"Jackson told me about that. I never knew you were such a player."

"I guess we protected you from that kind of thing back then. But seriously, I knew you would never feel that way about me."

"Did Jackson know?" she asked.

"No way. I've never told anyone but Natalie."

The fiancée from *the wedding that wasn't a wedding.*

"Seriously, don't look so sad," he said. "As close as you and I were, it was impossible not to be in love with you. No man's that strong. As close as Jackson and I were—*are*—it was impossible to ever let him know that something he felt or did caused me pain. You know how he is."

"But you told Natalie," Maggie said.

He shrugged. "Sure."

"What was she like?"

"Let me get the knife out of my back so I can describe her," he said.

"There was *something* there—enough you wanted to marry her."

"I was in love with her. Big time. But she broke my heart. So, here I am again. Playing it safe."

"By not asking Honor out on a proper date? Before you say anything, I already know you slept together."

"Total mistake. I should've stayed true to my monk-like existence." He shook his head as he stared up at the ceiling. "I swear, she makes me feel insane every time I'm around her. I never noticed her when she was still a kid working for my dad, but when I came back here three years ago to take over the bar, she blew me away. For one thing, she's smart as a whip. I can't resist a sassy mouth. And, she's sexy as hell. She's also the most dangerous woman on the planet if you're trying to keep your heart safe."

"She likes you," Maggie said.

"No, she likes what I did to her in bed. She's not capable of really liking someone."

"You don't know that."

"We're too alike to ever make it work," Zane said.

"Both in your safe corners?"

"That's right."

"She asked me to put in a good word for her," Maggie said.

"What's that now?"

"She said she's sorry for what she did and that she'd really like another chance. A do-over."

"Why hasn't she told me herself?" Zane asked. "Ever since that night she acts like she couldn't care less. Also demonstrated when she left without saying goodbye."

"Has it ever occurred to you that she might be scared?" Maggie asked.

He rolled his eyes. "No way."

"She had a rough time of it as a kid. Foster fathers are not always father-like."

Zane's gaze bored into her. "Really?"

"I think that's why she's so protective of her heart—why she only goes so deep with a guy. It could be the reason she sabotages things when she has real feelings. She had a crush on you when she was a teenager and worked for your dad."

He smiled. "That's funny. She was like ninety pounds soaking wet back then and seemed like a child. When I moved back here three years ago, I didn't even recognize her."

Maggie crossed her arms. "Ask her out on a real date. Not falling into bed after spending the night working downstairs. Okay?"

"Maybe."

"You're the most stubborn man I've ever met," she said. "Don't be so stubborn that you pass up an opportunity for a woman who pushes all the right buttons."

"And some wrong ones."

They were interrupted by a ping from Maggie's phone. "I have a new email."

She opened the message. "It's from her. Zane, it's her."

Dear Maggie,

Wow. I'm sitting here totally and completely freaking out. I think your suspicions are right. From the time I could understand, my parents told me I was adopted. I was left at Fire Station 38 in the early hours of December 22nd. An article in the newspaper prompted them to contact the hospital where they were put in touch with Child Protective Services. They were already approved to foster children, so I was able to go home with them. After almost a year of red tape, they adopted me. So, yeah. I think you're right. We're probably sisters. I have a billion questions. Where are you? Can I come see you? I'm assuming you know where my brother lives? Anyway, call me and we can talk. Or, just write back and tell me where to meet you. I live in San Francisco, but I can come to wherever you are.

Sophie

Maggie wrote back to her.

Hi again. First, I'd love to meet you as soon as possible. Would you be able to meet next Tuesday? We have a wedding to attend over the weekend, but we'll be free after that. Let me know when and where in San Francisco and I'll be there. I'll be coming from Cliffside Bay, which is north of the city by about an hour and a half.

To answer one of your questions, I do know where your half-brother is. In a rather long story, we only recently discovered that our parents were involved romantically. We were best friends when we were young and remain so. He would very much like to join us.

Maggie

Minutes later, a new email arrived from Sophie with a suggestion to meet at a Starbucks on Market Street.

"She wants to meet us on Tuesday," she said.

Zane grinned. "Here we go then."

"Fasten your seatbelt."

CHAPTER EIGHTEEN

Jackson

IN FRONT OF the church, Jackson steadied Maggie as she stumbled on an uneven section of the sidewalk in her high heels. Today, Flora and Dax would marry. Like Jackson and Maggie, Flora and Dax had been broken apart as teenagers. For forty years they lived without each other, making lives out of the empty spaces.

Jackson wrapped his arm over Maggie's shoulders. *Thank you, God, for bringing her back to me.* Twelve years had seemed a lifetime, but compared to forty, he knew how lucky he was to once more have her by his side.

"You're beautiful," he whispered as they made their way up the steps to the church.

"Thanks," she said. "I love the dress."

He'd bought it for her and surprised her last night, knowing that she hadn't brought anything appropriate for a wedding. To his delight, she'd fallen in love with the contours of the silky, sage green material and the scooped back.

He gently caressed the small of her back with his thumb and

felt her shiver. When they reached the top of the stairs, Brody greeted them with a handshake and hug. "Maggie, you look stunning," Brody said.

"You look nice too," Maggie said.

"Thanks. Kara dressed me." Brody grinned and tugged on his lavender tie. A white shirt and dark blue linen suit completed the look. "Two weeks until our wedding and she's already picking out my clothes."

"You don't seem to mind," Jackson said.

"Never," Brody said. "I'm a recovering idiot. Whatever she wants or needs, is what I do."

"That's sweet, Brody," Maggie said in a husky voice. Jackson glanced over at her to see a lone tear nestled in her bottom lashes.

"It took him awhile to figure it out," Jackson said.

"Thanks to this guy knocking sense into me when I needed it, I'm now the happiest man alive," Brody said.

"Where *is* Kara?" Jackson asked.

"Inside helping the bride with last-minute touches. But Honor's looking for you. The pianist has food poisoning or the flu. They need you to look at the music and see if you can pinch hit."

Maggie's eyes sparkled. "Pinch hit is one way to put it."

As Jackson prepared to guide Maggie inside, Brody stopped him.

"Before you guys go in, there's one other thing. Lance made it home last night. I wasn't sure he was going to make it with work and everything," Brody said. "But listen, things are a little sketchy. He looks awful and he says he quit his job. I think it's more than that."

"More?" Jackson asked.

"I think he had some kind of mental and physical breakdown."

"Lance? But he's the steadiest guy around," Jackson said. Alarm bells went off inside his head. What had happened?

"Something's not right. I'm worried about him," Brody said. "He said he's staying for the foreseeable future, which is not at all what he's been saying for the last few years."

Maggie squeezed Brody's arm. "Maybe the sea air will be just what he needs."

Jackson looked over at his precious date. "It agrees with you, that's for certain."

Kyle shouted out to them from the bottom step. A woman in high stiletto heels and a short red dress hung on his arm. Leave it to Kyle to find a last-minute date who would wear red to a summer wedding. Jackson waved to him and then ushered Maggie inside the church. No time to waste. Flora needed a songbird.

The moment they were inside, Lance Mullen grabbed him into a hug. "Hey, buddy. Good to see you." Lance, two years younger than the rest of the Dogs, had been an innocent freshman in need of the older boys' wisdom when Jackson had first met him. Now he was a heavy hitting hedge fund manager. Or, he had been anyway.

"You as well. It's been too long, prodigal son," Jackson said.

Lance had taken Maggie's hand. "And this beauty must be Maggie."

Pink flushed Maggie's cheeks. "It's nice to meet you. I've heard a lot about you from the other Dogs."

"Whatever they said is most likely a profound exaggeration," Lance said.

Maggie smiled and tucked her chin against her neck. "All good, I can assure you."

Honor and Kara rushed toward them. "Maggie, we need you. There's been a disaster with that flaky piano player," Honor said. "He says its food poisoning, but my guess is a hangover."

Kara nodded in agreement. "Can you play for us, Maggie?"

"Sure. I'm happy to help. Let me look at the music and give it a run through," Maggie said.

Maggie kissed him on the cheek. "I'll find you after the ceremony," she said.

"I'm proud of you, Bird," he whispered in her ear.

The women's high heels clicked on the hardwood floor as they scurried up the aisle.

Lance suggested they take a seat near the front. "Flora asked if we could sit on the right for her. Dax's family and friends are on the left."

They settled into a second-row pew.

"Brody said you're staying awhile," Jackson said. "Everything all right?"

"Let's call it a transition chapter," Lance said.

Jackson studied him. Lance had always been good-looking, almost pretty, with even features and thick brown hair he wore long on the top, so it fell just so over his forehead. Lance's forehead did not seem to be growing larger. However, his friend's face was drawn and thin. Dark smudges under his eyes hinted at long nights. "What happened with your work?"

"I had a slight physical breakdown." Lance spoke in his usual light-hearted manner, but his dark blue eyes had lost their sparkle.

"For real?"

"Yeah, man. It was embarrassing. I had a full-fledged panic attack in the middle of a regular workday. I thought I was having a heart attack. My coworker took me to the ER. Turns out it was just my shattered nerves and not a heart attack, thank God. It appears the endless hours and travel have taken their toll. My doctor said it was time to reevaluate my priorities. Translation, take some time off. So, I'm home for a bit."

"You made the right choice." Jackson put his hand on his shoulder. "But will you be all right?"

"You mean financially?" Lance asked.

Jackson nodded. Why was it always so uncomfortable to talk about money?

"Between work and investments of my own capital, not to mention Brody's, I've made enough to last a long, long time. You know the Mullen men. Frugal to a fault."

"Will you finally build your house here?" The plan had always been for Lance to move to Cliffside Bay and build a home on Brody's property.

"Brody wants me to. We'll see."

They were interrupted by a slender woman with dark blond hair. Jackson didn't recognize her, but he suspected she was Mary Hansen, daughter of the groom. Kara and Brody were not fans. Apparently, she could chill the warmest man's heart and had expressed distinct displeasure that her father was marrying Flora.

She stood at the side of the pew and held out her hand. "I'm Mary Hansen. You must be Lance."

"Yes, that's me." Lance stumbled to his feet and shook Mary's narrow hand. "Nice to meet you. I'm sorry I haven't had a chance to do so before this." Mary was a tall woman, but at six feet, Lance had a few inches on her.

Mary raised a perfectly arched eyebrow and peered at him with cornflower blue eyes. "I hadn't expected to. It's not like we're family." She pursed her small mouth and ran her hands down her pencil thin black dress. *Odd choice for a wedding.*

Jackson looked over at his friend. Lance didn't appear to be offended. In fact, he looked amused. All said, it took a lot to offend Lance. Always had. He was simply a nice person. Slow to anger or judgment, always giving people the benefit of the doubt and looking deeper than most to find the good in people. He might have to look really deep to find it in Mary Hansen.

"Flora's family to me, so that makes us family too," Lance said.

Mary turned to Jackson. They shook hands. "I'm Jackson. Welcome to Cliffside Bay."

She studied him for a moment before taking his hand. "You're Doctor Waller, I suppose? One of Brody's friends."

"That's right," Jackson said.

"I met your father at the Mullen's," Mary said as she turned to Lance. "He's dating your mother."

Jackson wasn't sure why this was a statement. It wasn't a secret that their parents were dating.

"That's right," Lance said. "We're still getting used to the idea. Isn't that right, Jackson?"

"Sure," Jackson said. "Especially Brody."

Mary's perfectly shaped eyebrows went up in a look Jackson

translated as surprise but could also be interpreted as disgust. "Really? Why's that?"

"Our father died a few years ago. He and Brody were close," Lance said. "It's hard for him to see our mom with someone else."

Mary's eyes softened for the first time. "I can understand that."

"My father's been alone for a long time," Jackson said. "Even though I'm happy for him, it's not exactly what I thought it would be like when I was a kid. I imagined having children with my mom right there."

"Exactly," Mary said.

Lance nodded sympathetically. "It's not easy to accept what *is* instead of wishing for what *was*."

Mary played with a heart locket she wore on a silver chain around her neck. "My mother died five years ago, but I still miss her so much." Her voice hushed to just above a whisper. "I can't stand it—seeing him with Flora. I know it's wrong of me. I hate feeling so petty and selfish. Not to mention, I suddenly have a new brother." She gestured toward the front, where a tall man in his mid-forties was talking with the pastor. "That's the golden-boy, Cameron. The son my father always wanted."

Lance smiled kindly at Mary. "I'm sure your father's immensely proud of you. My dad always told Brody and me that his heart had room enough to love both of us equally."

"I don't know. My father's agreed to move to California without a second thought about me." Mary smiled, but it appeared to come at a great effort like the muscles were pulled upward with toothpicks. "I followed him all the way out to Oregon from the east coast to have him move two years later, simply because of Flora and Cameron."

"I'm sorry," Lance said. "You feel left out and deserted. Anyone would."

Mary folded her arms across her narrow chest. "Thanks. It's nice of you to try and understand my feelings instead of assuming I'm a witch like Brody and Kara do."

"Surely not," Lance said. "They've said nothing but nice things about you."

Jackson stifled a smile. Even Lance couldn't make that statement sound true.

She smiled as she tucked a strand of shiny hair behind her ear. "You, Lance Mullen, are a liar. I'm tainted in their eyes. I wasn't nice when I first met them, which I regret, but I'm one of those people who can't seem to keep their feelings locked inside where they belong."

"It's not always a better choice. Sometimes all that stuffing results in a nervous breakdown that pretty much turns your life upside down." Lance's shoulders rose in a self-deprecating shrug. He smiled in that same way Mary had—like it hurt to do so. "Or so I've heard."

Mary cocked her head to the side, examining Lance like he was a mathematical equation to be solved. "Are you home for a while, then?"

"Something like that," Lance said.

"It's nothing to be ashamed of," Mary said.

"What's that?" Lance asked.

"Suffering," she said softly. "It happens to the best of us."

Mary's entire demeanor had changed in the few minutes they'd been talking. *Lance Mullen strikes again.* Even the Grinch or a sour woman couldn't remain brittle in the presence of such genuine kindness. No wonder Wall Street had eaten him alive. Lance was the last of the good guys.

"What're your plans?" Jackson asked Mary. "Will you go back to Oregon after the wedding?"

Mary shook her head. "I'm not sure. I'm between jobs right now—I'm a librarian and I was laid off a few months ago. I've been living with my dad while I try and find a job. It's not going so well."

"It happens to the best of us," Lance said.

"Anyway, it's good to meet you both, but I need to go find my dad. I want to make sure he doesn't need anything."

"It's good to meet you," Lance said. "I'm here if you need to talk."

"I won't, but thank you," Mary said.

"Sure thing," Lance said.

After she was gone, Jackson and Lance sat back in their seats.

"She likes you," Jackson said.

"You think? It's hard to tell."

"As much as she likes anyone. She's what my mother would call hard-shelled. But she seemed to soften under your charms."

"We're going to be seeing a lot of each other," Lance said. "So, it's best we try and get along."

"I missed you, man. Whatever brought you here, I'm glad you're back. Welcome home."

"You know, we really are going to be brothers now," Lance said.

A jolt ran through Jackson. "You're right. I hadn't thought of it that way."

"Stepbrothers, anyway."

"Bonus brothers," Jackson said.

Lance excused himself. "Have to get my 'walking a beautiful bride down the aisle' hat on."

Maggie, at the piano, began to the play Beethoven's "Moonlight Sonata." The rest of the guests trickled in and took seats in the pews. His dad delivered Janet before he excused himself to check in with Dax. They'd become close friends the past few months.

He noticed Zane and Honor were on the other side of the church next to Mary. Surely, they hadn't come together?

"I can't believe the musician didn't show," Janet said. "I thought Honor was going to lose it."

"We have Bird to cover now," Jackson said.

"She plays beautifully," Janet said.

"She does everything beautifully," Jackson said.

Janet smiled at him. "A man in love."

"A little," he said.

"I'm so very happy for you."

"Thanks, Janet." He looked into her dark eyes, so similar to Lance's. She and Brody shared the same intensity, but it was Lance who favored her in appearance.

"You'll come by the house sometime soon, won't you? I'd love to get to know her better." Janet played with the string of pearls around her neck.

"Soon. I promise."

"It's a crazy kind of blended family we're making here. Isn't it?" she asked.

"You could say that, yes." Jackson took her soft hand in his own for a moment. "I'm glad you're part of it. You make my dad very happy, and for that I'll always be grateful."

"Never in a million years would I have thought a second love was in the cards for me," she said.

"I don't think my dad did either," Jackson said.

"Did you talk to Lance? Something happened back there, but he won't tell me much about it. You know, mothers are always the last to know things."

"He didn't tell me details either. But he's home now. We'll fix him up. That's what we do here."

"You sound like your father," Janet said. "Both of you are such kind men. That's a rare thing these days."

"My mother made sure," Jackson said. "Her expectations were high in that way."

Jackson's father slipped in beside Janet. "All good with the groom. Other than he's shaking like a leaf."

Janet touched a tissue to the corners of her eyes. "I don't know if I'm going to make it through this day. When I think of all the years they were apart and now this."

Jackson's dad kissed the top of her head. "It's going to be a great day."

"Yes. One to remember for a long time," Janet said.

Everyone stood and turned to the back of the church as Maggie played the first notes of Canon in D. Cameron and Kara, best man and maid of honor, walked down the aisle arm-in-arm. Jackson scanned the guests to make sure no one had a camera pointed at Kara. They must have all gotten the memo. Wait. Other than Mary. She snapped photographs on her phone. Someone needed to stop her without making a scene.

He looked over at Zane and Honor. They'd noticed it too. "I'll get it from her," Zane mouthed.

Fortunately, Kara hadn't seemed to notice. She beamed as Flora and the Mullen brothers appeared the end of the aisle. Each held one of Flora's arms as they escorted her down the aisle.

Flora, in a cream-colored suit, smiled as brightly as the sunlight on the stained-glass windows. Her salt and pepper hair hung in tight curls around her face. Jackson fought tears of his own as Dax wiped his eyes. As they passed by, Flora blew a kiss to Janet.

Each Mullen brother kissed Flora on the cheek and settled next to Mary in the front pew.

Pastor Robbins held a bible in his weathered hands. Jackson wondered how many couples he'd married over the years. "We are gathered here today to witness the marriage of two people, long parted," Pastor Robbins said. "None of us can understand the mysterious ways of either God or love, only that there are some bonds that even time cannot break. Flora and Dax loved each other when they were sixteen years old. And now, over forty years later, they're finally able to get the happy ending they'd longed for so long ago."

Loved each other since they were sixteen. Happy ending. Finally.

I'm going to ask Maggie to marry me. Sooner than later. Time was not his to waste. They deserved to have their happy ending.

CHAPTER NINETEEN

Maggie

TUESDAY MORNING, MAGGIE and Zane arrived at the agreed upon Starbucks early and were already waiting at a table when Sophie walked through the door.

They knew her immediately from the photos. Tall, with long legs and an athletic frame, she wore faded shorts and a t-shirt from a rock concert. String bracelets with silver charms dangled from one wrist and a fitness watch encircled the other. She wore Birkenstock sandals on her tanned feet.

She headed straight for them. Her golden hair and light blue eyes were so like Zane's, Maggie almost gasped.

"Hi. I'm Sophie."

Zane popped upright and held out his hand. "Zane Shaw. This is Maggie Keene."

Sophie stared at him with a startled expression as they shook hands. "Hi Zane. Your eyes. Wow."

"Yeah," he said.

Sophie turned to Maggie. "Hi, Maggie."

"Hi." Maggie's voice caught in her throat. "Please, sit. Do you want anything?"

"God, no. I feel like I'm seasick, I'm so nervous." Sophie was taller than Maggie by a few inches. No freckles, and skin like Zane's, also tanned to a warm glow.

Sophie plopped into a chair and looked from one of them to the other. "So, where do we start? Do you guys want to know about me or should you tell me how you found me?"

"Let's start there," Zane said. "It's complicated."

Sophie clasped her hands in her lap. "I'm all ears."

Maggie launched into their complex story, including how she and Zane figured out their parents had once been lovers. She concluded with the story of Sophie's birth.

"So, wait. I was born in a bathtub with no doctor or anything?" Sophie asked.

"As far as I can tell," Maggie said. "You came while I was gone. That was maybe twenty minutes."

"And that's when your father came home? Right after I was born?" Sophie asked.

Maggie looked at Zane for help. No sound could penetrate the ache in the back of her throat.

Zane rescued her. "We believe so. All Maggie remembers is seeing her father at the top of the stairs holding a bundle."

"You," Maggie said.

Sophie smiled. "Me. Just born."

"That's right," Maggie said. "But I never saw you. You were wrapped in a burlap sack. I thought you'd died. All this time I lived under that assumption.

"Until you got the truth out of his wife," Sophie said. "Gosh, that's awful." Her eyes filled. "I'm so sorry."

"I only came home to find out what he did with the body. I wanted the two of you to be together."

They told her how Doctor Waller had insisted on a full search by the police but that they couldn't find any trace of a baby. "He's been sure all these years, as have I, that the baby died," Maggie said. "So, when I got the truth out of Darla, I could hardly believe it."

"But you told Zane what you learned, and you guys looked for me right away?"

"That's right. We couldn't wait," Zane said. "Neither one of us have much patience."

"Me either," Sophie said.

"There's another thing," Maggie said. "Another complication." How in the world did she explain that everyone thought she was dead?

Once again, Zane took over for her. "Maggie's dad's a psycho. Let's just start with that."

Sophie's eyes widened in horror as Zane told her what he'd done.

"This whole time, you thought she was dead and she was actually dancing on Broadway?" Sophie asked. "That's the craziest thing I've ever heard. Crazier than a baby being left at a fire station."

"Yeah. We're bringing the crazy," Maggie said. "We totally understand if you want this to be our one and only meeting."

"What? No way. I've wanted to know where I came from since I can remember," Sophie said. "I always knew I had siblings. I could just feel it in my bones."

"Tell us about your life," Maggie said. "We want to know everything."

"Well, it started at Fire Station thirty-eight."

Sophie told them how her parents heard the story on the news and rushed to the hospital in the hopes that they could foster her. "Even though it took a whole year to make the adoption final, I've been with them since I was two days old."

"Have they been good to you?" Zane asked.

"Oh my gosh, totally. They're like the best people ever. Not exactly what you might think, though. I mean, they're not your typical suburban parents. My dad's a music producer and a little out there. He's kind and gentle and super understanding, but he says groovy and bitchin' like they're still a thing."

"How old is he?" Maggie asked, imagining an aging rocker type.

"Mid-fifties. Young enough to know those are not what anyone says anymore. Not that he cares what anyone thinks. Like, he's this killer business guy, but you'd never know it by looking at him. I always tell him he's timeless. My mom's this mother of the earth type. A health enthusiast, as she calls it. She's a vegan and grows her own vegetables in the backyard, which is not normal given where we live. Think, like, gigantic houses and super snoots in the wealthiest part of San Francisco. I left her this morning out in the yard digging up carrots for the quinoa smoothie she wanted me to drink before I left. Seriously, I had to go to college to get a hamburger." Sophie grinned. "But they're cool, even though they're dorky. My dad started his own independent record label back in the early 2000s and now he's got all these successful bands. They're kind of folksy-blues types. Not mainstream, but with popular cult followings. You know, good music—not this junk you hear on the radio. But anyway, Maggie, what's super weird is that I'm a dancer, like you. I studied ballet, jazz, and tap when I was younger. I was on the dance team all through high school. It was my life."

"Past tense?" Maggie asked.

"Well, I still do it for fun, but I decided to focus more on academics in college. I graduated with a degree in restaurant and hotel management last month. I have no idea why, but I love the restaurant business. I'm a total foodie, despite my mom trying to ruin my palate with her vegan lifestyle. I'm home for a few weeks before going full speed ahead on the job search."

"Restaurant business, huh?" Zane asked. "Weird."

"Why?" Sophie asked.

"I own a restaurant. It was my dad's—our dad's place. Now I run it."

"No way," Sophie said.

"Yes, ma'am."

"Does your mother work, other than her garden?" Maggie asked.

"No, she focused on raising us. I have a little brother. They got pregnant after they adopted me."

"That often happens," Zane said.

"Right? It blew their minds after trying forever. Anyway, he's still in high school."

"It sounds like a great childhood," Maggie said, unable to keep the wistfulness out of her voice.

Sophie's expression turned sympathetic. "I'm sorry. I'm being completely insensitive to your feelings."

"No, I'm glad to know you've had such a good life. Our mom would be happy to know what a good family you ended up with." Maggie choked on the last words. Sophie reached out and squeezed her hand.

"Tell me about her, please. Anything you can think of. And then I want to hear about your dad, Zane. Our dad."

"She was a dancer too. Her dream was Broadway, which she passed onto me. When she married my dad, she gave up any hope of having a career. She was pregnant with me by the time she was your age. Life with my dad wasn't good."

"He was abusive?" Sophie asked.

"That's right. The night she died wasn't an isolated incident. I had a little spot under the stairs where she had me hide when he was on one of his rampages."

"I didn't know that," Zane said.

"Yeah," Maggie said. She'd never told anyone but Jackson.

"That's terrible," Sophie said.

"I'm not wild about small spaces."

"I still don't get it, though. How did our parents meet each other?" Sophie asked. "If our mom was still married to your dad?"

"I'm a little fuzzy on the details," Maggie said. "But my dad left to work on an oil rig in Texas. He was gone almost a full year. I didn't know it, but Mama started seeing Zane's dad. Cliffside

Bay's a small town. Mama and I used to go into the restaurant for dinner sometimes when we were low on food and money and he'd always make us a meal." Maggie smiled, remembering Hugh's gentle face. "I always ordered the cheeseburger."

"Lucky," Sophie said.

"We *do* have a veggie burger on the menu," Zane said.

"My mom will approve," Sophie said.

"They must have fallen in love at some point because they made you," Maggie said. "We're not entirely sure how long they'd been involved. I'm pretty sure it was serious though." She told Sophie what she remembered from the night her mother had told her about the baby. "She said we were going to have a new life with the man she loved."

"They never had a chance to make good on that promise," Zane said. "Looking back, I can see that my dad was devastated when Mae died. He and Doctor Waller spent months trying to figure out what happened to the baby. He assumed, like everyone, that Roger Keene had killed the baby out of spite."

"But no one could ever prove anything," Maggie said.

"Until now." Sophie tugged at a lock of her hair and looked out the window. "Now, there's proof. I'm here. I'm alive."

"Yes, it seems we've both come back from the dead," Maggie said.

Sophie squeezed Maggie's hand again. "All this time, we never knew we were dead."

They both laughed.

Zane grimaced. "It's really not funny."

Sophie clasped her hands together on the table. "Can I meet Hugh? My dad?"

"Absolutely. But, he's not all there most days," Zane said. "He probably won't understand who you are. We can try and explain and we might get lucky and catch him on one of his more lucid days."

"I would like to meet him, no matter what," Sophie said.

Maggie reached into her purse. "I almost forgot, we brought

photographs." She laid them out on the table. One was her mother's high school portrait. In another, she held baby Maggie.

Sophie held them close to her face, looking at each for at least a minute. "I'm glad to know what she looked like."

Zane pulled several of his father out of his wallet. "And here's Dad. He was handsome when he was young."

"He looks like you," Sophie said. "Or, you look like him."

"You're a perfect combination of them," Zane said. "His eyes."

"Mama's mouth," Maggie said.

"What were they like?" Sophie asked. "What did they like to do?"

"Dad was the quiet type. Loved to surf. Loved football," Zane said. "At the end of every night, he wrapped up any leftovers and sent them over to the church for the homeless. He loved his business. The bar was his pride and joy."

"And you," Maggie said.

"And me." Zane looked at his hands. "It was just the two of us. My mom left when I was a baby." He shot a glance at Maggie. "That's been the hardest part for Maggie and me to accept. Both Mae and my dad had such lonely lives. The thought that they might have been able to build a life together if they'd had a chance will haunt me the rest of my life. They deserved more than they got." He grabbed a napkin and brought it to his eyes. "I'm sorry."

"Don't apologize. My mom says people are always apologizing when they're emotional, as if it's a bad thing when what we need to do is embrace whatever we're feeling because it's part of what makes us alive. You're sad. I'm sad too." Sophie wiped her cheeks with her already damp napkin. "We had the chance to be a family and that was ripped from us."

Maggie nodded. "Because of one man."

"Was it hard to confront him?" Sophie said.

"Like going into a house of horrors," Maggie said. "But I had to."

"She's brave," Zane said. "Always has been."

"We found *you*," Maggie said to Sophie. "Which makes it all worth it. I only hoped for the truth."

"I've wanted to know about my parents since the moment I understood what adopted meant," Sophie said. "I didn't think there was much chance I'd ever know, given the way I was dropped. I assumed I wasn't wanted and that my mother just wished to forget I was ever born."

"I had no idea you were out there," Maggie said. "If I had known I would've done anything to find you. Zane too."

"You're here now. That's what we should focus on," Sophie said.

"Mama wanted you. You should know that. I can see her face the night she told me about you. She was so happy. So hopeful," Maggie said. "She fought hard to keep you safe that night."

Sophie nodded. "What do we do now?"

Zane crumbled his napkin between his hands. "I vote for making up for lost time."

"You could come to Cliffside Bay for a visit," Maggie said.

"We could show you around. I could take you up to see Dad," Zane said.

"I'd like that. Maybe I could even stay over, if you have room for me."

"Anytime," Zane said.

"Will your parents be all right with all of this?" Maggie asked.

"Totally. They already gave their blessing when I told them about your letter. Actually, it was more of a Native American chant with some incense, but you get my point." She glanced out the window for a moment before turning back to them. "They asked if you guys could come back to the house."

"Now?" Zane asked. Maggie almost laughed. He looked like he used to when a teacher announced a pop quiz back in high school.

"It doesn't have to be now," Sophie said. "Maybe next week?"

"We'd love to meet them today," Maggie said. "We're here and everything."

"Right. Sure. Bring it on," Zane said.

* * *

An hour later, Maggie and Zane were welcomed into the home of Rhona and Micky Woods. In the entryway of their Spanish inspired home, Sophie introduced them to one another, as if it was the most ordinary event in the world. "Mom and Dad, meet Zane and Maggie."

"We're pleased to meet you," Rhona said.

"You too, Mrs. Woods. Thank you for inviting us into your home," Maggie said.

"Please, no formalities. Call us by our first names," Rhona said. "We're going to be family."

Maggie wasn't sure what she'd imagined Sophie's parents to look like, but it wasn't this. For one, they were of Hispanic descent. For two, they didn't look old enough to have grown children.

"Yes, please. We don't do formal here." Micky Woods was of average height and weight, with sharp brown eyes and thick black hair. "We're tickled you had time to come by and meet us."

"Can you believe Zane's eyes?" Sophie slipped her hand into Rhona's. Sophie towered over her petite mother. Rhona was about five feet tall and couldn't weigh more than a hundred pounds. She wore a long skirt and a peasant blouse. Bare feet peeked out from under her skirt.

"I cannot," Rhona said. "I've never seen the exact color of your eyes on another person. Until now." Rhona's eyes were the color of dark caramels and framed with thick, black lashes.

Brown spiral curls swept her shoulders. Her skin glowed. Maggie might need to rethink veganism if it caused one to look like Rhona Woods.

"Follow me to the patio. This time of day is quite pleasant out there," Rhona said. "I've just made an iced herb tea and gluten free cookies."

Sophie made a gagging gesture to Maggie and Zane as they followed Rhona and Micky through the front room to the kitchen where a set of wide doors opened to a stone patio. Maggie repressed the urge to giggle. This little sister was the perfect kind of trouble.

Throughout, the floors of the house were made of large square tiles in the color of terra cotta pots. High ceilings and big windows let light in from every angle. Brightly colored furniture and art work hinted at the free, creative spirits who inhabited the house.

They took seats on the outdoor furniture arranged around an unlit gas fire pit. A canopy provided shade from the afternoon sun.

An azure swimming pool with Spanish tiles took up part of the large yard. Raised beds hosted a vegetable garden. Maggie recognized zucchini and green beans. Green tomatoes ripened on vines by the fence.

The conversation began with a summary of what they knew about the night Sophie disappeared from Cliffside Bay. Rhona, bless her, listened without interruption, other than touching a cotton handkerchief, provided by her husband from the pocket of his shorts, to the corners of her large eyes.

Maggie told the story with little emotion, until she reached the part about the baby. "When Jackson and I arrived in the house, my mother...she screamed this scream I'd never heard before—and I knew he'd done something to the baby."

Zane, sitting next to her, took her hand. "Mags, I can tell the rest."

"No, I can do it," Maggie said. "He'd stuffed her in a burlap sack. When he ran past me, she didn't make a sound. We all assumed she'd died." Maggie's voice broke. She fixated on an ant making its way up an aloe plant in the pot next to her chair. *Keep it together.*

Zane jumped in then. "Jackson's father, who happened to be Mae's doctor, tore the town and countryside apart looking for a body."

"But they never found one," Micky said.

"Because there wasn't one," Rhona said.

Maggie nodded and wiped her face. How could there be any tears still left?

Zane took up the story, describing what they recently learned from Darla. "Maggie and I've been best friends since we were little kids, but we had no idea of our parents' affair with each other. We were stunned to learn we shared a sister." He explained about Hugh's illness. "Unfortunately, he won't understand that Sophie's his daughter. Most days he doesn't remember me either."

"I'm sorry, Son. That's rough," Micky said. "I went through the same thing with my mother. It's heartbreaking every time."

"That's right," Zane said. "Maggie and I both wish we could ask him about his relationship with Mae. But we won't ever know the truth about what happened between them."

"We do know they wanted to be together. My mother told me that just before she died. But the divorce from my father wasn't final. And then, well, it was too late."

"We both knew immediately that we wanted to try and find our sister," Zane said. "And that brings us to today."

"What a pair of detectives you were," Rhona said.

"The internet made it easy," Zane said. "We were shocked by how easy it was to find her."

"Which made us wonder how it could've been that no one thought to look for her in the first place," Maggie said.

"We had no idea of any of this," Micky said. "If we'd known— as much as it would've hurt, we would never have wanted to keep her from her father."

Sophie left the loveseat she had been sharing with her mother to perch on the arm of her father's chair. She wrapped her arm around his neck. "Daddy, it's no one's fault except Roger Keene's. We've already established that."

"What kind of man would do this?" Rhona asked.

"A sick one," Maggie whispered.

"Poor lamb," Rhona said.

"My mother would've been happy to know what a good childhood she had," Maggie said. "I can attest to her character and that she was a fine, unselfish mother."

"How wonderful that you'll be able to share your memories with Sophie," Rhona said.

"Tell them about the rest, Maggie," Sophie said. "About how everyone thought you were dead."

"What?" Micky looked alarmed.

"It's a long story," Maggie said.

"Have another cookie," Rhona said. "We have all afternoon."

"When I got the call that my dad was dying, I got on a plane to confront him about my sister's death." She summarized her visit to the cemetery and what she found there and of Zane's sudden appearance.

"Goodness, you must've thought you were seeing a ghost," Rhona said to Zane.

"I did," Zane said. "Absolutely, I did."

"And here you were bringing flowers to your best friend," Rhona said. "Isn't it poignant?"

"Something like that." Zane smiled. "We had to sort through the mess, including that we were not seeing things, but that Roger Keene had set up quite a web of deceit."

Sophie squeezed her father's arm. "It turns out neither of us were dead."

"Two sisters whose deaths had been greatly exaggerated," Micky said.

They all laughed, except Rhona. She stared into space with her hands folded on her lap.

"Mom, are you okay?" Sophie asked.

"I just remembered something." She opened her mouth to speak, but no sound came out.

"Sweetheart, what is it?" Micky sat forward in his chair and put his hand on her knee.

Rhona seemed to gather strength from her husband's touch. "One time, when I was waiting for Sophie outside of her kindergarten class, there was a man across the street in a pickup truck. I noticed him because I knew most of the parents and I didn't recognize him. When the children started to spill out of the classroom, I got out of my car, as I always did, to greet her just outside the gate. As I did so, the man rolled down the window of his truck. Sophie ran out to the sidewalk and yelled to me, 'Mommy' and ran into my arms. When I rose to my feet and took her hand, the man was watching us. He wore a Giants baseball cap low over his forehead and dark glasses that covered his eyes. Still, I could see that he was crying. Tears glistened on his cheeks. I was frightened but also felt worried about him. Crying men always rip my insides to pieces. I asked him if he was all right—could I help him?" She paused to take in a shaky breath. Zane interrupted before she could continue.

"What kind of truck was it?" Zane's voice was no louder than a whisper.

"It was a Chevy. Early seventies," Rhona said. "Yellow."

"How do you know what year?" Zane asked in the same strange voice.

"My father had the same truck when I was a child. His was blue, not yellow, but I recognized the make and model," Rhona said.

Maggie's body had gone numb. Hugh's truck had been yellow. An old Chevy, she was certain.

"What did he say?" Zane asked. "What did he say when you spoke to him?"

"He looked at me for a second and then down at Sophie. He said, 'You have a beautiful little girl.' I said, 'Yes, I do. Thank you.' Before I could say anything else, Sophie interrupted." Rhona's hands shook as she pressed them together in her lap.

"What did I say?" Sophie asked.

"You said, 'My mommy tells me I should worry more about being kind than pretty.' And he answered, 'You have a very smart mama—a wonderful mama who loves you—a mama who waits for you to get out of school. Not everyone's so lucky.' "

Rhona glanced over at Sophie with a slight smile on her pretty face. "And Sophie said, 'Yes sir. She's always here. Every day. And sometimes my daddy comes too.' " Rhona's bottom lip trembled, but she continued through her tears. "He said, 'Your daddy's awful lucky to have such a sweet girl.' Then, he nodded at me and tipped his hat. 'You have a good day, ma'am.' And he drove off."

No one said anything for a good ten seconds. Maggie's heart beat so fast she thought it might explode. *Hugh knew. He knew about Sophie.*

"I hadn't thought of that moment for years," Rhona said. "But his jawline—it was like yours, Zane. Perhaps that's what jiggled the memory."

Micky glanced over at his wife. "He knew we had her, but he thought she was better off with us."

Maggie's body had gone numb. She shifted to look at Zane. "He knew."

Zane stared back at her. "Why, though? Why would he do that, knowing that she was his daughter?"

"Maybe he didn't know until then," Sophie said. "Maybe he didn't want to yank me out of a happy home."

"He could've discovered your existence later, I suppose," Zane said. "He wouldn't have wanted to hurt you by taking you away from your parents. That's not something he would've been able to do."

Just like that, she knew. "That's not why he did it," Maggie said. He'd known all along the baby had survived. He would have thought to look in the newspapers. No one like Hugh Shaw would have left any stone unturned. Hugh hadn't helped look for the baby because he saw the article in the newspaper or on the internet —he put it together that the baby was his. He hadn't told the Wallers about his relationship with Maggie's mother because he didn't want anyone to know the truth.

Hugh had done it to protect Sophie from Roger Keene. He'd sacrificed his little girl so that she could be safe.

Maggie addressed the Woods. "This has been bothering me from the first time we learned that Hugh was the father of my mother's baby. Why wouldn't he have thought to look outside the assumption that the baby had died? I knew Hugh well. He was smart—a street smart type of man. It would definitely have occurred to him to search the hospitals and news articles for a baby."

"He knew," Zane said. "He knew."

"He chose to give you a better life, Sophie," said Maggie. "One that didn't have the threat of Roger Keene in it."

Zane was as pale as the day he'd found Maggie at the cemetery. "I don't understand how he could let her go."

Micky spoke, his voice hoarse. "Because he was a father and he wanted what was best for his little girl."

"When you're a parent, you grow superpowers in self-sacrifice," Rhona said. "Suddenly, all that matters is protecting your baby from harm. Even if it means giving them up."

"My mother left us when I was a baby," Zane said. "He raised me by himself, always apologetic that I didn't have the love of a mother. It wasn't just that he was afraid of Roger Keene. He wanted you to have a good mother, Sophie. One who was always there when you came out of the school yard." He looked over at Rhona. "And you did. He was right. You have a wonderful mother."

"I can share mine," Sophie said, wiping her eyes. "I can share her with both of you."

"Everything about my wife is tiny, except her heart," Micky said. "She has room."

Rhona smiled and pressed her hands in the position of a prayer over her chest. "Lots and lots of room."

Zane smiled. "We know a few others who could use some motherly love. You have room in there for a couple of overgrown boys?"

"We should break her in gently," Maggie said.

* * *

A few days later, Maggie, in the passenger seat of Zane's truck, took in a deep breath as they parked in the visitor section at the memory care facility. About fifteen minutes from Cliffside Bay, the facility appeared new and well-maintained, with manicured lawns and shrubs. Flowers planted along the walkways bloomed in shades of red and purple. The weather was in the upper seventies and sunny with an occasional breeze that whispered around her bare legs.

Sophie had already arrived in her own car and was waiting for them under an awning by the front entrance. They hugged and exchanged greetings before walking into the lobby that smelled of coffee and vanilla. Warm wood and a high ceiling made it seem more like a hotel than a healthcare facility. Maggie sighed with relief. She'd been worried Hugh had to spend his last days in a building that smelled like split pea soup and urine, like so many. How was Zane paying for this?

The receptionist obviously knew Zane. She smiled and greeted him by name. "This isn't your usual day. And I see you brought visitors."

"This is my old friend Maggie Keene. She used to work for my dad back in the day," Zane said before pausing, clearly unsure how to introduce Sophie.

"I'm Sophie. A friend of the family."

"Well, how sweet of you both to come. I'm Frieda. I manage this facility, so I know all the patients and their families well."

"How is he today?" Zane asked.

"About the same as last week," Frieda said.

Zane nodded, his eyes flat. "Which means he won't remember me." He glanced over at Maggie. "He looks remarkably the same as he did years ago, but his mind isn't there any longer. Most of the time anyway."

Maggie nodded. Zane had already shared this with her. He was nervous she would be upset when she saw Hugh's decline for herself. She would be, whether he warned her or not. Her feelings couldn't be spared. "Can we see him now?" Maggie asked.

Frieda nodded. "Absolutely. They're just finishing lunch. Usually Hugh spends time outside on the lawn after his noon meal. But we can bring him inside for a visit."

They followed Frieda down a long hallway. "The patients' individual bedrooms are down this hallway. We encourage families to decorate their loved ones' rooms with photographs and even furniture from their former homes to nudge memory."

"Does that work?" Sophie asked.

"We're not entirely certain. It depends on the patient and how far advanced they are," Frieda said.

They were at the end of the hallway now and entered a sitting area, decorated in warm colors and comfortable furniture with picture windows that looked out to a rolling lawn. A staff member looked up from arranging a blanket around an old woman in a wheelchair to greet them with a smile.

"We only have room for twenty-five patients. For every two patients, there's one staff member."

Seriously, how was Zane paying for this?

Frieda used a key to unlock the glass doors that opened to a covered patio. "We keep everything locked up, so that no one wanders away."

"That's what made me realize how bad Dad was," Zane said. "He wandered out of our apartment one night. I have no idea what was in his mind, but I found him on the beach at sunrise with nothing but his boxer shorts on, about to dive into the water. I knew then it was time to find a safe home for him."

"As I've told Zane before, we love Mr. Shaw. Despite his memory loss, he's a sweet man. Very well-mannered and complimentary to the staff, even though he doesn't remember us from day to day. He's a charmer too. Sometimes, he thinks our Nurse Kelly is his girlfriend and picks flowers for her."

"He remembers all the lyrics from his favorite rock bands too," Zane said. "Frieda said it's common for Alzheimer's patients to remember songs and nursery rhymes longer than anything else from their past."

"Yes, and memories from their younger days seem to remain the longest. Whereas, that from the recent past is the first to go," Frieda said.

A dozen patients and almost as many staff relaxed in the shade of the patio. Maggie's heart pounded as she searched the old faces for Hugh.

Frieda pointed to a man by the rose bushes, just left of the patio. "There he is. He loves to smell the roses."

Maggie stole a glance at Sophie. She looked a tad green under her tan. Maggie reached out and took her hand. Standing together, they watched as Zane and Frieda crossed the lawn toward Hugh.

"It'll be all right. We can do this," Maggie said.

"I'm suddenly scared," Sophie said.

"Me too."

"They're all so old and sad," Sophie whispered.

"I know. But they're obviously well taken care of." Maggie glanced around the room, taking in the patients. They were all clean with combed hair. One staff member sat with a stooped patient on the couch and rubbed lotion into his hands. Another painted a shriveled woman's nails.

Zane had hold of Hugh's arm as they made their way across the lawn. When they reached Maggie and Sophie, Zane asked Hugh if he wanted to sit in his favorite chair by the bookshelf.

"Is that my favorite?" Hugh asked. Same throaty voice. Same face, older but still handsome. He looked over at Maggie and Sophie. His eyes, the same color as Zane and Sophie's, twinkled. For a split second, Maggie thought he remembered her. "And who are these lovely young ladies?"

"This is Maggie and Sophie."

"What pretty friends you have." Hugh looked over at Frieda. "Is this my son?"

"Yes, Mr. Shaw. This is Zane. He comes to see you twice a week."

Hugh peered at Zane as if he were trying with all his might to remember. "Sure, yeah. My son. Good looking kid, like his old man."

"Thanks, Dad." Zane spoke under his breath to Maggie.

"Sometimes he pretends like he knows me. Frieda says it's a common reaction."

"Come on, let's get you settled. Frieda said you can have some lemonade," Zane said.

"Lemonade. Good, yes. Wouldn't want a beer in the middle of the afternoon. Isn't that right?" Hugh allowed Zane to escort him over to his favorite chair. Maggie and Sophie, still clinging to each other, sat on the loveseat opposite. Frieda excused herself to fetch the drinks.

Hugh blinked as he gazed at Maggie. "Mae, you changed your hair. It looks nice."

Maggie bit the inside of her lip. *Mae?* Did he think she was her mother? He must. She caught Zane's eye.

"Dad, do you know who this is?" The hopeful tone in his voice broke Maggie's heart.

"Sure. The prettiest lady in town. Mae Keene."

"What do you remember about her?" Sophie asked.

Hugh blinked again. The alert expression in his eyes was gone, replaced by a vacant one. "I apologize, but I can't place you, young lady. Are you related to me?"

"I'm your daughter. Mae was my mother." Sophie pointed to her eyes. "See. We have the same eyes. Zane too."

"Daughter? I have a daughter?" He looked over at Maggie. "Mae?"

Maggie would play along. Perhaps it would jog his memory—get him to tell them something. "I had a baby girl, Hugh. This is her. Sophie Grace."

As Frieda brought the drinks, Hugh's face went slack, all hint of understanding vanished. He turned to Zane. "Young man, remind me who you are again? Did you work for me at the restaurant?"

"I did. Dad, it's Zane. I'm your son. I run the restaurant now."

"I had a restaurant? Was I the owner?"

"For forty years, Dad. In Cliffside Bay. Do you remember?"

"I apologize, young man, but I can't seem to place you. Did you work for me at the restaurant?"

Zane sighed and looked away. "That's right."

Maggie leaned closer to Hugh. "I'm Maggie. Mae Keene's daughter. Do you remember her?"

"Yes, ma'am," Hugh said. "Love of my life, Mae Keene." He closed his eyes. "She died. Broke my heart."

"She had a baby, Dad. We found her. Sophie Grace."

"It's me," Sophie said. "Zane and Maggie found me. I came to meet you."

Hugh scrutinized her for a long moment, like a man trying to place an old friend. "Yes, Sophie Grace. Oh, gosh, yes. My baby girl." His hand shook violently as he tried to set his glass of lemonade on the table, but it crashed to the floor. He clasped and unclasped his hands, clearly agitated.

Several staff members rushed over in an attempt to settle Hugh with soothing words. He didn't look their way; his watery eyes fixed on Sophie.

"I'm sorry I had to let you go, but it was better," Hugh said. "If Roger Keene knew you lived, he would've hurt you. I couldn't take that risk."

Sophie knelt next to his chair and laid her head on his knee. "I know. I've had a good life. I'm safe. You don't need to worry any longer."

Hugh placed his hand on the top of Sophie's blond head. "You looked very pretty at your high school graduation. I was proud. You had the best speech."

Sophie jerked upright. "You were there?"

"In the background, kid, but I was there. Lots of times, I was there."

"Where else?" Sophie whispered. "What else did you see?"

Just as quickly as lucidity had come, it was gone. The blank look returned to Hugh's eyes.

"He's gone," Zane said and cursed under his breath.

Sophie slid onto the floor and wrapped her arms around her knees. "But he was there, Zane. He said so. Lots of times."

* * *

Maggie, Zane, and Sophie sat under the shade of a maple tree in front of the memory care facility. After Frieda had taken an unsettled Hugh back to his room, they'd wandered outside. She didn't know about the other two, but Maggie felt nauseated.

"I know you feel robbed," Zane said. "But he loved you the best way he could."

Sophie nodded. "I got him for a second, though, which is better than I hoped for. I could get him again. Maybe."

"Sure," Maggie said. "He still comes in and out, obviously."

Sophie played with the tie at the waist of her skirt. "I've been thinking...I might stay awhile in Cliffside Bay. That way I could visit him as much as possible before he gets any worse."

"You can stay with me," Zane said. "As long as you want."

"I could work at the restaurant for my keep," Sophie said. "Waiting tables, washing dishes. Whatever you need."

"It's about time you learned the family business." Zane smiled. "I'm thinking more along the lines of assistant manager. You can put that degree to good use. Maybe teach me a thing or two."

Clearly, there is more to "nature" than "nurture." What were the odds that their sister would want to be in the restaurant business?

"Really?" Sophie's eyes were wide. "I promise I'll work hard."

"Technically, half the restaurant's yours," Zane said. "Anyway, it might be good for me to have a partner. I could actually have a life."

"But it's your baby. You've worked so hard to build it up to what it is," Sophie said. "I don't deserve to have it handed to me."

"It's not a handout. You'll work hard, I promise. I've worked seven days a week since I took over the place, just like Dad did. I don't want to end up alone like he has. Maybe I should concentrate on my personal life for a while."

He didn't say it, but Maggie hoped by personal life he meant Honor.

CHAPTER TWENTY

Jackson

THE NEXT FRIDAY night, Jackson and Maggie shared the table closest to The Oar's stage with Sophie's parents. Zane already had Sophie behind the bar making and serving drinks. The place was packed with locals and tourists. Jackson knew why. They'd come to hear Maggie sing. It had only taken a month for word to spread about the girl with the voice of an angel.

Rhona set aside her menu and wrinkled her nose. "I'm going to have to talk to Zane about getting a few vegan dishes on this menu."

"Good idea," Jackson said. "And some gluten free choices too."

Maggie laughed. "You two are a buzzkill. Here I was thinking of ordering a burger."

"Oh, dear, no," Rhona said. "Not a good idea. Not at all."

"See what I have to live with?" Micky asked.

Rhona reached over and patted her husband's flat stomach. "You should thank me every day for your hot body, darling."

Micky winked at Jackson. "It's better for men to marry early, so our wives can save us from ourselves."

"Or, the other way around," Maggie said.

Rhona turned her attention to Maggie. "Will you be returning to New York City soon?"

Maggie smiled over at Jackson. "No, I'm staying here."

"What about your career?" Micky asked.

Maggie explained about her knee and subsequent decision to move out of New York City. "Even before I came home and learned the truth about everything, I knew a change was in order."

"L.A., then?" Micky asked.

Maggie shook her head no. "I'm ready to retire from the business. It took twelve years of my life. I gave it my best shot, so I don't have to ever wonder *what if*. I'm not sure exactly what I'll do next, other than spend time with the people I love and sing here on the weekends."

"She writes songs," Jackson said.

"Really? Maggie, you didn't tell me that," Micky said.

"She'll sing some for you tonight," Jackson said.

"I will?" Maggie asked as she shot him a dirty look.

"She's shy about them, but they're really good," Jackson said. "I could see her selling them to the Nashville types. Maybe you know of an agent she could pitch to?"

"Jackson, stop. You're worse than a stage mom," Maggie said.

"I'd be happy to take a look at them," Micky said.

Jackson knew that look. Micky was only being polite. He must get a thousand appeals just like this one every month. But not everyone was Maggie. Not everyone could write great songs like his Maggie. And wait until he heard her sing.

"It must have been terribly hard to give up dancing," Rhona said.

"I shed some tears," Maggie said. "But I had to get back up and keep going. This is life, right?"

"I'm afraid so," Rhona said. "But when one door closes, another opens."

Maggie smiled at Jackson and his heart fluttered. "This is true."

Rhona looked over at her husband. "You two remind me of us. We were high school sweethearts too."

"Until she dumped me for a football player," Micky said.

"That's not how the story goes," Rhona said. "We went away to college and lost touch. It wasn't until I was back in town a few years after college that I ran into Micky at a bar."

"Like most stories, they begin in a bar," Micky said.

"It began in a high school cafeteria," Rhona said. "Anyway, we started talking. It was like no time had passed."

"Before we knew it, we'd closed the bar down," Micky said. "And I knew right then and there—I was never letting this woman get away from me again."

"I played a little hard to get. It's best, you know, for women to do this, but I knew the minute I saw him sitting at the counter that night. It's a thing—a chemistry between two people that one can't describe. But if it's there and it's meant to be—you *will* find your way back to each other."

"Even when one of you has to rise from the dead," Maggie said, grinning.

"I keep telling her it's not funny," Jackson said.

"You know what I've always found?" Rhona asked. "One can either choose to be bitter from regret or grateful for another chance. Everything's a choice. Choose happiness, I say."

"I'm an anxious type of person," Jackson said. "My mother used to tell me that the antidote to anxiety was gratitude."

"I think I would've liked your mother," Rhona said.

"I could see you two being great friends," Maggie said. "She was a great mother, just like you."

"She obviously did a fantastic job with this young man," Rhona said.

Jackson grinned. "It took some pointed concentration on her part."

* * *

Maggie had just finished her first set when Micky spoke quietly into Jackson's ear. "How in the world is this girl not a singing star?"

"You tell me," Jackson said. The last song of the first set was one of Maggie's originals. "What did you think of her original songs?"

"I'll tell you this. Normally, in a venue like this, cover songs are king. Without something they can recognize, most crowds' attention will wander. Not so in this case."

"That's good, I'm assuming?" Jackson asked.

"It's good, yes. How much original music does she have? Enough for an album?"

"She has enough for two albums, at the least. Although, she doesn't think they're all equally commercial."

"Interesting." Micky studied him. "What do *you* want, Jackson?"

"I'm sorry?"

"For your life—do you want a stay at home wife who raises your children? I won't lie to you—that's what I wanted. It sounds old-fashioned and it probably is. I would've backed down if Rhona hadn't felt the same way. Luckily, she did. When we were finally able to adopt, she quit her job the minute Sophie was in her arms. But your Maggie, she's a different type of woman. You understand that?"

"I've known her since she was a little girl, sir. So, yes, I do. Besides my friend Brody, she's the most driven person I've ever met."

"She'll be bored without something creative to do," Micky said. "I know the type."

"You're correct," Jackson said.

"Are you worried you'll lose her again if she pursues a career?"

Jackson scratched under the collar of his t-shirt. "Thankfully, I'm more evolved than I was at eighteen. I want what she wants. There's no way I'm letting my insecurity get in her way."

Maggie waved to them as she headed toward the restroom.

"You're prepared to let her spread her wings?"

"Yes sir. What do you have in mind for her?"

"I don't know if she told you, but I have my own independent label. I choose artists I like and I do things how I like. Not only do my artists have to be good, but they also can't be divas or jack-asses. I like singer/songwriter types."

"Like Maggie?"

"That's correct. I think I could make her a star. You think you can handle it?"

"It's not up to me," Jackson said. "What she wants is what I want."

"She'll be away for periods of time. On tour. Cutting albums. That kind of thing."

"How can you be sure she'll be a star?" Jackson asked.

"I know my stuff."

"She might think you're making the offer to make Sophie happy."

"She'll need to get over that and fast. Self-confidence is key," Micky said.

"New York tore her down for a long time."

"I have a partner. A young woman—tough as nails. Maggie will have to get past her, but I don't see that as a problem."

"Not if she has ears," Jackson said.

* * *

Jackson opened the kitchen door to let Honor inside. "Thanks for coming."

"What's up?" Honor asked.

"I have an idea. Something I want to do for Maggie. You said to go big, right? A Brody Mullen type of romantic gesture?"

"I did, yes." Honor sat at the island. "Are we talking the proposal night?"

"Sort of. I want to throw Maggie a prom. We didn't go to ours because my mom died."

"A prom? Doctor Waller, I didn't know you had it in you."

"Then, afterward, I'll take her down to the beach and propose," he said.

"No. Propose first, then bring her to the prom. That way, you can have an engagement party right then and there." Honor's eyes sparkled. "Leave it all to me."

"I want to throw it at The Oar in two days."

"Two days? You don't mess around," she said.

"You'll have to work with Zane."

She narrowed her eyes but didn't comment.

"Zane said we could close the place for the night," Jackson said. "I want to decorate it and everything with the theme we had for our Senior Prom."

Honor tossed her hair behind one shoulder. "Do you even remember what it was?"

"Yes. I was on the committee that planned it. Maggie and I both were."

"Of course, you were." Honor rolled her eyes. "Seriously, you two are such goodie-two-shoes."

He ignored her. "The theme was *Night of a Thousand Stars*," he said. "Maggie thought of it."

"And then you didn't get to go?" Honor asked, all hints of teasing gone from her expression. "That's so sad."

He explained how his mother had died unexpectedly that morning. "Even though my mom had made me promise to take her to the prom, no matter what, Maggie wouldn't go. We were not in any shape to go, either one of us."

"It's about time you kept your promise, then," Honor said.

"That's what I was thinking."

"Who do you want to invite?"

He grabbed the list he'd made from the desk in the corner. "Here."

"Awesome. All the gang," she said.

"The decorations were stars made out of tin foil and hung from the ceiling." He paused, remembering what the high school gym had looked like that morning. "And the tables were covered in shiny silver too, but everything else was purple. Dark purple like the sky on a summer night."

Honor was making notes on the list he'd given her. "Silver and purple. What about refreshments?"

"That's the beauty of a prom for grownups. We can have real drinks."

"We should have Zane make a special punch," she said. "Should we do bite-sized appetizers and have the staff pass them around during the party?"

"Sure. Whatever you think. It has to be classy, though. Maggie's kind of classy."

"I'm a total snob, so you're in good hands," Honor said.

"Wait, there's one more thing. I have to get her a dress."

"Oh no. You leave that to Kara and me. Finding the perfect dress is a job for a woman. What would she like, do you think?"

He thought for a moment. What *had* her dress looked like back then? Shiny and flowy. He seemed to recall sparkles. "She likes feminine but kind of simple since she's so tiny. The one she had was cut like this." He gestured at his waist to indicate a full skirt.

"A-line?"

"Yeah, sure. I think so. All I know is she looked like a princess in it. The most beautiful princess in the world."

Honor's eyes misted over. "Oh, Jackson, if only I had a man who loved me like you love Maggie."

He looked at her, surprised. Honor wasn't usually so vulnerable. "You could have one, you know. If you'd let anyone in."

"You sound like Kara," Honor said.

"Did you ever go to your prom?"

"Me. God no. I could never afford a dress, even if someone had asked me."

If he had to force him, Jackson was getting Zane Shaw to ask this pretty girl right in front of him to the prom. It might be just what they needed.

"But you can afford a dress now," Jackson said. "Think of all you've accomplished, all on your own."

"Not exactly on my own. I have Brody to thank. And, the rest of you Dogs for always looking out for me. Until I came here, I didn't know there were good men out there."

"Doesn't take away all your hard work," he said.

"Stop it. You're going to make me cry and I don't want to smear my makeup." She waved her hand in front of her eyes. "I'll send an evite to everyone tonight. The ladies will need a chance to get dresses."

"Thanks for doing this," he said.

"You kidding? I live for stuff like this." She waved the list in the air. "I've got to run. Kara and I have no time to waste."

* * *

After Honor left, Jackson found his dad downstairs in his study.

"Good, it's you." His father set aside the book in his lap. "There's something I wanted to talk with you about."

Jackson took the seat in the chair opposite. "What's up?"

"Couple things. One is I'd like your permission to ask Janet to marry me."

He stared at his father for a moment. "You don't need my permission, Dad." Jackson hesitated. Should he say something about Brody? While he was deciding, his dad beat him to it.

"I went out and saw Brody earlier. To ask his permission, so to speak."

"How'd that go?"

"Remarkably well. Kara's done a good job of softening him to the idea."

Jackson smiled, imagining the conversation she must have had with Brody. "She has a gift that way."

"Brody asked me to take good care of her, which of course, I will. But he said something else that really touched me. He told me how much his father liked me, and that he often told him that I was the type of man to emulate. He said his father would approve of Janet and me—that I was one of the only men he would have deemed good enough for Janet."

"Dad, that's really nice. Wow."

"Brody also said that he feels that way about you. That he will tell his own children, if you want to see a good man, look at Jackson Waller." His father choked up. "That made me prouder than I can express."

"I don't know what to say." Jackson examined his hands, embarrassed.

"Like men, we'll move onto another topic. I'm fairly certain Janet's going to say yes, and we want to spend some time traveling together before the grandchildren start arriving."

"Yeah?"

"And that means I need to retire for real. No more of this half-time stuff. Janet's ready to go wherever and whenever. I want to be too. With Kara at the office, you don't need me. The two of you can run it together."

Jackson wanted to be supportive of his dad's plans, but the whole idea had been for them to practice together for a few years before he retired for good. His disappointment must have shown on his face.

"I'm sorry my plans have changed, Son. But I think it's all for the best. Kara coming here was the catalyst for many things. Janet and me. The fact that you don't need me at the office. It's futile to resist change. When we try, it makes everything that much worse."

"Do you think that's what you did after Mom died?"

"Maybe. I remember a deep sense of wanting everything to be exactly as she left it, which is absurd when you think about it."

"Dad, you grieved in your own way. And now, finally, you have a chance to be happy with someone else. I'm going to miss the idea of us, but truthfully, you're right. We shouldn't resist change just because we had an idea of something. Whatever is coming might be that much better."

"For one, you won't have your old man bossing you around at work."

Jackson smiled. "If I can be half the doctor and father you've been, I'll be happy."

"Well, now, let's not get carried away."

"I have something to tell you too. I'm going to propose to Maggie." He told his dad about his idea for the prom.

"I always felt terrible you two missed yours."

"I need to scramble to get a ring." He chuckled. "I'm hoping they'll let me exchange the one I got for Sharon. Maggie will want something more traditional, don't you think?"

"Funny you should mention that." His father crossed the room and opened a desk drawer, from which he took out a small velvet bag. "Inside are your mother's rings. The ones I gave her on our tenth wedding anniversary. When we got married the first time I could barely afford a plastic one."

Jackson loosened the top of the bag. The engagement ring was a two-carat princess cut diamond with tiny diamonds on the edges.

"When your mother was dying, she asked me to save her rings for Maggie. She felt certain you'd marry sooner than later, and she wanted her to have them. That way, she said, a small part of her would be there for the wedding and with you as you made a life together. They would be good luck, too, because she'd been blessed with such a happy marriage."

So much for the pledge not to cry. Jackson couldn't stop the tears that spilled from his eyes. "I can't believe, after all this time, you can finally keep your promise to Mom."

"It's been a circuitous route."

"I'm overwhelmed," Jackson said. "Maggie will be too."

"There's one more thing. Reach inside the bag. There's a note hidden in there from Lily to Maggie. She's supposed to read it on her wedding day, but I think you could go ahead and let her read it when you propose."

"May I?" Jackson asked. Was it for Maggie's eyes only?

"Lily never said, so I think we're good. Read it aloud."

Jackson cleared his throat. If he could get through this without breaking down, it would be a miracle. "Dear Maggie. If you're reading this…"

CHAPTER TWENTY-ONE

Maggie

MAGGIE HELD HER breath when she knocked on the back door of her father's house. Darla answered seconds later. She looked like she'd aged ten years. The skin under Darla's eyes looked like raw dough. A wave of pity went through Maggie.

"What do you want?"

"May I come in? I want to talk to you."

"Fine." Darla stepped aside so she could enter.

Dishes were stacked on the counters, and the air smelled like rotting bananas and stale coffee grounds.

"I found her. The baby. My sister."

Darla stared at her hands. "Yeah?"

"She's good. She's had a great life. A great family adopted her. I can't help but feel gratitude toward you for saving her life."

"They rich?"

"As far as I can tell. What does that matter?" Maggie asked.

"It doesn't. But it figures."

"How's he doing?" Maggie asked.

"Not good. In and out."

"I want to see him."

"It'll just upset him." Darla's voice wavered.

"Would it surprise you to know I don't care?"

A muscle at the left of Darla's mouth twitched. "Please don't tell him about the girl."

"Why? He can't hurt you now."

Darla crossed her arms and leaned against the counter. "It's not that. I don't want him to know he didn't kill her."

Maggie stared at her. "I don't get it."

"He doesn't deserve to be let off the hook."

"That's a change."

Darla nodded. "I've been thinking about what you said. You know, about why I was with him. Feeling like crap about yourself isn't really an excuse to do bad things."

"As far as the baby goes, you did the only decent thing you could," Maggie said. "You're not the only woman who loved Roger Keene and accepted less than you deserved. You're not the only one who was afraid of him."

Darla rubbed under her eyes. "I can't sleep. I'm awake all night wondering why I let him do what he did. To me, that is."

"Has he hurt you?"

"Sure. He didn't save that brand of love for just your mother."

"You're almost free. And he'll go where he belongs," Maggie said.

"I'm sorry about your mother. She didn't deserve what happened to her."

"Abused women never do. Including you."

"I wasted my whole life," Darla said. "For a man who never loved me."

"He can't love anyone. That's on him, not you."

"I suppose you'll take the house from me," Darla said.

Maggie thought for a moment before answering. What had Darla ever had of her own? "I don't want the house. There's nothing but bad memories for me here. You can live here as long as you like. When you move on, I'll take it back."

"It was your family's house. Doesn't feel right."

"Think of it as a thank you for bringing my sister to me."

"Thank you." Darla looked away. "I don't deserve your kindness."

"I should see him now. This'll be the last time. I want to say goodbye."

Darla led her down the hallway to the living room. He was in the bed with his eyes closed.

"Roger, Maggie's here," Darla said.

She still loves him. I can hear it in her voice.

Her dad's eyes fluttered open. "You came back?"

"I came to say goodbye."

"You going somewhere?" he asked.

"No. But you are."

"That, yes."

"I'll never forgive you for the things you've done, but I'm not going to let you destroy my life any longer. I'm going to live a good, full life despite of all the ways you tried to destroy it. Not one single person will be sad you're gone. Me, on the other hand? I have so much love. So much to live for. Consider my living well the ultimate revenge."

He fluttered his fingers. "Get out. You ungrateful girl. I did everything for you and this is the thanks I get?"

"Goodbye, Roger Keene. May you rot in hell."

* * *

Maggie arrived at the Woods' home around ten the next morning. She grabbed her portfolio and guitar from the back of the car and headed up the walkway. Birds chirped in the maple tree as she knocked on the front door. *A good sign.* Good wishes from her bird friends. Micky opened the door and invited her inside.

He gave her a quick hug before getting right to business. "Let's head on down to the studio. My staff's waiting for us."

She followed Micky down steep stairs to the basement level of the house as he explained how he'd built the studio and made it soundproof. "The kids were still little when I built it, so there was a lot of racket going on up there. Nothing can penetrate this place."

When they arrived downstairs, Micky introduced her to Carlos, his sound technician. Carlos made up for the lack of hair on his shiny head with a bushy beard that touched the collar of his shirt. A young woman with spiked pink hair and tattoos on every inch of her arms waved to them from inside the recording booth.

Maggie had been in a recording studio before for voiceover work, but never one as sophisticated as this. Micky Woods didn't mess around.

When the young woman joined them, Micky introduced her as Lena Wheeler. "Lena works with our artists most intimately, both on the music itself as well as your brand and career direction."

"If we decide to sign you, we can help you find the right manager, publicist, and agent as well. We know who's good in this business and who isn't." Lena's articulate and resonate way of speaking surprised Maggie. She looked like she belonged on the back of a Harley. "From what Micky said, you don't have much experience in this side of show business. We're a family here. Unlike a bigger studio with lots of artists, we don't take many on, but the ones we do get our full attention. We win when our artists win."

"I've been in New York, mostly in chorus girl roles on Broadway," Maggie said. "I studied musical theatre at NYU. We had a lot of vocal training, obviously. But I've also worked with vocal coaches over the years. Some of the best."

"Cool beans, Chica," Lena said. "I prefer to work with people who have formal training. No matter if they want to sing rock and roll or opera, technique always shows in your voice. That said, singers who come from musical theatre usually can't transfer to pop music."

"I've sung in a lot of bars and coffee shops," Maggie said. That familiar feeling from auditions washed over her. Directors and casting agents loved to make you sweat. How bad do you want it? Can you defend yourself? Heck yes, she could. She'd been a New Yorker for twelve years. *Be tough. I can do this. I have the chops. This is finally my chance to prove it to someone who can actually take me somewhere.*

"Micky tells me you're kind of Norah Jones meets Trisha Yearwood," Lena said. "Which, if true, makes me wonder when you sold your soul to the devil."

"Micky's kind to say so," Maggie said.

"Kindness doesn't mean a flying squirrel in this business. It's all about the delivery. Let's see what you've got."

Micky, who had been fiddling with the equipment over with Carlos, looked up at them. "Lena, just have a seat. Maggie's got this nailed." He indicated for Maggie to follow him into the recording booth. Once inside, he lowered his voice. "Don't mind her. She's just testing you to see if you're tough enough. Once she hears you sing, she's going to be all over you. Now, I want you to choose one of your original songs and just play and sing like you did last night in front of the crowd."

He spoke into the microphone. "She's going to sing an original with just her guitar."

Lena nodded as she sat on one of the tall chairs next to the equipment.

This is happening. This is really happening.

"You been in one of these before?" Micky asked.

"Once or twice for voiceover work," Maggie said.

"Good. Then you know what to do."

A glass window encased the front of the booth so that she could see out to the engineer. As she took a seat on the stool, Micky adjusted a sophisticated looking microphone to the proper distance and level. "Sing *Deleted*," he said. "Lena won't know what to do with herself when she hears the vocals on that one."

"Whatever you say, boss," she said.

"Just nice and easy." Micky handed her a set of headphones. "Like you did last night. No reason to change a thing. Be you. Let it show through the music. Remember, you're good enough just as you are."

"Great. Thanks." *If* she could sing without shaking. As Micky stepped through the door, Maggie adjusted a few strings to get control of her nerves. Whatever she did, she must not show how jumpy she was. Pull out the old acting skills.

As if she were here, Lisa appeared in her imagination and repeated her favorite saying.

Be myself. Everyone else is taken.

This one's for you, Lisa.

Maggie slipped the headphones over her ears. Outside of the booth, Sophie bounded into the room and flashed her wide smile. "Good luck," she mouthed.

Buoyed by her sister's face, she took in a deep, centering breath. *Sing for all the women in my life. Sophie and Lisa. Mama and Lily up in heaven.* Maggie played the beginning chord on her guitar. *Sing for Jackson.*

From the other side of the glass, Micky gave her the thumbs up.

Maggie leaned into the microphone and began to sing.

I danced under a fallen moon,

And wondered where were...

* * *

When she finished, she glanced out to the studio. Sophie clapped and bounced up and down on her toes. Micky gave her the thumbs up. Carlos was bent over the equipment moving dials.

Lena had uncrossed her arms, but her facial expression was as stoic as before Maggie had started singing.

Micky pushed a button and his voice came through to the booth. "You did great, kid. Sing another. One of your originals, but with the piano this time."

Maggie set aside her guitar and moved to the piano. Intimidated by the size and quality of the instrument, her hands shook. This was nothing like her keyboard at her apartment or the one at Zane's bar. *I can do this. I can do this.*

She played the opening notes to the song she'd written last week. It had come out of her in an hour, like it wrote itself. Lena stood against the wall with her tattooed arms crossed over her chest.

I thought I saw you today,
By the flowers near the bay.
But it was only a reflection of the sea so blue,
Not the you of me and you.

* * *

Maggie looked out to where the others stood together by the equipment. As before, Sophie smiled and clapped. Micky motioned for Maggie to come outside of the booth. She did so.

Sophie hugged her and whispered in her ear, "Lena's impressed. I knew she would be."

Micky nodded at her before turning his attention to his partner. "Lena, what do you think?"

Lena remained by the wall with her hands stuck into the pockets of her jeans. "I think she needs an album."

"I'm thinking acoustic with just her guitar or piano," Micky said.

"Agreed," Lena said. "Raw and unfiltered."

"That could be the title," Sophie said.

"It's been done, sweetie," Micky said. "But we'll think of something even better."

* * *

Maggie and Jackson walked near the shore as the sun set before them in a blaze of orange. She hadn't yet told him her news, afraid of what he might think, afraid it would jeopardize their tenuous bond that time had so long impeded.

"You're quiet," he said.

"Am I?" Why would the words not come? *They want me. I'm going to make an album. I might have to tour.*

"I know where you went today," he said.

She gulped. "You do?"

"Micky told me last night that he wanted you to meet Lena—to sing for her." He squeezed her hand. "Tell me. Did it go well?"

She could feel him holding his breath as he waited for her answer. What was the right one? All those years ago, she had chosen her dreams instead of him. Would he be able to handle it this time?

"It went well. They want to sign me," she said.

"I'm a little offended."

"Why?" she asked.

"That you hesitated to tell me," he said.

She stopped and looked up at him. The orange light sparkled in his blue eyes. "There might be touring."

"I might not deserve it after what I did all those years ago, but you have to trust me. I'm not a boy any longer. I want what you want. I want it more for you than you even want it for yourself. Your dreams are my dreams."

"Months in the studio recording—publicity stuff. It's all part of the package."

"Will you always come back to me? Will you save the last dance for me?" he asked.

"Yes. Of course, I will."

"I'll be here when you get back. Every time. No matter how far you go."

"What about your dreams?" she asked. "This town, the house. Babies."

He was quiet for a moment. A wave crashed to shore, soaking their bare feet. "I know what it's like to live without you. I don't ever want to do so again. If that means I sacrifice so that you can

241

have what you want, then I will. I'll choose you every time. You say the word, and I'll pack up and go tomorrow."

"Knowing that you would means a lot," she said. "But you don't have to. It's possible to compromise. Look at Brody and Kara. His job takes him away, but they make it work."

"It's true," he said. "And they have the added pressure of her needing to stay hidden from the world."

"We have a village here," she said. "Your dad and Janet. The Dogs. Honor and Kara. They'll be there for us if we need them to help with kids."

"I agree."

"You're sure?" she asked.

"I am. We can make this work. We're us. Jackson and Maggie."

"Us," she said. "My favorite word."

He stood and held out his hand. "Now, come along. I have a surprise for you."

* * *

Maggie followed Jackson into Zane's apartment. It was nearing the dinner hour, so Zane was already downstairs getting ready for a busy night. Jackson asked her to follow him into her bedroom.

"You're acting very mysterious," she said.

"Wait here, by the bed. Close your eyes."

She did as he asked. Had he gotten her flowers to celebrate? No, he was opening the closet. She recognized the squeak of the door's hinge.

"You can open your eyes now," he said.

Jackson held a silver sparkling dress in his hands. A fitted bodice and spaghetti straps with an A-line skirt reminded her of a fairy princess in a ballet.

"What is this?" she asked.

"I had the girls pick it for you." He placed the dress on the bed as gently as he always touched her. It lay there, lovely and shiny.

The material sparkled like a million stars. The sweetheart neckline would flatter her small chest. "Do you like it?" he asked.

"It's beautiful, but what's it for?" she asked.

He stood before her and wrapped his hands around her waist. "Maggie Keene, will you go to the prom with me?"

She stared up at him, speechless. What was he saying?

"All these years, I've regretted how you didn't get to attend your prom or wear the beautiful dress you'd picked out." Tears dampened his face, but he didn't seem to notice. "Every woman should get to feel like a princess at least a few times in her life. I thought you'd died not even getting to feel that way one time. I hated it, myself, but mostly that you and my mom didn't get that day and those photographs for our hallway. I didn't get to pin a corsage on you like I'd planned since we were ten years old."

"It's fine. It didn't matter."

"It mattered to me. So, I got together with our friends and we planned a prom for you. Zane's shut the bar down for the night and we decorated it just like our prom."

"A Night of a Thousand Stars?" she whispered.

"Yes. Only Violet, Kara, and Honor made what we did look like chump change. Wait until you see the bar."

"I'm overwhelmed." She cried the ugly cry now.

He swooped her into his arms. "Don't cry, Bird. This is a happy day. A day we'll remember all our lives."

"I can't think of what to say."

"Say yes to the dress," he said.

She laughed through her tears. "You're ridiculous."

"I know. Ridiculously in love with you. Now listen, I'm going to leave you here with Honor, Kara, and Violet. They're waiting in the kitchen with wine and snacks and a full crew of folks to get you girls ready for the big night. Brody hired a whole team of hair and makeup people. I'll be back to pick you up at seven sharp. Okay?"

She nodded and sniffed. "Okay."

* * *

As promised, Jackson arrived right at seven. The girls were still there, all of them in their gowns toasting one another with glasses of champagne when he knocked on the door. Kara wore a light blue mermaid style dress with sequins and an illusion neckline that clung to her hourglass figure. Honor's dress was a silky red halter with an open back that plunged to her tailbone and a skirt with a slit that showed off one shapely leg. Violet had chosen a soft pink taffeta that swirled around her middle like frosting on the most beautiful cupcake in the world.

But the dress they'd chosen for her was the best of all. She was a princess.

Jackson stopped in the doorway and stared at her. He carried a corsage made of white ranunculus. "A princess. You're a princess."

He didn't look so bad himself in a dark blue suit and silver tie. "You're the perfect prince to take me to the ball," she said.

"I've been waiting twelve years for this," he said, as he leaned over to pin the corsage on her dress.

She was vaguely aware of their friends snapping photographs on their phones.

He offered his arm and they waved goodbye to the ladies. "See you all later," he said. "We have someplace to go first."

"Good luck," Honor called.

Luck? What did they need luck for? She didn't have time to think about it as Jackson scooped her into his arms and instructed her to close her eyes.

"I mean it," he said. "You're not allowed to see the back patio."

She laughed and squeezed them shut until he said she could open them. They were in front of the bar now. Jackson's truck was parked in the "loading only" zone.

"Where are we going?"

"We have a little business to take care of before the prom." He opened the door to the passenger side and set her inside. "Gather your skirt, so the door doesn't crush it."

She gathered the layers of the silky material into her hands as he shut the door. Sitting this high in a truck with a formal gown on made her chuckle. She looked up at Zane's apartment. Kara, Violet, and Honor waved at her from the window.

Maggie waved back and grinned at them. She had friends here that had her back and wanted the best for her. And a new sister. And Zane.

A recording contract. Her heart soared at the thought of the months ahead.

And Jackson. Mostly Jackson. Always Jackson.

This was a life. A big, fat, live-out-loud life.

They didn't talk as they drove down the main street of town to the beach. When they arrived, he parked his truck in the beach parking lot. "Wait, so I can help you down," he said.

He crossed in front of the truck fidgeting with his tie. For a split second, she was back to the morning of Lily's memorial. He'd worn a suit that morning and he'd fiddled with his tie as they walked up the steps of the church. The raw vulnerability of that gesture had caused her to stumble in her high heels. He'd reached out to hold her steady but instead they'd both fallen to their knees right there on the church steps. "I don't know if I can do it, Bird," he'd whispered. "I can't go in and say goodbye."

"I'm right here beside you." She had stood and helped him to his feet, surprised at her own strength.

She blinked away the memory. Tonight was joyous, not sad. They'd had enough sadness for a lifetime already. She shivered, knowing it was inevitable there would be more. To love means to suffer. Loss came eventually. At the end, would it be only memories?

Jackson opened her door and held out his hand. "Princess, may I escort you over to our bench?"

"Yes, please. These heels are wobbly." *If one stumbles, the other will lead the way.*

No breezes tonight. Good. Her hair would stay in place. The stylist had gone to great trouble to gather it into a complicated mass on top of her head. Teardrop diamond earrings that Honor had insisted she wear tickled her neck as they walked carefully over the uneven cement of the parking lot to the bench that looked out over the Pacific. *Their* bench.

Jackson had been here earlier because a blanket covered the seat. Only he would've thought about the slivers of wood snagging her dress.

She sat, making sure to gather her skirt so that it wouldn't soil in the sand and grass. "It's so beautiful," she said.

"Yes, you are." Jackson smiled down at her before joining her on the bench.

The sun was a finger's width from sinking below the horizon. Rays of orange light cast a spell over the entire coastline and glinted in the water like a thousand topaz stones. Was it real? *Can a scene be this beautiful and still be real?*

Jackson took both her hands into his lap. "We have a lot of memories on this bench. All the time we sat here and shared our secrets and dreams. Some are sad memories, but most are good. I want this one to be the happiest of all—the one to overshadow all the others." He reached into the pocket of his trousers and pulled a small velvet pouch from his pocket. What was he doing? Here? Now? Was it too soon? No. It was perfect. *He is perfect.*

Still, knowing what was coming, her heart beat with the wings of a startled sparrow. *Remember every moment.*

"When I was a kid, I told my mom I was going to marry you—I told her I'd ask you right in this very spot. You know, she never once laughed at me. She took it completely seriously, like it was the most normal thing in the world for a ten-year-old boy to say."

A petite sob rose from her chest but came out as a giggle instead. "You always were a romantic."

"Yes. But how could I help it when the most beautiful girl in the world loved me? I wanted nothing but to please you, to make you smile, to keep you safe. Every minute I spent with you made me a better person. After we lost you, I used to come here and sit and think about you. What I would've given to have the chance to sit here with you once more—believe me, I bargained with God many times. The day I saw you standing here, I thought I was losing my mind. All these years, I thought I saw you a thousand times. Even though I knew it wasn't you—couldn't be you—each time my heart leapt with hope only to be crushed with reality. Until that day, finally, it *was* you. Bird, I won't ever forget what it was like without you. Not ever. Not one day will pass that I won't fall on my knees and thank God for bringing you back to me." He kissed the palm of her left hand and held it against his mouth for a moment. "It's always been you. Before we were born, even, our souls were attached to each other. It might seem fast to some, but I've waited a lifetime already to ask you this."

This is the story we'll tell our children someday.

Jackson slid a ring from the pouch. She gasped. *This* ring. She knew this ring and the hand that had worn it. *Lily's ring.*

"My mother wanted you to have it," he said. "Only you."

"I don't understand."

"She asked my dad to save it for you—for when we got engaged." He lifted her left hand and held it against his chest. She could feel his elevated heartbeat. "He didn't think I'd ever have the chance to give it to you—to ask you, will you be my wife? But we were wrong. By a miracle, you came back to me. Bird, will you be my wife? Will you marry me?"

"Yes, yes," she whispered.

He slipped the ring on her finger. It fit perfectly. "I thought we might have to get it sized, but it's the perfect fit."

The diamonds sparkled even in the dim light. "It's too nice," she said.

"Nothing is too nice for you. My mom wanted you to have it so a part of her would be with us on our wedding day and for all the days of our marriage."

"With or without the ring, she's with me. With us." She tilted her face to him. "Kiss me?"

"You never have to ask," he said. He traced her bottom lip with his thumb. "You're more breathtaking tonight than I've ever seen you, and that's saying something." He leaned close and kissed her with the same tender touch of the muted rays of light.

When their first kiss as an engaged couple was finished, he drew a piece of folded paper from the pouch. "There's something else. There's a letter for you from my mom. She wrote it just before she passed away. I was supposed to read it to you on our wedding day, but there's no way I can do that." He pulled a folded piece of paper from the pouch.

She shook her head and clasped her hands together on her lap. "I can't. You have to read it to me."

His voice sounded gruff and shaky, but he didn't pause until it was finished.

Dear Maggie, if you're reading this then it must be your big day. I wish I could be there, but it wasn't to be. My seat will be from heaven. I imagine it will be with your mother and we'll hold hands and cry tears of joy. We'll be without pain then, Maggie, so do not cry for us. Just love my son and make a life with him that will make us proud.

I wanted you to have my rings not only because you love my son, but because you were the daughter I never had. I wanted more children, but it wasn't in God's plan. I have often thought how lucky we were to have each other after your mother died. You needed me and I needed you.

I can still see you and Jackson walking home together after the first day of school. You were holding hands and your clothes were all muddy and Jackson's face was red. I knew someone must have pushed you in the mud. Jackson's red face told me he probably beat the daylights out of whomever had done the pushing. But you were both laughing at something the other one said or did. In that moment, I knew, like a mother does, that there was something special about the two of you. No matter what, you would have each other. And, even during hard times, you would find something to laugh about. This, my dear girl, is as good as it gets.

I wish for you, my sweet Maggie, more joy than hardship, but I know that whatever comes your way, you will have my brave, kind boy by your side. Be happy. Keep singing.

I love you. Lily.

They were both in tears by the time he finished.

"She said to keep singing," Maggie said. "Not dancing."

"I hadn't thought of that, but yes."

"Isn't that odd?"

"There's not much about our story that isn't odd, Bird," he said.

They laughed. He took a tissue from his pocket and dabbed under her eyes. "Honor will be mad. I've caused your makeup to smear," he said.

"She gave me an emergency kit to take with me in my purse," Maggie said. "Like she knew what was coming my way."

He grinned. "Yes. Everyone knows. They're all waiting to celebrate with us."

"I wish your mom could be here," Maggie said. "And my mom too."

"Me too."

"The trouble is time," she said.

"Time?"

"The way it slips away. Nothing can hold it. There's no return to the beautiful moments. They're gone before we even realize what they were," she said.

"Except in here." He tapped the side of his head. "And, when it's a beautiful moment between us, we can recall it together in such a way that it lives forever. We have the rest of our lives to make more memories and to visit them. Think of it. All that waits for us."

"Whatever comes, I'll always save the last dance for you. No matter what."

"And I'll always be there."

She rested her head against his shoulder as the sun slipped below the horizon. Overhead, seagulls screeched as if to call one another home. Waves crashed to shore and backed out again in the dance of time. Time would not stand still. Not even for lovers.

But they had this moment. This memory. Time could not take that from them.

CHAPTER TWENTY-TWO

Jackson

THE BAR PATIO had been transformed into a fairytale. White lights twinkled from the rafters and railings. Candles in various sizes threw shadows with their soft flames. Tables had been arranged around a makeshift dance floor and covered with white cloths. More candles in mason jars and masses of ranunculus in bright colors decorated the tables. A theatre light had been set up with a screen that made stars on the ceiling.

Gratitude surged through him. Who had friends like this? He did. Maggie did.

Next to him, Maggie sighed and squeezed his arm so tightly he thought he might lose circulation. "Oh my God," she said. "How did they do this?"

"I have no idea."

No one noticed them for a moment. Zane and Kyle stood on the far end of the patio with drinks in their hands visiting with Micky and Rhona. Honor and Mary, a surprising duo, sat at a table together looking as if they discussed something terribly interesting.

"Did Mary decide to stay for a while?" Maggie asked.

"Indefinitely, from what I hear," Jackson said.

"Interesting," Maggie said. "It seems no one wants to leave here."

"I think it's more her dad she doesn't want to leave," Jackson said.

Sophie and Violet were over by the DJ talking animatedly, most likely figuring out how to save the world. Jackson's dad and Janet sat with Kara and Lance at a table. Flora and Dax were over at the dessert table, perusing the petit fours Honor had brought from the city. *Classy for Maggie,* Honor had told him earlier.

Staff passed around glasses of champagne. Brody came from behind them and wrapped Maggie in a hug before taking her left hand to peer at her ring. He patted Jackson on the back. "Got it done, I see."

"Yes sir," Jackson said as everyone surrounded them.

Maggie held up her hand. "I said yes."

The DJ had music playing, but Brody asked him to turn it down so they could toast the newly engaged couple.

Jackson's dad clinked his glass with a fork. "I want to say—" He halted for a moment, before gathering himself. "This day's been a long time coming. Jackson's mother and I always knew it *would* come, but we couldn't imagine all the twists and turns it would take to get here. I can't tell you how proud I am of my son or how happy it makes me to have Maggie back where she belongs. With us. Congratulations."

Brody clinked his glass next. "My turn, I guess. I'm not the best at giving speeches, as you can tell by my after-game interviews, but here goes. Maggie, from the day I met your future husband, he's been the rock in our friend group, as steady and solid as they come. No one could be a better or more understanding friend. There's no better man, period. But there was always a sadness in him. I wasn't sure it would ever go away. Until now. Seeing him with you—how happy you make him and how alive he is with you—maybe *alive* is the wrong thing to bring up, but you know what I mean."

Laughter erupted around the room.

Flushed, Brody continued. "The fact that you've come back and the way your love has blossomed as if no time had passed—well, it's the best I could've ever hoped for the man I think of as a brother. Welcome to our family, Maggie."

Zane raised his glass. "I'm next. Maggie, I'm sorry you missed our prom. Heck, I'm sorry we all missed it, but that's life, right? Some days are diamonds and some days are stones." He grinned. "I think that's a country song, but what I'm trying to say is—there have been times that have sucked pretty bad and times so good it almost hurts. This is one of those times." He shrugged and ran a hand through his hair. "So anyway. Congratulations. Yep, that's all. Just congratulations."

"All right, guys, save something for the actual wedding," Kyle said. "It's time to party like it's 2005."

"Thank you," Maggie said. "For all of this." She waved her hand around the room. "I'm overwhelmed and so touched by all of this and all of you. I don't even know what to say."

Jackson gave the cue to the DJ. He'd made sure to tell him which song they wanted for the first dance.

"May I have this dance?" he asked.

"Yes," she whispered.

He put his hand around her waist and took her other hand in his as the first notes of "Save the Last Dance for Me" filled the space. "I'll try not to step on your toes," he whispered.

"As long as you hold me tight, I promise not to notice."

* * *

Two days later, while between patients, Jackson checked his phone. There was a message from Maggie that she'd be home late.

Her meetings in San Francisco had run long and traffic was terrible getting out of the city. Nothing new there.

Around five-thirty, he and Kara were sharing the day's events. They had just finished their discussion about their last two patients when he heard the receptionist talking to someone in the waiting room. Figuring it was an emergency of some kind, he left Kara in the office and went out to the waiting room, expecting a kid with a broken limb or a sore throat.

But it wasn't a patient.

Sharon.

"What are you doing here?" he asked.

"I have something to talk to you about. In private, please."

"We can talk in my office."

Kara was heading down the hallway as they walked back to his office. She caught his eye as she passed but didn't say anything.

He closed the door behind them. "What's going on?" For her to come here unannounced in the middle of the week was strange. She'd only come to visit a handful of times when they were together. Had he been wrong that she was going quietly? Was this her plea to get him back?

"I'm pregnant," she said.

His stomach dropped. How could this be? She was on the pill. Or, so she said. "I thought you were on the pill?"

"As you know, there's that one percent chance," she said.

"How far along?"

"Ten weeks."

He sank into his chair behind the desk, too stunned to speak.

"I brought the pregnancy test to prove it." She pulled a wand out of her bag and set it on the desk. "Two pink lines. I took several of them because I couldn't believe it."

"Why didn't you say anything before now?"

"You mean, when you proposed? Before your long-lost love suddenly appeared and you dropped me?"

He flinched. "Sharon, this is…I don't know what to say."

"Well, it changes things. You can't just dismiss a baby like you did me."

Just when he thought happiness might finally be his. He had his Maggie back, and now this? What should he do? He couldn't be with Sharon simply because she was pregnant, especially since he loved someone else. But how could this work? The child would be raised by Sharon in L.A. and Jackson would see him or her on holidays and scattered weekends? This was not the kind of father he wanted to be. Not at all. What he wanted was to be the father of Maggie's children.

"I'm stunned," Jackson said. "But we'll work something out. It's a baby."

"We should go forward with our plans to marry," she said. "This baby's a sign that we're supposed to be together."

"I can't be with you when I love someone else. I'm sorry, but Maggie and I are getting married."

"Married? Are you insane?" The last word came out as a screech.

He flinched at the pain in her voice. "It'll be all right. I'll take care of you and the baby. We'll just have to have an unconventional arrangement."

"Which you hate." She started to cry and grabbed tissues from his desk. "I thought you wanted a family. That's all you ever talked about."

"I do."

"Just not with me."

"I care about you. I admire you. But when Maggie came back in my life, I knew that what I felt for her was what it's supposed to be like between two people."

"You can't dismiss me. I'm going to have your baby."

"People have shared custody." The contents of his lunch swirled inside his stomach. He took in a deep breath. What was he going to tell Maggie? How could he be the father he wanted to be if he and the child didn't even live in the same place?

"I don't want that. I want to get married. I want the life you promised me," she said.

"I'm sorry, but everything's changed." The guilt wanted to suffocate him, knock him out. "Please don't make this harder than it already is."

"That would be impossible."

"I'll share every aspect of parenthood with you. Money, whatever you need, I'll be here. But I can't be your husband."

* * *

After he finally convinced Sharon to leave, he sat in his office staring at the wall. He couldn't figure out what to do, what to think. He wanted to talk to Maggie, but first he needed to get advice from the most solid guy he knew. Brody Mullen.

Brody picked up on the first ring. Jackson couldn't get the words to come out of his mouth. "Can I come out to see you? I need to talk to you."

"Yep. Kara already told me Sharon was there. Come over now. I'm here."

Ten minutes later, Brody led him into the kitchen of his enormous home. Kara had gone to Zumba after work, so it was just the two of them. Jackson looked out at the view of the blue ocean that sparkled under the sun.

"Sharon's ten weeks pregnant."

"No. No, this can't be right. She's lying," Brody said. "A woman like that doesn't get pregnant unless she wants to."

"Maybe she wanted to."

"To trap you into marrying her, you mean?"

"She knew how much I wanted kids." He covered his face with his hands. "This is going to ruin everything with Maggie. I want to marry her and have children and grow old together, beside you and Kara. I don't want a baby with Sharon. It complicates everything."

"Listen, buddy, I know you like everything in neat packages, but life's not that way. Is this the ideal situation? No. But you can make it work. And, Maggie will understand."

"I don't know. She already feels like she's messed everything up by coming back. This might push her away from me. I can't lose her again."

Brody paced in front of the window. "You need to find out if she's really pregnant. I don't trust Sharon."

"She had a wand with two pink stripes," Jackson said.

"She could've gotten it from someone else. A pregnant friend?"

Jackson thought for a moment. She had a group of girlfriends she was close with. He went through them one by one. Was anyone pregnant? It was possible. Two got married last summer. One of them could be. His heart thumped with new hope. "Maybe she's lying. It's possible."

"Get her on the phone and tell her you want her to take a test at the clinic and Kara will give it to her. Tell her to meet us there in an hour and a half."

"And if she won't?"

"We'll threaten her with a court order."

CHAPTER TWENTY-THREE

Maggie

MAGGIE ARRIVED HOME a little after seven, exhausted but exhilarated. Today had been a series of meetings with her new manager as well as the agent Micky recommended for her. Although Micky had been by her side the entire time, the contracts and numbers and discussion of marketing strategies had left her feeling like a wrung-out dishrag.

Thankful she didn't have to perform that evening, she looked forward to a quiet dinner with Jackson. She tried unsuccessfully to get him on the phone, so she settled for a text telling him that she was home at Zane's and to come over when he was done doing whatever he was doing.

She'd just changed into soft jeans and a t-shirt when the doorbell rang. She ran down the back stairs, expecting Jackson. He must have forgotten his key.

A tall, blond woman stood on the steps. "Maggie?"

"Yes. Can I help you?"

"I'm Sharon Fox."

Maggie gripped the door. Sharon. This was Sharon. Why was she here? "Jackson's not here."

"I know. I came to talk to you."

Ice gushed through Maggie's veins. "I don't think that's a good idea." The woman had hatred in her eyes. *She wants to hurt me.*

Sharon shook her head. "You're so freckled. And, red hair. You're not at all what I expected."

"You're not at all what I expected either," Maggie said. It was true. She'd imagined a scholarly type with glasses and inquisitive eyes, not a walking Barbie doll. A woman that Maggie might like if the circumstances were different. But this woman was the opposite of what she would have imagined for Jackson. She looked fake—primped and polished to perfection and had eyes that shot daggers. She wore tight, cropped white jeans and a tank top. Red toes peeked out of high-heeled sandals. This was not the type of woman Jackson had ever liked. Natural is best, he'd always said. But this? No, not this woman. This was the woman Jackson had almost married? She couldn't understand how he'd fallen for her. Jackson liked authenticity.

And, the way she talked. It was as if she went to broadcasting school in England but didn't quite get the knack of a flawless British accent.

"I don't get it," Sharon said.

"Did you come to get a good look at me, or is there a message I can give Jackson?"

"Fine. I'll tell you here. I'm pregnant. Jackson's the father."

Oh, God, no. Not with this woman. Maggie's legs trembled. Why now, when they were so close to having the life they wanted? Together, without someone like this in their lives. Hadn't they gone through enough with her father's deviousness?

"I thought I should tell you myself, in case Jackson decides to keep it from you. He told me he wants nothing to do with me or the baby."

Sharon's eyes had looked to the right just now. She was lying. Maggie had taken enough acting classes with untalented people to know bad acting. Plus, Jackson would never say or do anything of the sort. He would never turn his back on a baby, no matter the circumstances.

If she lied about this, what else would she lie about? Being pregnant? Maggie had spent her entire adult life learning about motivation. In acting, you must always figure out what the character wants to play them well. What did Sharon want? To mess up things between them, so that Jackson would go back to her. It wouldn't work. Their bond was too strong now. They could weather this, just as they had every other obstacle that had come their way. It was too late now for anyone to mess them up ever again. They'd made their commitment to each other and nothing could pull them under. Not today. Not this. Nothing.

"I have two things to say to you, and then I want you out of my sight. Jackson would never say such a thing. Above everything, he's a man of integrity. He *will* do the right thing for his child, regardless of who the mother is. Secondly, I think you better get some solid proof that you're pregnant because I'm having a hard time believing that the woman who didn't want to leave her career to move here let herself get pregnant."

"Birth control can fail."

"Rarely, when used right. So, no. This just doesn't ring true. The thing is, I feel sorry for you. I really do. It's awful to lose someone you love. I know. The pain is awful and there's nothing you can do about it but suffer. I feel terrible that my return has caused you pain. But this is so desperate. Think about it, Sharon. What good can come from stirring up trouble like this? I know you think it will break us up, but we've been through hell and back and nothing, I mean, nothing will be able to pull us apart ever again."

"I'm not lying." Sharon crossed her arms over her chest as if to express authority. But her voice had wavered, and she'd once again looked up and to the right. Sharon better stick to medical research. She was a terrible liar.

"How long will you keep this up? Eventually, he'll know

there's no baby." Maggie snapped her fingers. "I know. You'll have a miscarriage. That's the plan, isn't it? Break us up and have Jackson run back to you, and then, all of the sudden, sadly, you're not pregnant anymore. But he's realized by then that he belongs with you. Honestly, it's like the plot of a bad television movie. You're better than this."

"Shut up. Just stop talking. Just stop."

"But I'm right, aren't I?" Maggie crossed her arms to hide the fact that her gut felt like it was being twisted like a wet dishrag. She must remain sure and confident, strike at this woman until she admitted the truth. "You made up the whole thing."

Without warning, Sharon crumbled and began to sob. "It's not fair. I had everything, and then you just came and took it."

"I know it's not fair," Maggie said. "But you don't want a man living a lie. It's better that you learned the truth."

"You don't know. You have no idea what it's like to have your life ripped away from you."

"I do, actually. But this is not the way to move forward. Wrecking Jackson's relationship with me isn't going to get you anywhere. Even if it worked, which it won't, when he discovered the truth, he'd hate you."

"Shut your face. Just shut it."

"Not until you tell me the truth," Maggie said. "You're not pregnant."

"Fine. You figured it out. Aren't you smart?" Her words came out in jagged spurts. Once perfectly applied eye makeup was now blue and black smudges. *Like a scary clown.* Maggie's heart softened. She *was* sorry for how it had all come down. It wasn't fair to Sharon, no matter how much she loved Jackson and he loved her. For Sharon, it was a nightmare.

"I'm sorry for your pain. Truly, I am. When you have love with the right man, you're going to see how wrong you and Jackson were. You're going to be so happy that it didn't work out with him."

"How dare you pity me. You're just a stupid whore. That's

what you are. Coming here and seducing him, like the past twelve years didn't matter. What did you do all those years in New York anyway? It's not like you have a career. Why should you get to come back and pick up where you left off? You're nothing. You're a two-bit actress that's not going to age well. I mean, look at your skin."

"You need to go now," Maggie said. "You're embarrassing yourself with every moment you stay."

"I told you to shut up." Sharon lunged at her.

Maggie, shocked, stepped back, but the stairs tripped her. She crumpled. A sharp pain shot through her head. Then, darkness.

CHAPTER TWENTY-FOUR

Jackson

JACKSON FOUND MAGGIE slumped at the bottom of Zane's stairwell. Blood spilled onto the stairs from a gash in her head. He pulled her into his arms. She didn't stir. He put his fingers on the pulse at her wrist. Strong. She was simply knocked out.

"You're all right," he whispered.

The sound of footsteps running up the stairs from the bar drew his attention away from Maggie.

Zane appeared around the corner. "Holy crap. What happened?"

"I don't know. I found her like this. She must have fallen. Her head's bleeding, but her pulse is strong."

Zane crouched next to them and felt Maggie's skull. "It's just a surface wound. Head wounds always bleed so much."

"Please, Bird, wake up," Jackson whispered as he cradled her against him.

She stirred and opened her eyes. "Jackson?"

"You okay?"

She gave him a feeble smile. "My head hurts."

"What happened? Did you fall?"

"Sharon was here. She lunged at me, and I fell backward. I think I hit my head. Is there blood?"

"Just a little," Zane said. "It's only a small cut, nothing major. Correct, doctor?"

"Sure, yes." A high buzz rang between Jackson's ears. Sharon had done this? How was this the same girl he thought he loved? Who was she? Had he known her at all?

"Come on, let's get her upstairs and put some ice on the wound," Zane said. "Give her a quick look to see if she needs stitches."

God bless him, Zane had always been good in a crisis.

Jackson didn't bother to ask Maggie if she could walk. He lifted her into his arms and carried her up the stairs. Zane ran by him to open the door. Once inside, Jackson set her gently on the couch while Zane ran to get ice and a towel for her head.

Jackson encouraged her to lay back with her head on a pillow. He knelt on the floor next to the couch and examined the cut. It *was* minor. Stitches wouldn't be necessary. She'd just been temporarily knocked unconscious. Zane was right. Head wounds tended to bleed more than other areas of the body. "No stitches needed."

"Good. I hate needles."

He gave her the same concussion protocol instructions he gave the young athletes who came into his office. "No football playing for you for at least two weeks. Or surfing."

"Yes, Doctor."

"You scared me." He brushed the hair away from her face and kissed her on the forehead. "I can't lose you."

"I'm tougher than I look," she said.

"You're the toughest person I've ever met." He hesitated. "Did Sharon tell you?"

She nodded. "But Jackson, it's not true."

"What?" he asked.

Before she could answer, Zane came back into the room with

the ice and towel. "What in God's name was Sharon doing here?" Zane asked.

"She came to tell me she's pregnant," Maggie said.

"No way. Can't be." Zane looked between them.

"It's true." A weariness leached him of the adrenaline that had propelled him up the stairs. He sank to the floor and buried his face in his hands. "I'm sorry, Bird. I had no idea."

Maggie's hand encircled his shoulder. "No, Jackson. She was lying. I got her to admit it. She shoved me because I guessed the truth."

Jackson thundered to his feet. "She admitted it?" It was a lie. Thank God, it was a lie. No longer weary, he could dance a jig or sing an opera. Brody's suspicions were correct. Why hadn't he seen through her? Why could others see what he couldn't?

As if he read his mind, Zane answered his questions. "Dude, you always see the best in people. That's a great quality."

"Until it isn't," Jackson said. "But right now, I don't care. I'm so relieved."

"It doesn't matter anyway. That's what you have us for," Maggie said. "Zane and I have your back."

"As do the Dogs," Zane said.

"And Honor and Kara," Maggie said. "You keep being you, and we'll keep being us, and it will all work out in the end."

"Right now I feel like the horse's behind," Jackson said. "I almost married her."

"But you didn't. You're going to marry me." Maggie's eyes blazed with a mixture of anger and triumph. "I'm ashamed at how much I enjoyed baiting her into the telling me the truth."

"I wish I'd seen that," Zane said.

"She admitted she came up with the story to break us up," Maggie said.

"What would she do when there's suddenly no baby?" Zane asked.

"Miscarriage," Jackson said. "It's the oldest trick in the book."

"I guess we were right about her," Zane said. "We sensed an instability and a cruelty."

"I should've listened to you guys," Jackson said.

"Honor saw it too," Zane said. "All along."

"She doesn't miss much," Jackson said.

"Smart *and* pretty," Maggie said. "Right, Zane?"

"Even a head injury can't keep you quiet," Zane said.

Maggie smirked and raised her eyebrows. "It's time, Zane."

"Time for what?" Zane asked. "Time for humiliation and heartbreak."

"Don't be ridiculous. You need to grab her before someone else snatches her up," Maggie said.

"Who says I want her?" A vein bulged in Zane's neck as he perched on the arm of the chair.

"You. Every time she walks in a room," Maggie said. "Maybe not with your words, but your body language tells a different story."

"What do you know about it?" Zane asked.

"For one, I've studied the physical expression of emotion almost all my life. For two, I've known you almost all my life. I know what I see. The question is why."

"Why what?" Zane asked.

"Why are you resisting her? And don't tell me she doesn't really like you, or she ran out on you in the middle of the night. Those excuses are just tired."

God, I love this woman. "I agree. It's obvious she cares about you," Jackson said. "You'd have to be blind not to see it. Every time we're all together, she can't keep her eyes off you."

"How did this conversation take such a devious turn?" Zane raised his hand in a gesture of helplessness.

"We love you, buddy," Jackson said.

"And we want you to be happy," Maggie said. "Whether you think so or not, you deserve to be happy."

Zane looked up at the ceiling for a moment. "I don't know if I can put myself out there. When Natalie left, it nearly broke me. I'm not sure I'm brave enough to try again. And, Honor, she's just so... so...special. She makes me feel crazy, but at the same time I've never met a woman I admire as much as I do her. When I think about what she came from and how she built a life out of nothing, it's pretty phenomenal."

Jackson felt a sudden insight flash before him. "Wait a minute. I know what's going on here. You don't think you're good enough for her."

"Maybe," Zane said, elongating the word. "I mean, c'mon. Look at me. I wear shorts to work."

"Who cares?" Maggie asked. "You're Zane Shaw, for heaven's sake. Town hottie."

Zane's mouth twisted into a pained smile. "Do you know the people she and Brody interact with daily? These are rich, powerful people with their own boats and jets and stuff. I own a bar I inherited from my dad."

"Who's killing it with his updated bar and grill?" Jackson asked.

"Who's making a profit in a really hard business?" Maggie asked.

"And who do Brody and Honor choose to hang out with? Who do they keep close?" Jackson asked.

"Who does she stare at every time we're all together?" Maggie asked. "Not some guy with a jet. You."

"You're the hardest working man in town. Not only does Honor admire that, we're so proud of you."

"So proud," Maggie said. "Sweetie, do you know what a phenomenal man you are? You brought your dad's place to a whole new level. You remodeled this place with your bare hands."

"You live your life with your own code, your own rules," Jackson said. "Honor sees that."

"She admires you as much as you do her," Maggie said.

"Also, it might not have occurred to you that inside that exterior of a self-confident woman is the little girl nobody wanted,"

Jackson said. "The little girl that suffered years of abuse. She's as afraid to get hurt as you are."

Zane studied Jackson with those eyes that had turned every woman's head other than Maggie's. "I never thought of it that way."

"Maybe it's time you do," Jackson said.

"Something to think about, I guess." Zane opened his mouth to say something else, then closed it just as quickly.

"What is it?" Maggie asked.

"It's just that—well, for as long as I can remember, it was always the three of us. We rode a lot of tough waves together, you know? And I wanted to say that it's good to be back together." Zane shuffled from one foot to the other. "I'm grateful. Mags, I'm grateful your courage brought Sophie to us. Grateful that you're finally going to sing for the world." He stuffed his hands into his pockets. "I don't know how to say it exactly. I love you guys. That's all."

"That's enough," Maggie whispered.

"That's everything," Jackson said.

"And now I'm leaving," Zane said. "I'll see you cats later."

After the door closed behind their friend, Jackson turned back to Maggie. He caressed her soft cheek and kissed her neck and lingered, breathing in the sweet smell of her skin. "Zane's getting soft on us."

She splayed her hands through his hair. "A little, yes. I want him to be happy. Like us."

"Me too."

"Jackson, look at me."

He left her delicious neck and stared into her eyes.

"There's something you need to understand. Nothing will ever pull us apart again. Not Sharon or my dad or anyone. Even if she'd really been pregnant, we would've figured it out and made it work."

"I have to admit, I was worried," he said.

"You're my favorite worrier." She placed her hands on the sides of his face. "But hear this. Tattoo it on your heart. Nothing can pull us apart. Nothing, do you understand?"

"Yes," he whispered.

"Do you know why?" she asked.

"Because we're us."

"That's right. We're Maggie and Jackson. Epic." She winced as she tried to straighten from her reclined position.

"How do you feel?" he asked.

Maggie nestled back against the throw pillow. "Like I'm going to have the mother of headaches." She smiled up at him. "I'll need a handsome doctor to look after me."

"I think that can be arranged." Jackson grinned. "My first prescription is for a good, long kiss."

CHAPTER TWENTY-FIVE

Maggie

A WEEK LATER, Maggie had one hand in Jackson's and the other around the handle of her guitar case as they walked through Brody's home to the back yard. "I love weddings," Maggie said.

"I especially love this one," Jackson said.

"Brody and Kara are enough to make anyone believe in love," Maggie said.

"Just like us."

"Just like us," she said.

Just after five in the afternoon, temperatures hovered in the low seventies. Muted sunlight filtered through the trees. In the distance, the ocean provided a pure blue backdrop. The lawn had been transformed into a wedding oasis, with rose petals for an aisle, and white chairs decorated with dusty pink hued sashes. A small tent had been erected on the other side of the lawn, near the pool where the reception feast would be served.

Maggie and Jackson were the first guests to arrive. After she set her guitar on the table near the altar, she joined Jackson near the chairs. Besides the wedding planner and the four string musicians, they were alone on the lawn. Kara and Brody had invited so few people that almost half of the guests were participating in the wedding. Honor and Lance were maid of honor and best man, respectively. Because Kara had no family, she'd asked Zane to walk her down the aisle. He was the first person she met when she came to Cliffside Bay and, according to Kara, the reason she and Brody met in the first place. Maggie had been asked to sing. Of the Dogs, that left only Jackson and Kyle without a job. Neither appeared to mind, promising to give great toasts instead.

"I'm worried they're having this outside," Jackson said. "What if it gets out and they have helicopters circling overhead and taking photos with those long-range lenses?"

"Honor said there's no way that's going to happen," Maggie said. "No one even knows he's engaged, let alone having a wedding."

"I hope she's right."

Maggie nodded. "Me too." She also hoped the firm Honor had found to accompany them to Europe for the honeymoon was as good as they said they were. She hated to think what *that* was costing Brody. *No price is too high to ensure my bride's safety,* he'd said last night at the rehearsal dinner.

Maggie and Jackson sat. Kyle arrived a few minutes later and sat in the seat next to them as the string quartet began playing a piece by Bach.

"You look gorgeous this evening," Kyle said as he kissed Maggie's hand.

"Keep away from her," Jackson said. "She's mine."

"If you say so." Kyle winked at her and grinned.

She blushed. "I'm wearing a new dress." The shop in town had a surprisingly good selection, including the one she'd chosen for the wedding. Since the wedding was at night, she'd decided on a sage green halter dress. No worries about getting burned tonight.

"You would look good in a plastic bag, my dear." Kyle kissed her cheek. "Congratulations on your recording deal."

"Thank you," Maggie said. "Who knows, though. I might be a bomb."

"Doubtful," Kyle said with a wicked twinkle in his eyes.

"I worry, but not about that," Jackson said.

"Speaking of Jackson's worries, I went out to the house earlier and the crews are making great progress. You'll be in by the end of September."

"You're kidding?" Maggie asked. "That soon? But we haven't done a thing to pick out interiors."

"I'll set you up with my designer," Kyle said. "She's the best."

"Great, yes. We'll need all the help we can get," Maggie said.

"We'll go out tomorrow, if you guys want and look at the progress," Kyle said. "You won't be disappointed."

At that moment, Violet arrived and ventured over to them. "Hi Jackson. Maggie." She narrowed her eyes as she addressed Kyle. "Mr. Hicks, I'm surprised you could take a day off from scarring the land to celebrate your friend's wedding."

Kyle's dark eyes flashed. "Perhaps you could take a day off from harassing me and allow me to enjoy my buddy's big day in peace."

"I could, but that would be a disservice to my cause." Violet wore a sleeveless lavender dress that complemented her golden skin and the blond highlights in her honey colored hair. *She does have the loveliest skin.*

"I'm surprised you didn't bring your picket sign as your date," Kyle said.

"I wouldn't ruin Kara's day by causing a scene." Violet tapped her foot. A few more inches and she would stomp Kyle's foot. His designer loafers would be no match for the heel on Violet's sandal. "But you can bet I'll be back Monday morning."

"How's your business staying afloat when its owner spends more time getting in the way of my workers than running it?" Kyle asked.

A muscle in Violet's jaw twitched. She crossed her arms over her narrow torso. "That is none of your concern, Kyle Hicks. I'll keep trying to save the earth while you go about destroying it."

"We're even then," Kyle said without a hint of amusement in his usually playful face.

Violet excused herself and crossed over to sit in the section on the other side of the rose petal aisle.

"Damn if she doesn't have the most gorgeous legs," Kyle said. "Such a pity they're wasted on a woman with the vilest personality in the state of California."

Methinks he doth protest too much.

Doc and Janet arrived, followed by Flora and Dax with Mary trailing closely behind.

The sun hung low in the sky and shot beams of light through the trees as Brody took his position on the right side of the altar. The pastor wore a long black robe and held a bible. A wooden arch entwined with ribbons and pink roses contrasted with the blue of the ocean in the distance. Brody looked dashing in a dark blue suit and white tie, other than the fact that his face had bleached of color.

"Brody looks a little wobbly," Jackson said.

"Totally," Maggie said.

"You don't think he'll faint, do you?" Kyle asked. "Maybe I should go up there just in case."

"No. He'll be fine the moment he sees Kara," Maggie said.

"How do you know?" Jackson asked. "Because he looks terrible."

"Women know these things."

The music changed. Time to stand for the wedding party to walk down the aisle. Maggie shivered. What a beautiful, perfect night it was. They all stood and turned to watch as Lance walked Honor down the aisle. The best man also wore a blue suit. His tie matched the blush pink of Honor's dress. *He looks like a model, not a hedge fund manager. How was this guy still single?*

Her gaze didn't linger long on Lance. He was no competition to the angel on his arm. Maggie had never seen Honor look so pretty, which was saying something. Her blond hair fell in soft waves down her back. The makeup artist had emphasized her large, brown eyes with smoky shadow. Her pale pink dress was made of chiffon, a plunging V-neckline, cinched waist and A-line skirt. Like pale pink clouds, the material flowed about her ankles as she walked. A sash tied at the back wrapped her like a precious gift. She held a bouquet of pale pink and white anemones. Maggie knew from the rehearsal dinner the night before they were Kara's favorite flower.

When Lance and Honor were in place at the altar, the string quartet began to play the traditional wedding march. From behind the temporary partition, Kara and Zane appeared. The guests all let out a collective sigh of appreciation. Kara was breathtaking. Her wedding dress was sleeveless with a heart shaped neckline combined with illusion material that reached her neck. The skirt's underlayers were chiffon, but several layers of tulle made the skirt seem like a crown. The same tulle created a modest train. A rose gold crown sat upon her shiny brown hair which she wore in a low bun at the base of her long, slender neck. Her bouquet was a mass of pale pink and white anemones and roses that dangled from her hands.

On Zane's arm, Kara floated down the aisle and past them.

Maggie turned back to look at the groom. Tears streamed from his eyes as his bride made her way to him, their gazes locked.

When she reached the arch, Kara handed her bouquet to Honor and the women embraced. Kara turned to Brody, who had managed to compose himself. The pastor smiled. "We gather here today to celebrate the love and marriage of Brody and Kara. They have written their own vows."

Kara reached up to wipe a tear from Brody's cheek before she began. Her voice was remarkably steady. "Brody, I was in a dark and lonely place when I arrived in your little town. My life as I knew it had vanished. I was more frightened than I'd ever been and sure I'd never be happy again. That is, until I walked into this house. From the moment I laid eyes on you, I felt an instant connection, even though I spent years cursing at you on television."

Everyone laughed, including the groom.

"As the days unfolded, I began to truly understand the extraordinary man you are. You're a faithful son, loyal friend, and loving brother. You're generous and caring to those in your circle and beyond. There's no finer man on this earth. I fell so completely in love with you, I didn't know what to do with myself. You're the only man who's ever made me tongue-tied, jealous, and infuriated. No one makes me laugh harder or challenges me more or makes me happier to be alive. I love you more than you could ever know."

Brody took in a shaky breath before he spoke. "I *do* know how much you love me because I love you that much if not more. I heard once that the way to know if you're truly in love is by gauging how you feel about yourself when you're with them. Kara, you make me feel like a superhero. Until I met you, I never felt that special or talented or worthy of all the phenomenal things that had happened in my life. I was just an ordinary man with an extraordinary job who worked harder than anyone else and happened to be blessed with the best family in the world. But now, with you at my side, I feel like the man you think I am. *You* make me feel extraordinary. *You* make me want to be better. I'll do my best to give you as much joy as you give me and to be the man you think I am. I don't deserve you. I get that. But I'll die trying." Brody let out a shaky breath. Kara once again wiped his cheeks.

Maggie rose from her chair walked up to the microphone. The bride had asked for "Bless the Broken Road" by Rascal Flatts.

Please, God, let my voice be worthy of this couple.

She walked up to the microphone and picked up her guitar. For a second, she simply breathed in and out, conjuring the muse that hovered so near these days. She strummed the first chord. *Sing from your heart.* Her first voice teacher at college had given this instruction before they performed. The inane direction had made them laugh. What other way was there, after all? But tonight, gathered with this group of people to celebrate a great love between two people, she understood the sentiment in a way she never had before. Music was not only about conquering vocal technique. To sing well was an extraction and expression of the soul's deepest longings. Every note and lyric should arise from the human heart's immense capacity for love. Without the willingness to sing from the deepest part of your soul, it remained a craft instead of art.

She was ready now to be an artist. How it happened that of all the people in the world, she was blessed with the gift of song, she could not guess. She knew, only, that she was grateful. Not only for her voice, but for every moment that had come before this. Yes, even for the ways the world had broken her. Without that brokenness, she could not heal others with her song.

I was given this *gift for* this *night.* A bird's throat. A poet's tongue.

Her own broken road had led her to this exact moment. These were her people. Her tribe.

And so, as she opened her throat and let her heart ring out into the open air, she watched as the notes washed over her people in waves as powerful as the ocean itself.

When the last note echoed into the still of the evening, even Kyle wiped the corners of his eyes.

Mission accomplished.

"And now for the rings, please," the pastor said as Maggie returned to her seat.

Lance and Honor handed the rings to the bride and groom.

Kara slipped the ring on Brody's finger. "I pledge to be your partner, best friend, loyal wife, and greatest love from this day forward, through all the joys and trials that will come our way. I promise to love you all the days of my life."

Brody took her hand in his. The band's diamonds sparkled in the sunlight as he slid it onto her finger. "I promise to always take care of you, to consider you above all else. I promise to keep you safe from harm and to love and cherish you for all the days of my life."

"Do you, Brody Mullen, take Kara Eaton to be your lawfully wedded wife?"

"I do."

"Kara Eaton, do you take Brody Mullen to be your lawfully wedded husband?"

"I do."

The pastor turned his gaze to the guests. "Brody and Kara shared with me how important it is to them that their friends be an active part of this ceremony. They, even more so than most couples, will need their friends and families support in the years to come. They are asking you now on this sacred day to pledge to always be there for them, to protect them from harm, and to be the family Kara has always wanted. If you agree, say I do."

The chorus of I do's filled the evening air.

"Well, then, without further ado, I pronounce you husband and wife. You may now seal your promise with a kiss."

Everyone cheered as they kissed.

* * *

The pool deck had been transformed into a dance floor. Paper lanterns and tiny white lights hung from invisible strings. Music came through speakers set up by the hired DJ.

As twilight gave way to a purple sky, Maggie followed Jackson out to the dance floor. "May I have this dance?" he asked.

She smiled up at him and softened into his embrace.

"What kind of wedding do you want?" he asked.

"Smallish. Only at the church like we always said we would," Maggie said.

"What about the reception?"

"At our house?"

"Our house. That just gave me butterflies."

"Good ones?" she asked.

"Good. Very good. Even though I'm still nervous if we made the right decision."

"Kyle wouldn't have let us buy it without feeling confident it was a good move," she said.

"I still can't believe it's really ours," he said. "The Arnoult house."

"Soon to be the Waller house," she said.

"I like the sound of that."

"I'd given up on dreams coming true," she said.

"What about now?"

"Coming home made them all come true," she said. Monday, they would begin recording her first collection of songs. It was heady and beguiling. "I'm scared out of my mind. Everything I ever wanted is starting to happen. Is it weird to feel this way?"

"You're asking the biggest worrier on the planet if it's weird?" He chuckled. "I'm going to say no, it's not weird. It's perfectly normal to be frightened. But, Bird, you're going to kill it. I know."

"If I don't, you'll still be here." She didn't phrase it as a question. "And that's more than enough. Even if I'm a dismal failure."

"You're not going to be, but yes, I'll be here no matter what."

They danced in silence for a few minutes. "I want to get married sooner rather than later," he said.

"Like how soon?"

"After we move into the house. Early October?"

"When the weather's still nice, but crisp," she said.

"We can have a reception and an open house on the same day." She grinned up at him. "Won't that be something?"

"Yes. Yes, it will."

"I want your dad to give me away," she said.

"Ah, Bird."

"It has to be him," she said. "Will you ask Zane to be your best man?"

"It has to be him."

"I want Lisa and Pepper for bridesmaids. And Kara and Honor." Two bookends. Her east coast sisters and her west coast sisters. "And my sister."

"We don't have enough Dogs for them all," Jackson said. "Your sister will have to be a flower girl."

Maggie laughed. "Sure, she'll love that. The world's oldest flower girl."

"Whatever you want, you shall have," he said.

"Really?"

"Yes. I want you to have the world," he said.

"Ranunculus?"

"I'll talk to Clayton."

As Jackson turned her, she noticed that Zane and Honor danced together on the other side of the dance floor. *They're dancing together. It's about time.* They looked good together, so blond and gorgeous, like they were made from sunshine.

Zane had taken off his jacket and rolled up his sleeves. He whispered something in Honor's ear. She threw her head back and laughed like she wanted to savor every succulent second of this sweet night.

Honor and Zane were right together, if only they could be brave enough to let themselves be vulnerable, to let themselves love without fear. Maggie wanted for them what she had with Jackson. *Every person deserves to be loved like this.*

Please God, help them shed their jaded pasts and find refuge in each other.

"Honor and Zane are dancing. Do you see them?" Maggie asked.

"I mostly have eyes for you, but yes, I do."

"It won't be long before we're at their wedding."

"You really think so?" Jackson asked.

"After our wedding, of course. We have to take turns."

Jackson chuckled. "They have to actually have a date first."

"They will. I have faith."

Jackson and Maggie danced together without much movement, swaying as softly as the scent of roses in the night air. No need for fancy footwork when you're resting in your soulmate's arms.

The moon appeared in the purple sky, full and fat and made for lovers. Maggie sighed with happiness and rested her cheek against Jackson's hard chest. She closed her eyes and let the music enter through her pores and penetrate the center of her heart. *Home.* She was home at last. It was not just the sea air and the small, familiar town, but the people in it that made it so. Mostly, Jackson.

Jackson was her home and always would be.

"Do you remember much about our trip to Italy?" Jackson asked.

She nodded against his chest. "Yes. I think I remember every moment of it. When I close my eyes, I see the view from our apartment as clearly as if it were right in front of me."

"I want to take you there for our honeymoon. To the same apartment we stayed in if I can find it."

"Oh, Jackson, really?"

"Where else could we go that would mean as much?"

"It was one of the happiest two weeks of my life. Your mom's too. Did she ever tell you that?"

"She didn't have to." He tightened his grip around her waist. "We're going to have so many more, Bird. So many more happy times. Moments to hang on the walls of our home."

"And behind my eyes," she said.

"Yes, behind your eyes."

She didn't have to explain what she meant to Jackson. He knew the passages and paths of her heart. He knew the cost of her losses and who and what she loved and wished for and despaired over. Since the day he held her muddy hand on the way home from school, he'd seen her like no one else had. Really *seen* her. Was this love, then? A familiarity with another's secrets and longings and missteps? Or was love simply too mysterious to assign words? Even in a song?

Maggie breathed in the scent of the sea and Jackson's neck and looked around at the glow of candlelight on their friends' faces. This would all too soon be a memory—one to hang on the walls and carry behind her eyes. Time stopped for no one, not even lovers.

An image of her mother and Lily flashed before her. In the kitchen of the Waller's home, laughing over some shared joke. Now, their voices, as clear as a recording from Micky's expensive equipment, echoed through her mind.

First her mother. *Don't miss one precious moment of your life, my Maggie.*

Then, Lily. *Gobble every succulent second of this sweet world.*

I promise, I will.

She wrapped her arms tighter around Jackson's neck and looked up to the purple sky. Two stars hovered near the moon twinkled down at her. She raised her left hand from Jackson's neck and let Lily's diamond twinkle in return.

I'll take care of your boy, Lily. I'll love him with all my heart.

I got the truth, Mama. We found Sophie.

She'd come home to get the truth. That truth had not led her to vindication, but to redemption. Love, not hate, had redeemed her. She was strong now, like the earth and sky. Her strength, built from the ashes of hardship and loss, had readied her for the most courageous act of all—to love without reservation. Because to love as she loved Jackson exposed her heart to the devastating possibility of loss. She *knew* how loss hurt. For twelve years she'd lived without him. Knowing this and choosing to love him anyway was the most courageous choice she would ever make. But what else was there that mattered as much? What else had there ever been but this man who saved the last dance for her? *Jackson Waller.* The man she'd loved all her life. The man with whom she would make a lifetime of memories.

She moved her gaze to Jackson's face and fought the urge to hold him tighter, to protect him from harm. But no, this was not the way. Fearful was not the path with which to relish life and love. No, she must let go and breathe as if no harm would ever come to them.

"Jackson," she whispered.

"What is it, Bird?" he asked.

"Did you ever notice the sky's purple this time of night?"

"Only because you showed me," he said.

"There's never going to be enough time. I'll always want one more day with you."

"Me too."

"But we have right now," she said.

"Yes. We have this one perfect moment. Nothing can ever take that from us. Not even time."

"Us. My favorite word."

"Now, shush, so I can kiss you and make it a little more perfect," he said.

And so she did.

The end.

ABOUT THE AUTHOR

Tess Thompson writes small-town romances and historical fiction. Her female protagonists are strong women who face challenges with courage and dignity. Her heroes are loyal, smart and funny, even if a bit misguided at times. While her stories are character driven, she weaves suspenseful plots that keep readers turning pages long into the night.

Her desire is to inspire readers on their journey toward their best life, just as her characters are on the way to theirs. In her fiction, she celebrates friendships, community, motherhood, family, and how love can change the world. If you like happy endings that leave you with the glow of possibility, her books are for you.

Like her characters in the River Valley Collection, Tess Thompson hails from a small town in southern Oregon, and will always feel like a small town girl, despite the fact she's lived in Seattle for over twenty-five years. She loves music and dancing, books and bubble baths, cooking and wine, movies and snuggling. She cries at sappy commercials and thinks kissing in the rain should be done whenever possible. Although she tries to act like a lady, there may or may not have been a few times in the last several years when she's gotten slightly carried away watching the Seattle Seahawks play, but that could also just be a nasty rumor.

Her historical fiction novel, *Duet for Three Hands* won the first runner-up in the 2016 RONE awards. *Miller's Secret*, her second historical, was released in 2017, as were the fourth and fifth River Valley Series books: *Riversnow* and *Riverstorm*. The sixth River Valley book will (hopefully) release in the latter part of 2018.

Traded: Brody and Kara, the first in her new contemporary, small town romance series, Cliffside Bay, released on February 15th, 2018. The second in the series, *Deleted: Jackson and Maggie* releases May 7th. The subsequent three Cliffside Bay books will release every couple months in 2018.

She currently lives in a suburb of Seattle, Washington with her recent groom, the hero of her own love story, and their Brady Bunch clan of two sons, two daughters and five cats, all of whom keep her too busy, often confused, but always amazed. Yes, that's four kids, three of whom are teenagers, and five cats. Pray for her.

Tess loves to hear from you. You can visit her website http://tesswrites.weebly.com/ or find her on social media:

facebook.com/AuthorTessThompson

twitter.com/tesswrites

pinterest.com/tesswrites

bookbub.com/authors/tess-thompson

CPSIA information can be obtained
at www.ICGtesting.com
Printed in the USA
FSHW02n0534090518
47805FS